THOMAS DUNNE BOOKS ST. MARTIN'S PRESS ≈ NEW YORK

This is a work of fiction. All of the characters, organizations, and events portrayed in this novel are either products of the author's imagination or are used fictitiously.

THOMAS DUNNE BOOKS.
An imprint of St. Martin's Press.

www.thomasdunnebooks.com
www.stmartins.com

Designed by Anna Gorovoy

Library of Congress Cataloging-in-Publication Data

Names: Kroese, Robert, author.
Title: The big sheep / Robert Kroese.
Description: First edition. | New York : Thomas Dunne Books, 2016.
Identifiers: LCCN 2015051260 | ISBN 978-1-250-08844-4 (hardcover) |
    ISBN 978-1-250-08845-1 (e-book)
Subjects: LCSH: Private investigators—California—Los Angeles—
    Fiction. | Conspiracy—Fiction. | Cloning—Fiction. | BISAC:
    FICTION / Science Fiction / General. | GSAFD: Science fiction. |
    Mystery fiction.
Classification: LCC PS3611.R625 B54 2016 | DDC 813/.6—dc23
LC record available at http://lccn.loc.gov/2015051260

Our books may be purchased in bulk for promotional, educational, or business use. Please contact your local bookseller or the Macmillan Corporate and Premium Sales Department at 1-800-221-7945, extension 5442, or by e-mail at MacmillanSpecialMarkets@macmillan.com.

First Edition: June 2016

10 9 8 7 6 5 4 3 2 1

FOR VIVIAN. SHE'LL KNOW WHY.

AND ADRIAN MONK
        FOR INSPIRATION.

ACKNOWLEDGMENTS

With thanks to: Julian Pavia at Crown, who took notice of a book I wrote called *Starship Grifters*; my agent, David Fugate, who believed in this book when it was still just a title and a fuzzy idea; and my editor at Thomas Dunne, Peter Wolverton, who made invaluable suggestions for improving the manuscript. This book never would have happened if it weren't for the timely intervention of all three of you.

Thanks also to my mom, who kept me alive over the past two years with love and lasagna.

Strange how paranoia can link up with reality now and then.

—PHILIP K. DICK, *A SCANNER DARKLY*

ONE

"That's a really big sheep," said Erasmus Keane, his observational powers functioning as flawlessly as ever.

The woman in the lab coat nodded curtly. "He's a Lincoln Longwool," she said. "Largest breed of sheep in the world." She had introduced herself as Dr. Kelly Takemago, Director of Research for the Esper Corporation. We were standing in her lab, a vast white room filled with the low humming of vaguely terrifying machines that hung from the ceiling like colossal clockwork bats. Poised in the middle of the room was the sheep in question, which Keane and I were regarding with professional interest. The sheep, in turn, was regarding us. It didn't appear impressed.

Keane, holding his chin in his hand, began walking around the sheep in a stooped posture that reminded me of a waddling duck. The sheep was nearly as tall as he was, and was looking back at Keane with scientific detachment. It was hard to say who was the odder-looking specimen, the quadrupedal area rug standing in stoic silence on the tiled floor of the lab or the lanky, balding biped creeping awkwardly around it.

"Can I touch it?" Keane asked, after completing his circumnavigation of the creature.

"Of course," said Dr. Takemago, seeming mildly annoyed at the question. "Sheep don't bite. They're very docile creatures."

Keane reached out nervously, his hand gradually disappearing into the beast's lush fleece. He gave an excited yelp, which startled Dr. Takemago but had no appreciable effect on the Longwool's equanimity. "You gotta try this, Fowler," he said. "It's like sticking your hand into Narnia."

I demurred.

"They produce the heaviest and coarsest fleece of all the long-wool sheep varieties," said Takemago, as if reciting from an encyclopedia article. "That isn't why the Esper Corporation keeps them, of course. This one is male. There are two others. John and Paul are downstairs."

"John and Paul?" I asked. "What's this one's name, Ringo?" There was a tag on the sheep's ear, but all it had on it was the number eight.

"Mark," said Dr. Takemago.

I nodded, as if that had been the other possibility.

"Biblical, not Beatles," mused Keane. He continued, "'All the nations will be gathered before him, and he will separate the people one from another as a shepherd separates the sheep from the goats. He will put the sheep on his right and the goats on his left.'" He grinned at me, as if expecting recognition of some sort.

I shrugged noncommittally.

"That's from Matthew," he went on. "The apostle, not the sheep."

I turned back to Dr. Takemago. "So the missing one . . . ?" I ventured.

"Mary," replied Dr. Takemago.

"Of course," I said. "And did Mary by any chance have a little lamb?" Very unprofessional of me, I know. But you can't lob a softball like that at me and expect me not to take a swing.

"No," Dr. Takemago said without cracking a smile. I couldn't tell if she was irritated by the joke or if the subtlety of my wit had eluded her. I got the impression Dr. Takemago didn't go in much for jokes. She was short and stocky, and wore her straight black hair cut so short that it required constant effort to remind myself that she wasn't a twelve-year-old boy. Her expressive range seemed to encompass only detached bemusement and mild irritation.

"So they are sterile?" asked Keane, now with both of his hands sunk deep within the long-suffering animal's fleece. The sheep bore this indignity with aplomb.

Dr. Takemago shook her head. "No, in fact the plan was to breed them. Unfortunately, Mary is the only female of the group."

"And she's been missing since yesterday?" I asked.

Dr. Takemago nodded. "Mary was gone when I arrived, shortly after seven. The security system had been overridden. The cameras didn't catch anything. All the animals wear a GPS tracking device on their collars, but Mary's stopped transmitting at four twenty-nine a.m. while she was still in the lab. Whoever did this knew what they were doing."

"Who else has access to the building?"

"To the building? Several hundred people. But the research area is only accessible to about fifty."

"We'll need a list," I said. "As well as details on your security system."

"Of course," said Dr. Takemago.

"You've called the police?"

Dr. Takemago was silent for a moment. "The executives didn't feel that the police would appreciate the nuances of this case."

I nodded as if this were a perfectly reasonable answer. Keane had extracted his hands from the fleece and was holding them in front of his nose with a slightly revolted expression on his face.

"You said you don't keep the sheep for their wool," I remarked. "Why *do* you keep them?"

"Genetic research," Dr. Takemago said.

I raised an eyebrow at her. Now she was being downright evasive. After a moment she sighed. "Organ transplants," she said. "The idea is to raise genetically modified sheep specifically for the purpose of being hosts for organs that can be transplanted into humans. Livers, kidneys, even hearts and lungs. This is confidential, of course."

Just at that moment the sheep let out an impassioned bleat that sent a shiver down my spine. It sounded precisely like the frightened cry of a small child. I turned to see Keane kneeling in front of the sheep, staring intently into its eyes. The sheep backed away, appearing frightened.

Dr. Takemago didn't look pleased.

"Stop spooking the sheep, Keane," I said, by way of mollifying her. I had no real hope of having any effect on Keane's behavior.

Keane continued to stare, and the sheep retreated, bleating its horrible bleat.

"What are you doing, Mr. Keane?" demanded Dr. Takemago.

Keane didn't answer, continuing to stare at the terrified sheep. Then he stood and turned to Dr. Takemago. "I have taken measure of this sheep's soul," announced Keane. The room was silent except for the low hum of the machinery for some time before I realized Keane wasn't planning to elaborate.

"And . . . ?" I asked at last.

Keane remained silent for several seconds more. "Inconclusive," he said at last. With that, he wandered to a corner of the laboratory and began staring at the wall. Dr. Takemago shook her head, clearly dubious about the Esper Corporation's decision to hire Keane to find its missing sheep.

"He's an unconventional thinker," I explained without enthusiasm. "But he gets results."

"One thing needs to be made clear," said Dr. Takemago, turning to face me. "The vice president of research and development left instructions to be cooperative. But hiring a two-bit private investigator to locate the missing specimen seems misguided, and frankly Mr. Keane's attitude is doing exactly nothing to allay those concerns. That sheep is absolutely critical to the life-saving research Esper Corporation is doing, and if it isn't found—"

"Phenomenological inquisitor," I mumbled.

"Excuse me?"

"Mr. Keane doesn't like being called a private investigator," I explained. "He prefers the term 'phenomenological inquisitor.'"

"Delusions of grandeur, too," noted Takemago coldly. "In what way does a 'phenomenological inquisitor' differ from a two-bit private investigator?"

I was ready for that one. "Phenomenology," I began, "is the philosophical study of the structures of experience and consciousness. The methods of a phenomenological inquisitor differ from those of a typical investigator in that the phenomenological inquisitor regards each case as a matter of resolving the tension between the appearance of things and things as they actually are. Further, the phenomenological inquisitor does not limit his understanding of the 'real' to mere physical phenomena, accepting that consciousness, memory, and experiences are no less real than, for example, chairs, automobiles, or"—I glanced at the sheep—"farm animals." I had this speech memorized, but I liked to occasionally improvise depending on the situation. Returning to the script, I went on, "Finally the phenomenological inquisitor differs from a scientist in that he does not attempt to isolate himself from his subject or to observe reality under artificially created laboratory conditions, preferring to seek out apparent anomalies and explore them on their own terms rather than reduce them to preexisting categories."

"That sounds like bullshit," said Takemago.

I shrugged. To be honest, it sounded like bullshit to me, too.

"Any idea who would want to steal your sheep?" I asked.

"The most reasonable hypothesis?" said Takemago. "One of the other biotech companies. Competition in this industry is cutthroat. Mary represents the culmination of a decade of top-secret research."

I frowned. I was no scientist, but something about that didn't seem to jibe. "You think they're going to dissect Esper's sheep to learn its secrets? Wouldn't it make more sense to steal the research? Not to mention that it's a lot easier to smuggle out a terabyte of data than to kidnap a sheep."

Dr. Takemago nodded. "Security is looking into the possibility that research data was stolen as well. Stealing Mary may have been only one part of their plan."

"Be sure to contact us if you find anything out," I said. "If we're going to solve this case, it's vital that you not withhold any information."

"Of course," Dr. Takemago said after a slight hesitation. I glanced at Keane to see if he had picked up on it, but he was oblivious, seemingly transfixed by the wall of the lab.

"What about someone needing an organ transplant?" I ventured.

Dr. Takemago shot me a dubious look.

"You said these sheep are engineered as hosts for organs intended for transplant. What if someone was desperate for a transplant and couldn't get an organ through legal channels for some reason?"

"Not a chance," said Dr. Takemago. "Anybody with the resources to pull off a theft like this could easily have gotten hold of a black-market kidney."

I furrowed my brow at her.

"Black-market trade in human organs from the Disincorporated Zone is well-documented. It wouldn't be difficult for a motivated person with adequate resources to get their hands on a viable human kidney." She was right of course, but something about the way she said it creeped me out. Takemago had a strange, clinical way of speaking that made me feel a little like I was conversing with a machine.

"What about a liver?" I asked. "Nobody's going to sell their liver on the black market."

"No one's *own* liver, no," Dr. Takemago said.

I nodded. She was right. You could get anything in the DZ if you had the money. "Still," I said, "it would help if we knew a little more about the potential uses for a sheep like Mary."

"There seems to be a bit of a disconnect here, Mr. Fowler," she said. "There are no 'uses' for a sheep like Mary. Her only value is as a subject of research. This is undoubtedly a case of corporate espionage. If the involvement of a 'phenomenological inquisitor' in this matter is unavoidable, then that's where such a person's efforts should be directed."

"Humor me," I said. "When you say the organs are meant for transplanting into humans, do you mean the sheep actually have human organs inside them?"

"More or less," Takemago said. "Their hearts, kidneys, and livers are designed from a subset of chromosomes common to sheep and human beings so they can be transplanted from one to the other with minimal complications."

"Minimal complications," I said. "Not *no* complications."

I watched as Keane spun around and approached the sheep again. He sank his hand into the top of its fleece once more, and the sheep gave a quick bleat as it felt his presence. Dr. Takemago frowned, clearly agitated.

"There's always the risk of complications with any transplant operation," she said, her eyes on Keane. "Particularly cross-species—even if the animal is specifically designed for the purpose. That's why it makes no sense to steal a sheep like Mary for her organs when one could more easily purchase a human organ on the black market. It's always better to stay within the same species, if at all possible. Not to mention that these sheep are still experimental. There's simply no advantage to harvesting organs from a sheep."

"Then why breed them in the first place?"

"Because," Takemago explained irritably, "Esper Corporation isn't selling organs on the black market. The idea is to supply usable organs through legitimate channels, without anybody having to die in the process."

"Except for the sheep," I said.

"Of course," said Takemago to me. "But better a sheep than a human being."

I nodded. "Why do you use such a large breed of sheep?" I asked. "Even allowing for the volume of its fleece, that one has to weigh close to three hundred pounds. I would think its organs are too large to fit inside a person."

Takemago nodded, still watching Keane anxiously. "Another reason it wouldn't make sense to harvest organs from Mary. But in answer to the question, Esper uses several different breeds. These specimens are all experimental. Size is one of the easiest variables to control. Once the problem of organ viability has been solved, the next step is to breed a version with a mass approximating that of an average human being. What are you doing, Mr. Keane?"

Keane seemed oblivious to the question. He was running his hands through the sheep's fleece, pulling away loose fibers and regarding them with apparent fascination.

Dr. Takemago turned to me. "What exactly is Mr. Keane doing?" she demanded.

I watched Keane impassively for a moment. "Woolgathering," I said, eyeing Dr. Takemago for her response. Crickets.

She continued to watch Keane for some time, clearly agitated. Her hands were clutched in fists at her sides. I saw her lips quivering as if she were preparing for a confrontation. She took a deep breath and said, "Mr. Keane, you have had adequate time to observe that sheep. If you have no other questions, I am going to have to ask you to leave."

Keane mumbled something incomprehensible.

"Excuse me?" said Dr. Takemago.

"I said, 'You'll do no such thing,'" Keane remarked.

"Oh?" said Dr. Takemago, rising to the challenge. "And why is that?"

"Because I'm your only hope to keep your job."

Dr. Takemago snorted derisively. "And how is that, Mr. Keane?"

Keane sighed. He straightened, facing Dr. Takemago, his hands tucked behind his back. "Other than the three of us and Mark here," he began, "this lab—which could easily accommodate twenty or more scientists and technicians—is empty. Not even a wrangler to help you with the sheep. I can't imagine all your research has ground to a halt simply because one of your subjects has gone missing, which means that the lab has been intentionally cleared of personnel for some reason. Not on your orders, I assume."

Dr. Takemago didn't reply.

Keane went on, "It's possible that they're trying to hide the theft of the sheep—or some other detail about the case—from the other employees, but that seems unlikely. They aren't going to be able to keep the sheep's disappearance under wraps for long, and you haven't told us anything I couldn't have learned from any low-level employee. Speaking of which, my fee is high enough that ordinarily when I'm hired by a corporate client like Esper, I'm met by one or more board members. Corporate officers uniformly possess an exaggerated sense of their own understanding of the strategic business realities affecting a case. This leads them to believe I couldn't possibly solve the case without their input. But rather than being called into a meeting with the vice president of research and development, who ostensibly hired me for this case, I was directed to speak only to you, a lowly researcher. No offense."

Dr. Takemago scowled.

"And then there's the fact that nobody has called the police. Perhaps, as you intimate, this is because the matter is too sensitive to be handled by the civil authorities. Or perhaps it's because your superiors didn't see the need."

"What is your point, Mr. Keane?" demanded Dr. Takemago.

"My point, Doctor, is that your bosses have already determined who is responsible for your missing sheep. They set up this meeting with the sole purpose of seeing how you would react—to see if you would attempt to steer us away from suspecting you. This room is monitored, I assume. I'd wager that the VP of R and D—assuming he really did hire me—is watching us right now. You'll be followed when you leave the building as well. If you don't incriminate yourself during this meeting, they're hoping to spook you into making a mistake, like trying to contact your coconspirators."

Dr. Takemago's mouth had fallen open in shock. "But I . . . I didn't—"

"What your superiors fail to take into account is that if you were the sheep thief, you'd have anticipated suspicion and surveillance. In fact, given that you're the obvious prime suspect, you'd likely have planned a strategy of misdirection, deliberately inviting suspicion in order to demonstrate your innocence and utter guilelessness. If you had conducted this heist directly under your superiors' noses, as it were, the last thing that would spook you into making a mistake is some eccentric detective poking around your lab, asking silly questions. This is one of the hazards of being an eccentric detective, by the way. Clients tend to rely on my reputation while discounting my ability. Esper hired me not to solve this case, but to put on my dog and pony show in your lab in order to flush you out. In addition to being completely misguided and doomed to fail from the outset, there's one major flaw with this plan."

"I didn't steal the sheep," said Dr. Takemago.

"No," Keane said. "You didn't."

"How do you know?" I asked.

"Do you see this sheep?" asked Keane, walking over to Mark and patting it gently on its head. "The poor thing is terrified."

"So?" I asked.

"Sheep are herd animals," said Keane. "They hate being separated from their herd. It's a little hard to tell, but this beast is having the sheep equivalent of a panic attack right now. Simply because it's standing alone in this lab, a place where it's probably been a hundred times before."

The sheep let out a low bleat, and Keane scratched its ear comfortingly.

I held up my hands, indicating I wasn't following.

"Well," he said, "imagine how *Mary* feels. She's in a strange place, alone, separated from her flock. She must be out of her mind with fear."

I was about to interject, asking if he was going to get to the point sometime this week, but then I saw Dr. Takemago bite her lip, and I caught a glimpse of the picture Keane was painting.

"Dr. Takemago's surly demeanor is a cover," said Keane. "She loves these sheep. She empathizes with them. You can tell by the way she fidgets when I approach it. It pains her to see poor Mark standing here, alone in the lab, being harassed by a strange man. Maybe at first they were just research subjects, but she's come to have strong feelings for them. She would never willingly remove Mary from her herd. I suppose it's possible that Dr. Takemago assisted the thief under duress, but it's hard to imagine what sort of leverage the thief might use."

"The usual, I suppose," I offered. "Threaten her family, or—"

Keane shook his head. "Dr. Takemago tends to avoid eye contact and personal pronouns, engages in the bare minimum of personal grooming, lacks social graces, presents a virtually asexual affect, and demonstrates an abbreviated range of emotions. These characteristics, along with her chosen career in a highly technical, specialized scientific field, indicate that she possesses traits of autism and social anxiety disorder. I expect she has no friends and no close family. This job is her entire life, and those sheep are the closest things she has to friends. To get Dr. Takemago to betray her employer and cause suffering to one of her sheep, the thief would have had to threaten to take away something she values more than her job and her research subjects. There isn't any such thing."

Dr. Takemago stared at Keane with something that was either annoyance or awe.

"So," I said, "this whole meeting has been a waste of time."

"Not at all," said Keane. "We've accomplished two important tasks. One, we've eliminated Dr. Takemago as a suspect and saved her job. Two: we've demonstrated that I'm the only person in this building smart enough to find the real thief." Keane craned his neck back and addressed the ceiling. "So," he said, "if it's all the same to you, I'll get to work on that."

TWO

The Case of the Lost Sheep was to be the eighteenth investigation Keane and I worked together. My association with Keane had begun three years earlier, on the Case of the Mischievous Holograms. At the time I had been the head of security for Canny Simulations, Inc., a company that creates artificially intelligent holograms of celebrities. CSI had the rights to most of the big names: Elvis, Michael Jackson, Beyoncé, Sheila Tong, the Weavil Brothers. A hacker had managed to get into our code base and was projecting our celebrities all over town: at strip clubs, children's birthday parties . . . Bette Midler showed up at a bowling alley in Van Nuys. The hacker didn't seem to be particularly malicious, but the CSI board of directors was understandably concerned that having unlicensed versions of our biggest names crashing bar mitzvahs in Glendale was diluting our corporate brand. The feds had pretty much given up on trying to enforce piracy laws by this point (this was shortly after the Collapse, so the feds had their hands full with more important things, like domestic terrorism and the threat of Chinese invasion), and the LAPD couldn't be bothered to expend much effort to catch someone who was essentially a high-tech graffiti artist. The board hired Erasmus Keane over my stringent objections, and I insisted I be present at all Keane's interactions with CSI personnel. I ended up accompanying Keane during most of the investigation, and spent much of the next three days thoroughly documenting his unprofessionalism, lack of social propriety, neurotic behavior, inability to execute mundane tasks, and poor hygiene. He was like an idiot savant without the savant part. At one point during the investigation, he locked himself in a bathroom stall for over three hours. After I'd gathered what I thought was more than enough evidence to get Keane fired, I asked to address the next board meeting. When I got there, Keane was already in the conference room, laughing it up with the CEO and the rest of the board. With him was a fourteen-year-old kid named Julio Chavez, who was conversing animatedly with Obi-Wan Kenobi, Teddy Roosevelt, and Greta Autenburg, who was the latest teen sensation at the time. Keane had not only found the hacker, he'd convinced the kid to come work for CSI. He's the director of simulation development now.

I'd been so humiliated by this turn of events that I quit my job on the spot. Truth be told, I'd been bored stiff by the corporate security gig; I was basically a glorified mall cop. I'd only taken the job because it seemed like a cushy gig after three years of running security details for VIPS on the Arabian Peninsula. Anyway, it paid better than civilian law enforcement, and at the time I'd had some thoughts of planning for the future. But then Gwen—my girlfriend at the time—disappeared, and . . . well, by the time dead celebrities started showing up around town, I'd pretty much given up on the future.

Three months after I quit, Keane showed up at my apartment with a job offer, saying I'd been "invaluable" on the hologram case. I almost punched him, thinking he had shown up at my door with the sole purpose of making fun of me.

Taking my reticence as a bargaining tactic, he upped his offer by twenty grand. When I balked at this, he offered me five grand for my notes on the hologram case. That was when it finally penetrated that he was serious.

I still probably wouldn't have taken the job, but Keane's timing—by chance or design—was fortuitous. I had spent every waking moment since leaving CSI investigating Gwen's disappearance, and had come up with exactly nothing. One day she simply hadn't shown up for work. I'd talked to her the previous night, and she had sounded fine. We were planning to see Sheila Tong at the Orpheum, and Gwen was complaining that she couldn't stay out late because she had to work most of the weekend. She worked for the city planning department, and they had been short-staffed ever since the Collapse, so she often took work home. She had called me on the way home from work on Wednesday night, and as far as I could tell, that was the last time anyone had talked to her. It was unclear whether she ever made it home that night; her last documented location was the parking garage down the street from her office. I had talked to friends, family members, coworkers, neighbors . . . but nobody had a clue what had happened to her. She had vanished into the proverbial thin air.

In any case, by the time Keane showed up with his offer, I was out of leads, nearly out of money, and rapidly sinking into hopelessness and depression. I'm still not certain whether I took the job because I thought Keane could help me find Gwen or because I thought working with him would be an effective distraction from what I knew to be a lost cause.

My official title was Director of Operations, but it became clear in short order that my function was essentially to be Keane's tether to mundane reality. Keane's mind dealt in concepts and abstractions; when it came to routine tasks like keeping case notes or doing laundry, he was hopeless.

He subsisted entirely on Lucky Charms, Dr Pepper, and instadinners. He dressed in rumpled, mismatched clothing he bought by the pallet directly from a Chinese wholesaler; he wore a set of clothes for a week and then threw it out. Ironically, my first task as Keane's employee was to locate the funds for paying my own salary. Keane possessed a bewildering array of bank accounts and investments, the value of which I eventually established at nearly a million new dollars, but for those first few weeks I was basically writing myself checks and holding my breath. Even after spending three years sorting out his accounts, it wasn't uncommon for us to be two or three months in arrears on our lease. Currently it was closer to four. Hopefully the Case of the Lost Sheep would bring us close to being current, if I could keep Keane from spending the money on a new aircar.

There was little doubt that Keane needed me, but I never did figure out exactly how I was so "invaluable" to him on the hologram case. I think maybe it helped him to have a sane person around to bounce ideas off. Either that, or he just liked having an audience. When we weren't on a case, I felt like a babysitter for a manic-depressive eight-year-old. When we were on a case, I alternated between feeling like I was chaperoning a chimpanzee on acid and having flashbacks to Mr. Feldman's advanced calculus class, where I'd been placed in tenth grade, despite my lack of mathematical aptitude, as a result of a computer error. Life with Erasmus Keane was not a low-stress existence, but on most days it beat the hell out of the boredom of a corporate job.

"What do you make of Dr. Takemago?" asked Keane on the way back to the office.

I took a deep breath. Questions like that were often tests. Keane had come to some conclusion and wanted to know if I'd reached it as well. Not so much to confirm his own hypothesis as to determine how much of it, with my feeble neurotypical brain, I had managed to piece together. "Well," I said, "she's clearly hiding something."

Keane let out a derisive sigh.

"Something about the missing sheep," I tried.

"Yes?" Keane said.

I thought for a moment. "Hang on," I said, feigning a need to concentrate on my driving. There weren't many other cars in the air at this time in the afternoon, but we were nearing a notorious bottleneck. Unlike in many areas of the city, where you could make a beeline to your destination, traffic in the downtown area was routed along a few narrowly defined channels. Sometimes when traffic got really bad, I would take a shortcut over the DZ, but we were in no hurry, so there was no point in risking some bored banger taking a potshot at us. I eased the car into the eastbound channel and put it on auto. A light went on, indicating that the car had successfully synced with the city's traffic routing system, and it settled into a comfortable niche between two other eastbound vehicles. I'd take back control once we were clear of Downtown.

This channel lined up more or less with the old I-10, which was basically an automotive graveyard at this point. The freeways had gotten so hopelessly snarled with traffic during the Collapse that nobody'd ever been able to unsnarl them. In fact, nobody had even really tried. There seemed to be sort of a general agreement that the Los Angeles freeway system was an experiment that hadn't really worked out, like nuclear power or rap metal. These days, if you wanted to get somewhere in LA, you had to take the surface streets; pay to drive on one of the privately funded, ultrafast expressways known as Uberbahns, which had been constructed on top of the old highway system; or—if you had the means—take an aircar. Thanks to the occasional deep-pocketed client like Esper, Erasmus Keane had the means, barely. His car was an old Nissan, one of their first aircar models, but it was in rea-sonably good shape and beat being stuck on the surface streets.

"What about the sheep?" asked Keane impatiently. He was sitting, his seat reclined as far as it would go, his feet up on the dash, his eyes closed.

"It's just a sheep," I said finally. Keane sighed again and put his palms on the top of his head, as if trying to shield his brain from my stupidity. "No, wait," I said. "What I mean is that it's just a sheep, for Pete's sake. Even if it's got some magic transplantable organs in it, so what? Why do they care so much? If they made one magical sheep, they can make an-other, right? It's not like it's irreplaceable. It's not the goose that laid the golden egg. It's a sheep."

"Good," said Keane, taking his hands off his head and opening his eyes.

Encouraged by this indication that I was not, after all, a complete moron, I went on, "As I see it, there are two possi-bilities: either there is something unique about that sheep that they aren't telling us, or there is some reason why they really don't want that sheep to fall into the wrong hands."

"Or both," said Keane. He sat upright and stared straight ahead.

"Right," I said. "Either way, there's something about Mary they aren't telling us. Are you certain we're even still on the case? I thought you said they hired us only to provoke Take-mago."

"That was when they thought Takemago was behind the theft," said Keane. "Now that I've cast doubt on that hypoth-esis, they'll need someone to conduct an actual investigation. In any case, Esper is contractually obligated to pay us through the week."

"Do you think they'll call the police?"

"No," said Keane. "Even if they were certain Takemago

was the thief, they'd have involved the police if there weren't some pressing reason to keep them in the dark. They didn't hire me simply because I put on a better show than the police. They hired me because there's something they don't want the police to know."

"Like what?" I asked.

Keane didn't respond, and I didn't press him. When Keane was done talking, he was done. Unlike most detectives, Keane rarely brainstormed about a case out loud, preferring, except for the occasional question, to ruminate silently. He believed that the process of translating abstract thoughts to language was "unavoidably reductionistic," which I took to be a bad thing. That was another reason why I could never quite figure out how I had helped him on the hologram case. Or any other case, for that matter, other than preventing him from getting hopelessly lost or killed, which were admittedly prerequisites to solving any case. We rode the rest of the way to the office in silence.

The office was a rundown three-story building bordering the Disincorporated Zone. The DZ, as the zone was commonly known, was a conglomeration of areas that, like the freeway system, had been disowned by the civil authorities. LA had nearly gone up in flames during the Collapse; the city had survived by virtue of a sort of municipal triage process. The LAPD and National Guard had been instructed to protect and fortify "vital areas" of the city, but LA was so spread out that in the end it was easier to bottle up the bad areas of the city than to defend the parts considered worth saving. A vast swath of the city, including South Los Angeles, Compton, and Huntington Park, became essentially a free-range prison. Faced with massive riots, arson, and looting, the powers that be chose to preserve the financial infrastructure while allowing the rest of the city to go to hell. Temporary police barriers became concrete walls topped with razor wire, and any pretense of equality under the law evaporated. If you had the misfortune to live in the DZ post-Collapse, you were automatically suspect. The breakdown of the freeway system made it easy to control movements in and out of the DZ; checkpoints were set up with the ostensible purpose of identifying terrorists and other criminals and to stem the flow of illegal drugs and weapons. The drugs were usually coming out of the DZ; the weapons were going in.

It took almost a decade for the legal formalities to catch up to the harsh reality of the situation: the majority of the residents of the DZ at the time of the Collapse were undocumented immigrants, and the legal status of tens of thousands of others was thrown into question by the loss of records during the Collapse and subsequent years of near anarchy while the state and federal governments were reconstituted. In many areas of the country the legacy of the Collapse was little more than a temporary lapse in government services, with local governments and ad hoc civilian organizations picking up the slack. But in the DZ, the Collapse was near-total. Income taxes went unpaid, vehicles went unregistered, children were born without birth certificates. Criminal enterprises burgeoned. By some estimates, over 90 percent of economic activity in the DZ was off the books. By the time anyone started to get a handle on the scope of the problem, there was neither the will nor the means to reincorporate the DZ into American society. Los Angeles had given birth to a third-world country within its borders, and nobody seemed to know what to do about it. There was a lot of blame to go around, and a lot of people in the city government lost their jobs, but the impression I got from Gwen—who had a privileged vantage point from her position in the city's planning department—was that pretty much everybody in the city was doing everything they could just to control the chaos.

Erasmus Keane's response to these events was as brilliant as it was perverse: he leased a rundown office building that was literally on the border of the DZ and Los Angeles proper. It was located in an area known as Boyle Heights, just east of Downtown. The front of the building was inside LA proper, while the back door exited into an alley inside the DZ. (We couldn't legally enter the building that way; the authorities had boarded up the back of the building to prevent anyone from sneaking through.) Keane's theory, as I understood it, was that human-created borders, particularly ones as stark and arbitrary as the ones between the DZ and LA proper, were unnatural things, akin to a sort of societal psychosis. Setting up shop as a private investigator (or phenomenological inquisitor) at such a juncture was the equivalent of being an immunologist at ground zero of a viral outbreak. Keane figured he could just sit back and wait for the symptoms of the disease to present themselves. For better or worse, he was right. Over the past three years, we'd had no shortage of clients, and while most of them tended to live in the protected areas of LA, more often than not there was some connection to criminal elements in the DZ.

I parked the car on the roof and followed Keane into the building. His office was on the top floor, and I knew he'd want to be left alone to think, so I continued downstairs. Keane lived on the second floor, and my quarters had been cobbled together out of the offices on the first floor behind the lobby. It was a fairly dismal place to live, not least because the windows facing the alley were boarded up, but you couldn't beat the commute. I took a seat at my desk, with the intention of doing some research on Esper Corporation's genetic-engineering work. I supposed Keane might be doing the same thing upstairs, but it wouldn't hurt to educate myself a bit. Keane tended to play things pretty close to his vest, and in any case he's what you might call a big-picture thinker.

That's a nice way of saying that details tended to elude him, and keeping track of those details was one of the reasons he kept me around.

I had barely gotten halfway through the About section of Esper's website when I was interrupted by a knock at the front door. I sighed, grabbed the SIG Sauer nine-millimeter I kept in the top drawer of my desk, and made my way down the hall toward the lobby. My ability to handle a gun—as well as just about any other weapon—was another reason Keane kept me around. The SIG was my gun of choice; there had been a lot of technological advancements in firearms over the past twenty years, from biometric authentication devices to smart bullets that could go around corners, but for my money nobody in the past hundred years had really improved on the basic idea of making a hunk of metal go really goddamned fast in a straight line.

Am I paranoid? Maybe a little. But as I mentioned, while the front of our building was technically in LA proper, it wasn't exactly what you'd call a nice neighborhood. Whoever was knocking on the door was probably just a religious freak or a guy selling vacuum cleaners, but it didn't hurt to be careful. The knocking became more persistent.

"Coming!" I shouted, strolling across the threadbare carpet of the lobby. The whole building was in pretty sad shape, but the lobby was like the waiting room for Hades. The carpet, which must have been hideously ugly even before it faded to a sort of dusty plum color that didn't match any of the four layers of paint peeling off the walls, was so worn in spots that you had to be careful to lift your feet completely off it or risk tripping on loose fibers. The walls were dotted with vaguely sconcelike light fixtures that required a type of light bulb that was no longer legally available anywhere in North America, and in any case at least two of them had failed catastrophically during a lightning storm at some point, leaving impressive scorch marks on the walls. Minimal sunlight filtered in through small frosted windows on either side of the front door, just enough to give you a good sense of the unrelenting oppressiveness of that room. I swear, you could stand in the middle of that lobby and actually feel your soul being sucked out. I walked briskly.

The knocking had become a banging. Whoever was out there was really laying into it now. That was either a very desperate vacuum cleaner salesman or a couple of very motivated religious fanatics. Whoever it was, they were going to be disappointed. Both our carpets and our souls were beyond saving.

"Look," I said, opening the door a crack, holding the nine-millimeter in front of me, "you don't have to pound the door off its . . ." I trailed off, having momentarily lost touch with the language center of my brain.

The girl was gorgeous: flawless brown skin, long wavy black hair, big blue eyes that made you want to dive into one and come out the other. She wore a sleeveless brown T-shirt, a denim skirt, and knee-high brown suede boots that left just enough skin uncovered to give rise to a sudden montage of really bad ideas. Some primordial part of my cerebellum, just above the brain stem, urged me to throw my arms around her waist, toss her over my shoulder, and seek shelter in the nearest cave. Higher brain functions countermanded this order just in time, and I stood there for a moment, awaiting further instructions from my nervous system.

"You gonna let me in?" she said impatiently, and I realized I had been standing there for a good ten seconds, the door still open.

"Of course!" I managed to say. I opened the door wider and stood to the side as she walked in. I smelled cherries and vanilla.

I recognized her, of course. Priya Mistry, darling of Holly-

wood, star of the smash drama *DiZzy Girl.* She had a decid-
edly more uptown appearance in person than she did on
the show, but there was no mistaking that face. I managed
to close the door behind us and smile in what I hoped was a
nonthreatening manner.

"Are you him?" she asked.

"Haa?" I said, momentarily baffled. "Oh no," I managed
after a moment. "He's upstairs."

"Can I see him?" She was growing impatient, and I sympathized. I wondered if all her interactions with men went
like this. What might it be like, going through life so beautiful that the males in your vicinity are all reduced to drool-
ing dullards? I wanted to hug her, reassure her that it wasn't
her, it was us. Apologize on behalf of my gender, for all the
inconveniences she had suffered at our hands. She hadn't
asked to be born beautiful, after all. Cruel fate, cursing such
a delicate creature with—

"Hello!" she shouted. "Mr. Keane. Can I see him?"

"Yes!" I shouted back, inadvertently startling both of us.
"Sorry. Yes. Of course you may see him." Of course! Except
that I was fairly certain Keane wouldn't want to be disturbed.
In any case, it was my job to vet any potential clients before
letting them talk to Keane. Why had I violated protocol for
this girl? Another glance at Priya, and the answer was obvious. Her face was like logic Kryptonite. I was struck by a
brief impulse to make a run for it, dash past her out to the
street, and wait for her to leave while things sorted themselves out. But that was my low brain talking again, the lizard
brain. Fight or flight. This situation called for a third alter-
native: finesse. I would handle the situation as delicately as I
could and hope for the best.

"Listen, Miss Mistry—" I said.

"Priya is fine," she said.

"Okay, Priya," I said. I found that if I focused on the wall behind her, she became a vaguely attractive blur, albeit a blur with a voice like an angel who smelled like cherries and vanilla. "Here's the thing: Mr. Keane is a brilliant investigator, but he tends to be a bit, uh, scattered. I find it helps if I interview any potential clients before they meet him, to ascertain the core facts of the case."

She said nothing. I'd have wagered she was regarding me dubiously, but I didn't dare take my eyes off the wall sconce just over her right ear.

"I don't mean to be presumptuous," I babbled on. "You are looking to hire Mr. Keane, correct?"

The blur nodded.

"Okay," I said, feeling like I was gathering some momentum. "Why don't you come with me to my office?"

The blur shrugged, which I took as agreement. I turned and led her to my shabby little office behind the lobby. The room was small and filled with mismatched office furniture and bookshelves lined with paperbacks, mostly pre-Collapse crime novels. The décor was only a couple of steps up from that of the lobby, but it wasn't an entirely unpleasant place, owing largely to the nonbarricaded window behind my desk that looked out on the alley on the side of the building. The brick wall of the building next door didn't provide much of a view, but at least there was some natural light and you didn't feel like you were in a prison cell.

I took a seat behind my desk, and the blur that was Priya Mistry sat in one of the plush vinyl chairs across from me.

"So, what brings you to the offices of Erasmus Keane?" I asked, looking intently at the door hinge just over her left shoulder.

Priya took a deep breath. "I . . . I think someone is trying to kill me," she said.

Something about the way she said it gave me chills. This wasn't the first time I'd heard those words from a potential client, but with Priya there was a weird sort of detachment behind them. It wasn't that I thought she was lying (and I'm pretty damn good at telling when someone is lying to me), but she gave me the impression that being afraid for her life was the least of her concerns.

I risked a glance at her face, and was surprised to find myself looking at a scared little girl. It's odd how physical perfection can blind you to a person's basic humanity. Now that I looked at her—really looked—I could see there was more to her than her beauty. She had a sort of haunted sadness that reminded me a little of Gwen. Gwen was blond, though, and older. She'd just turned thirty when she disappeared. Priya was what, twenty-six? Twenty-seven? Her entire adult life had been lived in the bubble of Hollywood. She spent most of her time pretending to be someone she wasn't, and the rest surrounded by obsessed fans and sycophants. You had to wonder how that sort of artificial reality affected a person's mental and emotional development. Did she have any sense of what the real world was like? This wasn't a mere academic question: it was one thing to have a client who lied to you or withheld information; it was quite another to have a client who was delusional. Was her life really in danger, or was that some paranoid fantasy? After all, paranoia was just the flip side of narcissism: it's a short walk from "everybody loves me" to "everybody is out to get me."

"What makes you think someone is trying to kill you?" I asked.

She reached into her purse and pulled out a sheet of paper that had been folded into fourths. "I found this in the pocket of my jacket yesterday." She unfolded it and handed it to me. It was a handwritten letter addressed to Priya. The first line read:

SOMEONE IS TRYING TO KILL YOU. TRUST NO ONE.

I nodded. "Well, that's fairly conclusive," I remarked. A few lines below that warning was the entreaty:

FIND ERASMUS KEANE

It was signed *NOOGUS*.

"Any idea who Noogus is?" I asked.

Priya shook her head.

"Hmm," I said. It wasn't much to go on. And frankly, it looked more like a cry for attention than an actual warning. The letters were all uppercase, so it was a bit hard to tell, but it looked like a woman's handwriting.

Apparently sensing my skepticism, Priya hurriedly went on, "It's not just the letter. I've had this feeling for a while now that I'm being watched. People are following me. Like, I'll see a homeless guy down the street from where we're shooting, and then later on we'll be shooting in a different area of town, and I'll see the same guy. And he'll be looking over at me, and talking to himself. Stuff like that happens all the time."

I nodded slowly. Could this girl really be that oblivious to her effect on men? She had rendered me incoherent just by showing up at my door, and I was a relatively high-functioning member of society. There was no telling what her presence might do to some schizophrenic misfit living on the streets in the DZ.

"I'm not crazy," she said, the crack in her voice not helping her case. "I know how this sounds, but I'm not. Please, just let me talk to Mr. Keane. He's the only one who can help me."

"Don't you have bodyguards to worry about these sorts of things for you?" I asked.

"I have a bodyguard, yes. And Flagship Media has security guards who are supposed to keep us safe on location. But they all answer to Élan, and I don't know if I can trust him."

I nodded. Élan Durham, the creator and producer of *DiZzy Girl*, was something of a golden boy in Hollywood these days. He had been a pioneer of the DZ drama, finding an untapped well of commercial potential in the post-apocalyptic conditions of Los Angeles' backyard. *DiZzy Girl* was the most successful program of all time, and it had inspired dozens of knockoffs. Few of these programs were actually filmed in the DZ, of course. Only a producer with Durham's clout could convince a production company to negotiate with a DZ warlord for rights to film on his territory. The knockoffs were filmed mostly in Bakersfield, Fresno, or sound stages set up to look like the DZ. Despite the popularity of DZ culture, it was simply too dangerous to film there unless you could negotiate some kind of protection deal with one of the DZ warlords. It was only three weeks ago that production on a reality program, *Surviving the DZ*, was shut down after a car bomb killed three of its stars.

Whatever else could be said about Élan Durham, he was a smart businessman, and he knew the success of *DiZzy Girl* was in large part due to the appeal of Priya Mistry. I tried to broach the matter gently.

"I don't know Élan Durham personally," I said. "But he seems like a smart guy. He's not going to let anything happen to you."

"But the note says not to trust anyone," she replied.

"The note from Noogus," I said.

She bit her lip.

"I wish I could help you, Priya," I said, allowing my gaze to linger for a moment at the hint of cleavage visible above the dip in her shirt. Man, did I wish I could help her. "But frankly, this isn't a lot to go on. My guess is that somebody is playing a joke on you. Noogus is probably one of the other actors on *DiZzy Girl*, someone with too much time in between scenes. Or maybe some bitter actress who you once beat out for a part. You know how this town breeds crazies. They're mostly harmless, though. And if there's ever a real threat, well, that's what the security is for. If they work for Flagship Media, they're pros. They're not going to let anything happen to you." I tried not to think of some of the knuckle-draggers who had worked security for me at CSI.

Priya leaned forward and put a hand over her face. As her shoulders began to bob slightly, I realized she was crying.

"Hey," I said, by way of comforting her. I couldn't think of anything to say after that, though, so I just said it again. "Hey."

"Maybe I am going crazy," she said, sobbing. "Like you said, this town breeds crazies. Maybe I'm just one of the crazies."

I felt like hugging her, but something told me that would be wildly inappropriate—not to mention logistically difficult, since she was hunched down in a chair on the other side of my desk. "You don't seem crazy to me," I said. "You're probably just under a lot of stress. I know how it is, shooting a hit show like *DiZzy Girl*. We worked this case once for this producer who was being blackmailed by . . . well, I can't really go into details, but—"

"Have you seen that commercial for that face cream, Prima Facie?" she asked, taking her hand from her face and looking up at me. Her cheeks were wet with tears.

"Probably a hundred times," I said. "'Approach life the way I do: face first.'" I did my best to muster the sort of enthusiasm Priya had evinced in the ad. She made a compelling pitch: I'm pretty sure I wasn't the target audience for the ad, and even I had given some thought to buying a tube of the stuff.

She burst into tears again, sobbing loudly into her hands.

Her reaction confused me. "I thought you were great," I said sincerely. "Are you worried about having sold out or something? Because I don't think there's anything wrong with—"

"I never made that commercial," Priya said, continuing to sob.

I wasn't sure what to make of this. "You mean they misrepresented what you were going to be selling or . . . ?"

"No!" she exclaimed, looking me in the eye. "I . . . never . . . made . . . that . . . commercial!"

"Oh," I said. "Wow. It's an amazing simulation, then. Like I said, I've probably seen that thing a hundred times, and I never noticed it was a sim. And I used to work for Canny Simulations, Inc., so I've seen a hell of a lot of them."

"It's not a sim," said Priya. "It's me."

"But you just said—"

"I know! I don't know how to explain it, but that's me in the commercial, even though I never made it. Don't you think I would know?"

"Know what? That it's you, or that you never made it?"

"Both!"

I sighed. I wanted to help her, but she wasn't making any sense. This girl didn't need a private investigator; she needed a psychiatrist.

"I did sign a contract with the Prima Facie people a while back," she was saying. "But I never agreed to have my likeness used in any advertisements. They can't legally use a sim of me to sell anything."

"Hmm," I said. "Well, using unlicensed sims to sell products isn't unheard of, although it would be rare for such a high-profile advertising campaign. There was probably some misunderstanding about the licensing. If your attorney—"

"You're not listening!" Priya shrieked. "It's not a sim. It's *me*. I can *tell*."

I threw up my hands. I'm a pretty patient guy (witness my ongoing tolerance for Erasmus Keane), but continuing in this vein was pointless. "Listen, Priya," I said. "You seem like a really nice person. Honestly, a lot nicer than I would have expected. Smart, too. Not to mention without a doubt the most beautiful woman I've ever met. But, sweetheart, I can't help you. Erasmus Keane can't help you. Your life isn't in danger. Men stare at you because you're gorgeous. You get weird letters because you're famous. You don't remember every commercial you've made because you're exhausted from filming too many commercials. Mystery solved. I'll see you to the door." I got to my feet. She did not. I sighed.

"Noogus," she said, "was my teddy bear."

"Eh?" I said.

"When I was little. His name was actually Nicholas, but I couldn't pronounce it, so I called him Noogus. Nobody knew about that except my mother. I lost Noogus shortly after my mother died, when I was four."

"Huh," said a voice from behind her. I had left the door open a crack, and I now noticed Erasmus Keane was standing there, just outside my office. Priya stood, turning to face him.

"Wow!" Keane said, taking a look at Priya. He walked into the office and began to duckwalk around her the way he had with the sheep. "You should be a model," he said. "For humanity, I mean."

"Erasmus Keane," I said, "meet Priya Mistry, the internationally acclaimed star of *DiZzy Girl* and numerous television commercials she may or may not have actually made." Priya scowled at me, and I shrugged. "I was just about to show her out."

"What on Earth for?" said Keane, still staring at Priya. "She's gorgeous. And completely crackers, judging by the conversation you two were having."

"How long were you standing there?" I demanded.

"Long enough to know that this little chickadee has gone around the bend. Classic narcissist with paranoiac tendencies. She's on the verge, this one."

Priya bore this assault with quiet dignity, which had the unfortunate effect of reminding me of Mark the sheep.

"Stop objectifying the poor thing," I snapped at last.

Keane shrugged. He stood up straight and held out his hand to Priya. "We'll take the case," he said.

"What?" I growled. I turned to Priya. "Give us a moment, please." She nodded uncertainly. I grabbed Keane's arm and pulled him into the hallway, closing the office door behind me.

"Why the hell would we take her case?" I demanded. "You just said she was nuts!"

"Oh, she is, most definitely," said Keane. "But she's also receiving letters from her teddy bear, and that's worth looking into."

THREE

There had been no talking Keane out of taking Priya's case, which he had taken to calling the Case of the Concerned Teddy Bear. I had suggested this be amended to the Case of the Concerned and Surprisingly Literate Teddy Bear, but Keane preferred pith to thoroughness. So now we were working two cases simultaneously, trying to find a lost sheep and trying to protect Priya Mistry from probably imaginary assassins. I didn't like the idea of double-booking cases, but I had to admit I was a little relieved not to have to kick Priya to the curb. The desire to save damsels from dragons was so deeply ingrained in males of our culture that even the ordinarily oblivious Erasmus Keane seemed to possess it. The fact that the dragons in this case were almost certainly imaginary made little difference.

I flew Priya to the Ritz-Carlton, where she had been staying while working on *DiZzy Girl*. I handed her over to her bodyguard, a massive Samoan who was pacing in the lobby. The bodyguard was either beside himself with concern about Priya or he was an Oscar-level actor. I thought the guy was going to burst into tears. The letter Priya had shown us had said to trust no one, but I found it hard to imagine that this man meant her any harm. For a split second I entertained the insane notion that this was Noogus himself, all grown-up and returned to watch over his beloved Priya. In any case, if her bodyguard was going to kill her, he'd presumably have done it already.

Priya feigned being drunk and claimed she just needed to sneak out to spend some time with a friend. I played the part of the friend, which mostly consisted of me quaking in fear and apologizing profusely to the Samoan. The role came naturally to me. I suspected I'd be able to outmaneuver the bodyguard if it came down to it, but there's something primally terrifying about a man that size. Priya shot me a fearful glance as she walked to the elevator with the giant man, and I gave her what I hoped was a reassuring nod. I'd told her that Keane would have her under surveillance for her safety, but I could tell she had her doubts. She might have been reassured to know that the small nondescript man who entered the elevator along with her and the Samoan was in Keane's employ, but we found it was generally better in these cases for the client to remain unaware of the identity of our operative.

Pavel Kratchovil was comically diminutive next to the Samoan, and I had to suppress a laugh until the elevator door closed. Pavel's unobtrusive nature was an asset, because it was Pavel's job to remain unnoticed. He would exit the elevator with Priya and her bodyguard and enter the room across the hall from hers, which he had reserved per Keane's instruction. He would spend the night, staring at a monitor connected to a peephole camera pointed at Priya's door, so he would know if anyone entered or left her room. If anyone did, he would alert Keane. In the morning, he would follow Priya to the set of *DiZzy Girl* and do his best to keep tabs on her while she worked. It would be difficult to keep a close eye on her during the shoot, but Keane figured it would be pretty unlikely for anyone to try to kill her on the set, with hundreds of people around, and if somebody was trying to kill her, then it would be a lot easier to flush them out if our operative remained incognito. I don't think either of us really believed she was in any danger, but we had taken the job, and that meant doing it right. The first priority was to ensure Priya's safety as best we could. While Pavel kept an eye on her, Keane and I could look into the threat, such as it was.

My role in this was to consult with one April Morgan, an intellectual property lawyer I had met while working at CSI. April and I had dated a few times, but that was shortly after Gwen disappeared, and it was pretty clear that things weren't going to work romantically between me and April anyway. We remained friends, though, and occasionally I relied on her legal expertise on cases. Sometimes this meant hiring her as a consultant; usually it just meant bribing her with dinner. Keane had retrieved, from some dimly lit alcove of his brain, the fact that April's old law firm, Ballard and Greene, had once represented Marcus and Shea, the advertising agency behind the Prima Facie commercials. He wanted April to find out whether Ballard and Greene had processed a contract for Priya to appear in the ads. I figured I could probably get this information from April for the price of dinner.

I had called April before taking Priya back to her hotel, and she had agreed to pick me up at six P.M. When I got back to our building, Keane was ensconced in his office, presumably meditating on errant sheep or sympathetic teddy bears. I had just enough time to change my shirt, wash my face, and put on a second coat of deodorant. April drove us to a local Thai place she liked, and we sat outside. It was unusually warm and humid for January, though not unpleasantly so. We spent half an hour catching up. I told her of the day's events, doing my best to present a professional account of my meeting with Priya Mistry, but April clearly wasn't buying it.

"Is she pretty?" April asked.

I hesitated. I was fairly certain April no longer had any romantic intentions toward me, but women can be funny about this sort of thing. Best to tread lightly.

"You know," I said, "there are some faces that look good on TV, but not so much in person."

"Uh-huh," April said. "So you're saying Priya Mistry is not attractive in person?"

I shrugged in a heroic effort to appear nonchalant. "Well, she's not *un*attractive. She's just a kid, really. You don't really think about how young she is when you see her on television. It's hard to think of her as an actual person."

"You don't think of her as a person? What do you think of her as?"

I spread my hands in a gesture of supplication. There was a point at which silence was the best tactical response. April stared at me for some time, her face completely expressionless. Then a smile crept across her lips. She broke into a laugh. "God, you're easy," she said.

"Heh?" I replied.

"Relax," she said. "I'm just having some fun with you. Priya Mistry is gorgeous. Any chance you can introduce me?"

I sank into my chair and exhaled, feeling like I'd just gone ten rounds with a sparring bot. "No," I grumbled irritably. "Not a chance in hell."

"Oh, stop," April chided. "You should have seen the goofy look on your face when I picked you up. You looked like you were in love. Frankly, I'm relieved to find out it's not the sheep."

I couldn't help but laugh at that. I really need to give April more credit.

"So, what's she like?" April asked. "Don't tell me she's a total bitch offscreen. I love her character on *DiZzy Girl*. Lie to me if you have to."

"She's nice," I said. "Honestly. Surprisingly levelheaded. Except . . ."

"What?"

"Well, I think she might be crazy."

"You just said she's levelheaded."

"Yeah, she's the levelheaded sort of crazy. The kind of crazy that looks you in the eye and tells you in all seriousness that she's getting letters from her teddy bear."

"Letters from her . . . ?"

"I don't have the energy to explain," I said. "Honestly, I don't understand it myself. She's obviously in distress, though. I feel bad for her. She thinks someone is trying to kill her, but it's all in her head."

"But Keane took her case?"

"Well, yeah," I said. "I guess he thinks there's more to it."

"This poor girl is imagining she's in danger, and Erasmus Keane is taking her money to protect her?"

I shrugged. "You know Keane. It's not about the money. It's about the puzzle."

"But you said yourself the puzzle is in her head. Does Keane think he's a psychologist now too?"

"I don't know what Keane thinks," I said irritably. "He doesn't tell me anything."

"I guess I hit a sore spot," said April.

"Sorry," I said. "I go a little nuts, dealing with him all day."

"I understand," said April. "I'm just worried Keane is taking advantage of Priya."

"You and me both," I said. "Keane can be a real asshole. But to be fair, I've never seen him intentionally hurt someone just for his own amusement. If Keane agreed to take this case, it's because he thinks there's a mystery to be solved. And you have to admit, there's no one better at solving mysteries. You've seen the good he's done."

"Hmm," said April. "It seems to me that the good he does

is mostly incidental. What Keane does is find interesting situations to insert himself into, and then alter things to suit his sense of . . . I don't know, aesthetics, or whatever it is."

"What about the hologram case? He found that kid, Julio Chavez, and brought him to justice."

"Technically, he got Julio Chavez a job with CSI," she said. "And got you to quit. Not two weeks later you were Erasmus Keane's employee. Keane manipulated that case to get what he wanted. Hell, for all I know, he put that Chavez kid up to it in the first place. And he still hasn't done a thing to help you find Gwen."

"Wow," I said. "And I thought Priya sounded paranoid. Just so I know I've got this straight: you're saying Erasmus Keane incited a fourteen-year-old kid to engage in intellectual property theft so CSI would hire Keane, which would allow him to humiliate me, causing me to quit so he could then offer me a job? So the entire hologram case was a big scam of Keane's to . . . what, get somebody to make his coffee for him?"

"You do make a mean pot of joe," said April.

"Be serious."

"Seriously?" said April. "I don't think Keane is evil. But I don't completely trust him either. You know what he did before he set up shop on the DZ border."

I sighed. This was a favorite topic of April's. She's something of a conspiracy theory buff. "Can we not talk about Keane anymore? I have to deal with him all day, and then—"

"Precrime," said April. "He worked for a secret unit of the LAPD whose purpose was to predict and stop crimes before they happened."

"You're being dramatic," I said. "First of all, this is all rumor and hearsay. Second, *if* that unit existed, its goal was primarily to predict social unrest. Riots and that sort of thing."

"Sure," said April. "That's how it started. Then, after Santa Monica, they started getting funding from the Pentagon to develop ways of predicting terrorist attacks."

"Rumors and unfounded conjecture," I said, without much enthusiasm. April and I had had this argument before, and I wasn't really interested in going through the motions again.

"I was working at Ballard and Greene at the time," April said. "I heard things. I remember when I first heard the name Erasmus Keane. Nobody knew who he was. The LAPD claimed he didn't exist. And I suppose they were telling the truth, in a sense. There are no records of any Erasmus Keane before he set up shop as a private investigator."

"Phenomenological inquisitor," I said, more out of habit than an attempt to be contrary. "Look, I know 'Erasmus Keane' is a pseudonym. He's made no secret of that."

"But he hasn't told you his real name."

"No. Nor has he told me his hat size or favorite Weavil Brothers song. Are you going to help me or not?"

"Of course," said April, with a smile. "I'll find out whatever I can about Priya Mistry. Just promise me you'll watch out for her."

I promised.

FOUR

It was still early when April dropped me off, so I decided to recommence my research on Esper. Keane was still holed up in his office, and I had no idea what he planned to do in the morning. Evidently, Priya's case was at the forefront of his mind, so in the interest of not duplicating our efforts, I figured I'd spend my time on the lost sheep.

I spent the next four hours browsing articles about the Esper Corporation, genetic engineering, and organ transplantation. I didn't learn much of interest, although I ran across some fascinating speculation on a few conspiracy websites about illegal research occurring shortly after the Collapse. During the Collapse, law and order largely broke down, which led to a surge in criminal activity. Many large corporations were known to have taken advantage of the lapse in enforcement to engage in a variety of illegal and unethical behavior, from insider trading to corporate espionage. Most of these transgressions were likely opportunistic; large corporations tend to be creatures of habit, fearful of change, and slow to take advantage of sudden changes in their environment. But certain sorts of research flirted daily with the legal and ethical constraints separating *what is* from *what if?*, and those pushing the boundaries didn't have to be told twice that the federal government was going to be busy putting out fires (often literally) for a few months. A few months turned into three years, and rumors abounded that certain companies, Esper among them, had engaged in some very questionable activities during the law enforcement holiday. Research into human cloning, animal-human hybrids, and illegal bioweaponry were all rumored to have taken place, and in some cases the rumors were confirmed by federal investigations conducted post-Collapse. A mere handful of cases made the news, but only the most naïve observer believed this was a reliable indicator of the scope of the misconduct. Other than a few rumors, Esper had managed to keep its alleged infractions out of the news. Whether this was because they had ceased any illegal activities or had been smart enough to cover their tracks was unclear.

I knocked off a little after midnight, knowing Keane would likely want to start early the next morning. I dreamt of a frightened sheep in a laboratory. Keane was there, grinning at me. "I have taken measure of this sheep's soul," he announced, and then stepped aside and swept his hand toward the sheep, as if introducing it. I saw that the sheep was completely shorn, and its wool lay in piles around its feet. Keane shook his head, and I saw he was holding a pair of shears. "There's never enough wool," he said. "No matter how much you give them, they always want more."

"Someone is trying to kill me," said the sheep. "Trust no one."

"I think I can get a bit more," said Keane, snicking the shears together and turning back to the sheep.

The sheep screamed.

"I know you're in there," said Keane, and the snick-snick of the shears had inexplicably morphed into a deep thudding. "Fowler!" Keane shouted. "You hear me? I know you're in there!"

I opened my eyes in the dull gray light of my bedroom, and the sparse rays poking through the boarded-up windows told me it was dawn.

"Yeah, I hear you!" I yelled back. "Give me a minute."

I took a quick shower, shaved, brushed my teeth, and threw on some clothes, all while Keane banged on the door to my quarters about every forty-five seconds or so. In between these percussive bursts he said something about conducting interviews with employees of Esper Corporation. Evidently, he'd gotten a call from Esper's vice president of research and development, Jason Banerjee, who was eager to have Keane continue his investigation now that a "key suspect has been eliminated." They'd lined up interviews with all the employees who had access to the lab.

We got to Esper just after eight A.M. A security guard ushered us into a conference room, outside of which three lab coat–wearing employees were already waiting in the hall. None of them looked particularly happy to be there, and their demeanor wasn't improved by Keane insisting that the interviews be delayed until the room had been adequately stocked with Dr Pepper and Circus Peanuts. It was almost eight thirty when we finally started.

We had forty-six employees to interview, and I didn't hold out much hope of getting through them all in a day. Fortunately, the interviews went quickly, with Keane disqualifying most of the prospective sheep thieves with only a question or two. He didn't even bother to interview several of the employees on the list; Esper had provided dossiers—complete with criminal records, employment histories, and credit reports—on all the suspects, and Keane had evidently been able to eliminate many of them based on this information.

He seemed to have a fairly solid idea of what a sheep thief was—or at least was not. I had to trust his judgment on the matter, but when we'd completed the interviews without identifying a likely suspect, I began to wonder whether he'd been too quick in his assessments.

There was only one employee who seemed to interest Keane at all, but I found it hard to imagine she was our thief. Her name was Stephanie Kemp, and she was a cute, plump brunette in her midtwenties. She was a lab technician with good credit, no criminal history, and a spotless though unremarkable work history. Working for Esper was her first job out of college. Keane had allowed me to handle most of the interviews while he wandered around the room, chewing on Circus Peanuts and occasionally interjecting an impertinent question, but he definitely took an interest in Stephanie Kemp. He spent a good ten minutes asking her about everything from her taste in music to her hair color.

"What was that about?" I asked when he finally dismissed her.

Keane shrugged.

"You don't think she's our thief."

He laughed. "Not a chance."

"So, what's with the grilling?"

"Just playing," said Keane, with a grin. "Such a sweet girl. Very cooperative."

I sighed and let in the next subject. We interviewed three more employees after Stephanie, but Keane showed no interest in any of them. It was nearly six P.M.

"Next!" Keane yelled.

"That's it," I said. "Unless you've changed your mind on some of the ones you dismissed out of hand."

Keane shook his head. "We're missing somebody." He slumped into a chair and began riffling through the dossiers again. "No. No. No. No. No. Wait, what about this guy? Hugo

Díaz. Lab tech. Lousy credit. Eyes of a sheep thief. I didn't dismiss this guy."

I took the file from him and pulled out the last page, which I handed to Keane. I pointed at the relevant line. It read:

DECEASED JAN. 18

"Two days before the sheep disappeared," I said. "Went home early on Friday afternoon, complaining of heartburn. Was found by his wife, dead of a heart attack early Saturday morning. The sheep theft occurred sometime Sunday night."

"Hmm," said Keane.

"I'll admit the timing is a little suspicious, but there just isn't any way Díaz could have stolen the sheep."

"But he could have been in on it. Working for a third party. The deal went wrong, and he ended up dead."

"The police found no evidence of foul play. And we know whoever overrode the security system was someone with access to the lab. Someone who could pass Esper's biometric scans: voiceprint, fingerprint, and retinal imaging. So unless someone physically dragged Díaz's corpse down to Esper, I can't see how he could have been much help in the theft. If there's an inside man, it's someone else."

"Hmm," said Keane again.

"What?" I asked. "He's dead, Keane. He didn't do it."

"Perhaps," said Keane.

"No, Keane," I said. "Not 'perhaps.' Death isn't a detail you can overlook. It's a hard and fast category. Dead men don't steal sheep."

"I just don't think we should dismiss him so quickly, is all," said Keane.

"You dismissed one woman because her shoes were too tight!" I exclaimed in exasperation.

"*Three sizes* too tight," said Keane. "That's a woman who

is willing to live in near-constant pain in order to maintain the illusion that her feet are slightly smaller than they are. She's not what you'd consider a creative problem-solver. She lacks the ambition and the imagination to execute a crime of this scope."

"So does Hugo Díaz," I said. "On account of his being *dead*."

"Convenient, isn't it?" said Keane. "Is there going to be an autopsy?"

"I highly doubt it," I said. "The man was forty-eight years old and sixty pounds overweight. He left work complaining of chest pains. His wife found him dead in bed the next morning. It's not exactly what you would call a suspicious death."

The door opened, and a slightly built, well-dressed man walked into the room.

"Mr. Keane," he said. "Mr. Fowler. I'm Jason Banerjee, Esper's vice president for research and development. I understand you're done with interviews for the day. Late for another appointment?"

I shook his hand. Banerjee looked to be in his late thirties—which meant, for a man in his position, he was some combination of brilliant, politically savvy, and phenomenally wealthy. Probably all three. He was dark-skinned and handsome, with cruel, clever eyes.

"Nope," said Keane. "We've talked to all the employees we need to."

"You have a suspect then?"

"Working a case like this is an iterative process," said Keane. "Speaking of which, we need an autopsy for Hugo Díaz."

"Díaz? The technician who had a heart attack? Why?"

"Alleged heart attack," said Keane. "And if I knew why I needed the autopsy, I wouldn't need it."

"Díaz was our employee. We don't have the authority—"

"Next of kin?"

"Wife," I said, examining Hugo's file. "Jessica."

"Convince his wife it's necessary," said Keane to Banerjee. "Bribe her if you have to. I need to know what killed Hugo Díaz."

"I'll see what I can do," said Banerjee. "This better not be a wild-goose chase. I need that sheep back as soon as possible. So, what's next?"

Keane checked his comm display. "*Now* we're late for another appointment."

FIVE

Priya had given us her complete schedule for the next several days, which consisted almost entirely of leaving her hotel early in the morning to go work on the *DiZzy Girl* set and then returning to the hotel sometime after dark. Tonight, though, she was supposed to make an appearance at a party at Élan Durham's house in the Hollywood Hills. When she mentioned it, I told her I didn't think it was a good idea to go to any unfamiliar places if she thought she was in danger, but Keane thought it was best to keep up appearances. He'd asked her to get us added to the guest list so we could keep an eye on her.

We made the trip mostly in silence, but as we neared Élan Durham's house, I decided to bring up something that had been bothering me.

"Do you actually think Priya is in danger?" I asked.

"Absolutely," Keane answered without hesitation. "I wouldn't have taken the case if I didn't think she was in danger."

"We have no evidence anyone intends her harm, other than her own testimony."

"You're forgetting the letter from Noogus," said Keane.

"Seriously?" I asked.

"You saw the letter with your own eyes. She didn't imagine it."

"You realize it's not difficult to write a letter to yourself, right? It's a short step from imagining somebody is trying to kill you to writing yourself a letter warning you about it."

"It is a step, though."

"I don't follow."

Keane sighed. "A letter is a physical projection of an idea. Paranoia is inward-focused and self-reinforcing. Your classical paranoiac isn't going to write a letter to herself warning about the conspiracy. There's no need. The paranoiac has all the evidence she needs. It's everywhere she looks."

"But she's not using it to convince herself. She's using it to convince *us*."

"Perhaps. But that doesn't fit the standard model of paranoia either. A paranoiac isn't going to seek out strangers to tell them about the conspiracy. And she certainly wouldn't manufacture evidence of the conspiracy to convince them. That's a complete inversion of typical paranoid behavior."

"So you don't think she's paranoid."

Keane shook his head. "No, she's clearly paranoid. But she's something else, too."

"What?"

"There are two possibilities, as far as I can tell," said Keane. "Either she's genuinely in danger, or . . ." He trailed off, seemingly lost in thought.

"Yes?" I prompted.

"Huh?" said Keane, apparently unaware of having left his rumination unfinished.

"She's in danger or . . . ?"

"Oh, or she's a whole new kind of crazy." He grinned at me. "Either way, though, it's exciting, isn't it?"

I shook my head. I was starting to think April was right. Priya Mistry needed professional help, and not from a phenomenological inquisitor. God knows how much damage Keane might do to the poor girl's psyche by the time he had tired of toying with her. On the other hand, it wasn't like I had the power to stop Keane from pursuing Priya's case—and there was a possibility she really was in danger. Probably the best thing to do now was to follow Keane's lead and try to step in if things got out of hand.

We caught up to Pavel at the foot of the driveway. His beat-up Suburban, parked on the side of the winding mountain road, was completely out of place in this neighborhood. I gave him a quick debriefing, which didn't amount to much: he had followed Priya's limo to the *DiZzy Girl* set, hung out there for the day, followed it back to her hotel, and then followed it to Durham's place. Security wouldn't let him up the driveway, so he had parked and waited.

Pavel was one of a handful of ad hoc operatives who were occasionally employed by Keane to do surveillance and other tedious legwork. Pavel was Keane's favorite, because the man had no ambition whatsoever. The way Keane figured it, no ambition meant no complications. Pavel never asked for a raise, and there was never any serious threat he'd fall prey to a bribe or blackmail. Other than the occasional check from Keane and a little income from selling synthetic drugs on the beaches around Malibu, Pavel had no visible means of support. He slept in his car and spent the vast majority of his time surfing. He used the occasional assignment from Keane as an opportunity to test whatever black-market synthetic stimulant had recently come into his possession. That was another reason Keane liked him: when Pavel was on an assignment, he didn't sleep. I sent him home, or wherever it is that he goes when he isn't working for Keane.

We pulled into the driveway. There followed an anxious few seconds during which I was convinced Priya didn't have the presence of mind to remember to have us added to the guest list, but the guard at the foot of the driveway waved us on after a cursory check of our IDs. We pulled up the long driveway toward Élan Durham's massive multilevel compound. Keane tossed the keys to a valet who did an admirable job of hiding his dismay at having to park a fifteen-year-old Nissan aircar, and we went inside. The house was suitably capacious, impressively appointed with expensive-looking abstract sculpture, and populated with scores of rich and beautiful people. I began to feel underdressed and out of place.

"So, now what?" I asked, scanning the attendees. "Wait for somebody with a lead pipe to lure Priya into the conservatory?"

"You keep an eye on Priya," said Keane. "I'm going to poke around a bit." With that, he snatched a glass of wine from a tray as a waiter passed, and then disappeared into the throng. I sighed and shouldered my way through the crowd, looking for Priya. It didn't take me long to find her. A sort of nexus had formed around her, with lesser celebrities loitering in her gravitational pull. A strange dynamic seemed to have asserted itself, with Priya's presence simultaneously attracting and repelling other guests according to some unconscious but inexorable social hierarchy, each guest finding his or her own place in relation to Priya. She looked stunning as always; tonight she wore a tight-fitting strapless red dress. Her long black hair was down, and she wore diamond earrings that glittered in the dim light of Élan Durham's vast living room. It was difficult not to stare.

I didn't intend to talk to her; Keane had made it clear we were to remain incognito, and he'd instructed Priya to play dumb if she ever saw us. My plan was simply to get close enough that I could keep an eye on her and intervene if I thought she was under threat. It was a little silly, since I didn't really believe she was in any danger, and couldn't possibly have protected her from every potential attacker in that room anyway, but maybe it would do her mental state some good to see me there.

As I got close to Priya, though, I began to feel uncomfortably self-conscious. It was bad enough I was underdressed and out of my element; I was also conspicuously alone. I told myself to pretend I was some eccentric investor who didn't need stylish clothes or the company of other people, but it was no good. I managed to get ahold of a drink, which at least gave me something to do with my hands. I felt the eyes of my societal betters boring into me, and while I didn't dare look, I was certain Priya herself was staring at me, those bottomless eyes demanding I account for my presumption. It made no sense: yesterday Priya had been on the verge of collapsing into my arms, but today I couldn't get within ten feet of her. One thought dominated my brain: I didn't belong there, and everyone knew it.

An opportunity to save my dignity presented itself as a balding executive type extracted himself from a conversation with a pretty young redhead in a green dress who was now drifting awkwardly at the periphery of the nexus. I walked over to her and whipped up one of my best lines.

"That dress looks really good with your hair," I said.

"Um, thanks," she said, eyeing me uncertainly. Under the guise of grabbing her a drink from a passing waiter, I maneuvered to where I could see Priya, who was chatting with TC Gemmel, a supporting actor on one of Flagship's other big shows, *Hal Correia, Street Doctor*. I held out the glass to the redhead.

"I don't drink," she said. "Are you a writer?"

I shrugged and took a swallow of the wine. "No," I said. "Why?"

"Well," she said, "you're not dressed like a producer. And . . ."

"I don't look like an actor," I said, picking up on her drift. "I'm a consultant. Working with Élan Durham on a new detective show." I figured it was a harmless lie. I'm sure I wasn't the only guy at this party bullshitting about working on a show with Élan Durham. At least my motives were pure.

"Oh, how exciting!" she exclaimed. "Is it going to be casting soon? I just did a three-episode guest spot on *DiZzy Girl*, and I'm ready for what's next."

More like desperate, I thought. Poor thing. She was probably a beauty queen in Podunk, Missouri, but in LA she was just another aspiring starlet waiting tables in between bit parts.

"We start casting on Monday," I lied.

"Really?" the girl asked. "I didn't see anything in the trades."

"Closed auditions," I said. "But if you're interested, I can see if I can get you in."

"Wow, that would be great!" she gushed.

"Sure, just toss me your info. I'm Blake, by the way."

"Gina," she said. "Nice to meet you, Blake."

"You too," I said. "So, you worked on *DiZzy Girl,* huh? What was that like?"

"What do you mean?"

"Oh, you know, working with a big star like Priya Mistry . . ."

The enthusiasm drained from her face. "God damn it," she said. "Are you even really a consultant?"

"Sure," I said weakly. Damn it. I had pushed her too fast, and she had seen right through me.

"What's the name of the show?"

"*Street . . . Detective,*" I managed. Clever, Fowler.

"You must think I'm pretty pathetic," she said. "Well, maybe I am. But I'll have my own TV show before you get in Priya Mistry's pants." With that, she turned and stomped away. I hate parties. Serves me right for lying to the girl, but what was I going to do? Tell her I was on the lookout for signs of a vast conspiracy against Priya Mistry?

As I mulled this, I became aware that Priya's conversation with TC Gemmel was becoming animated. Heads began to turn. "... can you forget something like that?" TC demanded. "I thought I meant something to you!"

Priya was backing away helplessly, sputtering half explanations about being under a lot of pressure and not getting much sleep. I could tell, though, that this guy wasn't going to let it go. He was trembling with anger and hurt, and it looked like it wouldn't take much to make him turn violent. I started walking in his direction, but then I saw Priya's massive bodyguard, the All-Grown-Up Noogus, moving to intercept him. *Fine,* I thought. *Let Noogus handle it.*

Priya looked like she was on the verge of a breakdown, and I was tempted to go to her, make sure she was okay. But there wasn't much I could do for her, and Keane had wanted me to remain incognito. So for the moment I just stood and watched as All-Grown-Up Noogus got TC Gemmel in a half nelson and escorted him away from Priya. But then two men in suits approached Priya, trying to calm her down. They were both over six feet tall; one looked like a Filipino, and the other was white, with bright red hair pulled back in a ponytail. All eyes were on Priya, so nobody noticed Red was pulling a syringe from his pocket. Nobody but me, anyway.

I dove forward, grabbing Red's wrist tightly and then twisting his arm behind his back while squeezing hard. The syringe dropped to the floor. Priya was now screaming and crying, trying to free her arm from the grip of the second man. I gave Red a shove between the shoulder blades, and he stumbled into his friend. The second man released his grip on Priya, and the two men fell in a heap on the floor. So far, so good. Now to get Priya somewhere safe. Out of the corner of my eye, I saw Keane approaching, a concerned look on his face. "Fowler!" he yelled, as if to warn me.

Then something hit me on the back of the head, and everything went black.

SIX

I came to on a couch inside a luxuriously decked-out office. My head throbbed.

I sat up and saw I was not alone. A few feet away, facing a large walnut desk, sat Erasmus Keane. Behind the desk sat Élan Durham.

"Good morning," said Durham, with a smile. He was nursing a drink.

"Priya," I managed to grunt.

"Priya is fine," said Durham. "That drama queen TC Gemmel got her a little worked up, but she's resting in a bedroom down the hall."

I glanced at Keane, who gave me a slight nod.

"Would you care for a drink, Mr. Fowler?" Durham held a half-empty tumbler in his hand, and I noticed Keane was working on one of his own. A very large man in tan slacks and a black turtleneck, who had at first escaped my attention, stood stock-still against a wall to my right. I wasn't sure how long I'd been unconscious, but it didn't seem like it had been more than a minute or two.

I shook my head and immediately regretted it. "Maybe some water."

"Sure," Durham said. The large man disappeared for a moment into an adjoining room and came back with a bottle of water, which he handed to me. He returned to his post without a word. The guy had to be six-foot-four, an inverted mountain of muscle. He moved like a wrestler and wore a gun in a shoulder holster. My own gun seemed to be missing. I wondered if I could get across the room and disarm Turtleneck before he could react. *Maybe,* I thought, *if the pounding in my head would stop for five seconds.*

"Sorry about your head," said Durham. "My security people are very protective of Priya. Brian may have gotten a little carried away." Turtleneck, whose name was evidently Brian, gave a little smirk. "Now, would one of you gentlemen care to explain why you've been sniffing around my house, asking questions about Priya?"

Neither of us said a word.

Brian took a step forward. He was squeezing his knuckles in his thumbs, cracking them one by one. You could see his muscles moving even under the fabric of the sweater. I imagine this was supposed to intimidate me. It did, a little.

I leaned forward on the couch, rubbing the base of my skull with my right hand. Brian was maybe fifteen feet away. I rolled my shoulders, then twisted my spine until it gave a satisfying crack. I straightened my legs, then bent them again. I leaned forward, spreading both of my palms out on the carpet. The throbbing in my head got exponentially worse. I leaned back and closed my eyes.

"Nothing to say for yourself, Mr. Keane?" said Durham. "I thought you were the brains of the operation." He turned to me. "I suppose that makes you the brawn, Mr. Fowler. What a pathetic operation you two are running. I've stumped the brain and incapacitated the body."

"Let me explain something to you," I said, opening my eyes and fixing them on Durham. "If you want to know why Mr. Keane and I are here, you have to understand what it is

I do for Mr. Keane." Flex muscles, release. Get the blood flowing. Fifteen feet. Could I do it? If I didn't black out from the pain in my head, I thought I could.

"You're stalling, Fowler," said Durham. "If you like, I can have Brian give you a reminder of the seriousness—"

I leaned forward again, mimicking my hunched-over stretching pose of a moment earlier. Except this time I dropped into a sprinter's crouch. Held it for just long enough to get my balance, then shot forward, making a beeline for Brian. My legs were rubbery, but they held. I'd done my best to get the blood moving to my extremities, but there was a pretty good chance the sudden movement would cause me to black out. And any second now the pain in my head would register.

It hit just as I reached Brian, like a grenade exploding at the base of my skull. I was relying on momentum now, coasting on a wave of agony. I brought my right hand back and made a fist. Brian saw it and bobbed to his left, which is what I was counting on.

Here's the thing about bodyguards: they weren't born bodyguards. They did something else first. Most are ex-military or civilian law enforcement. But the really high-paid ones, the ones who work for people like Durham, tend to be heavyweight boxers or wrestlers, for the simple reason that they look impressive. Appearances are important, particularly in Hollywood.

That isn't to say Brian was incompetent. I'm sure he was well trained; he could probably hit a dime at twenty-five yards with that Glock .40 on his chest. But he had a weakness, which was that he was at heart a wrestler. You could tell from his neck muscles and the way he walked, his arms hanging in front of him as if he expected any moment to have to drop on all fours. So when a crazy man threw a punch at him, he reacted like a wrestler: bob to the side and try to take advantage of the attacker's loss of balance. Solid tactic, if this were a wrestling match. It wasn't.

Brian grabbed my wrist with his right and twisted hard. It probably would have hurt a lot if I didn't already have Hiroshima going off between my ears. He slammed me against the wall behind him, grinding my wrist into the middle of my back. Point to Brian. He had me in an unbreakable hold. Unfortunately for Brian, I was now pointing his own gun at his abdomen. I'd wager that until he felt the cold steel of the barrel creeping up under his turtleneck, he'd completely forgotten he even *had* a gun. I'd slipped it out of its holster with my left while he was focused on my right. Wrestlers.

It was an incredibly awkward position to be in, my face smashed up against the wall and both of my arms twisted behind my back. But I held the trump card. Brian could break my arm, but I could perforate his colon and possibly paralyze him from the waist down. Hard to make a living as a bodyguard in a wheelchair.

The only problem with this plan was that I was rapidly losing consciousness. My eyes were watering from the pain in my head, and I could feel my vision darkening around the edges—not that I could see anything with my nose smashed against a wall. I couldn't feel my fingers, and it was all I could do to keep the gun barrel pressed up against Brian's belly. My only hope was that Brian's wrestler brain would finish its cost-benefit analysis of the situation before I collapsed. As an added bonus, I was pretty sure that if I passed out before Brian loosened his grip, he'd rip my arm right out of its socket. So that was a whole new sort of pain to look forward to, if I ever woke up again.

"Brian!" I heard Durham yell. "Get him under control!"

I'm not sure what he was expecting Brian to do exactly, but Brian was frozen with indecision. Evidently, Durham didn't realize I had a gun on Brian. I did, didn't I? I couldn't feel my hand anymore.

As my vision blurred, my thoughts did as well. Where was Keane? Hadn't he been in the room with me? Why wasn't he helping? We had come here on a case, I seemed to recall. Something about a sheep. Someone was trying to murder a sheep? That didn't sound right. Where was *here*, anyway? Some kind of party? It didn't feel like a party. It was no use; I wasn't going to be able to make sense of it. I just needed to lie down. Lie down and sleep.

A moment of blackness, then:

I was sitting on the floor, my back against the wall, the Glock about to slip out of my left hand. Brian, standing a few feet away, looked like he was about to make a move for the gun.

"Uh-uh," I muttered, managing to get a slightly tighter grip on the gun. I don't think I could have pulled the trigger if I tried, but evidently I appeared threatening enough to make Brian rethink his plans. I took a deep breath and shifted the gun to my right hand. My head still felt like a bass drum at the Rose Bowl parade, but feeling was coming back into my fingers. Brian must have made the right choice—and just in time, too. I didn't remember turning around or sliding down the wall, but some part of my brain must have been functioning well enough to keep the gun pointed more or less in Brian's direction.

"That," I said with as much bravado as I could muster, "is why Keane keeps me around."

Durham glared at me a moment and then broke into a laugh. "Well done, Mr. Fowler. I guess you do earn your keep after all."

Keane finished his drink and turned to face Durham. "Now how about you tell us what's going on with Priya."

"Put down the gun, and I'll tell you what I know," said Durham.

"Nice try," I said.

"You've made your point, Mr. Fowler," said Durham, with a touch of irritation. "You're not going to murder me in my own home. Drop the gun, and we'll talk things over. I have nothing to hide."

"I'll give Brian his gun when I get mine," I said. I got to my feet, still pointing the Glock at him, while doing my best to ignore the sheet-metal-stamping plant operating in my skull.

Durham nodded at Brian, and he turned and walked to a portrait that hung on the wall. I recognized the subject as Selah Fiore, the ex-actress who was currently the CEO of Flagship Media. The picture was from her glory days, some thirty years ago, when she was still quite the looker. Brian removed the portrait, tapped a combination on a wall safe, and opened the door. He picked up the gun and handed it to me, handle first. I returned the favor. I waited for him to holster his gun before I did the same.

"All right," said Keane. "Tell us what you know about Priya."

Durham shrugged. "I'm not sure what you mean."

"Bullshit," I growled. "The girl is scared out of her mind. You parade her in front of strangers at parties like she's some kind of prize animal. Meanwhile, you've got men standing by with syringes, for Christ's sake."

Durham sighed. "What's going on with Priya is that she's a frightened little girl who became famous way too fast. I don't 'parade' her in front of strangers; I invite her to parties, and I encourage her to attend because it's good for her to meet people away from the set. And yes, I have people looking out for her safety. Occasionally she has panic attacks, and sedatives help calm her down. Her personal physician recommended these measures."

"Who does this physician work for?" I asked. "Flagship Media?"

"Who do *you* work for?" said Durham.

"We're asking the questions, remember?" I said.

"We have Priya's best interests at heart," said Keane. "If you really are looking out for her, we've got no quarrel with you."

"I'll tell you what," said Durham. "Come down to the set tomorrow. Observe Priya all you want. Talk to whoever you like. If Priya hired you, then clearly she doesn't trust me. Maybe if you poke around for a while and don't find anything, it will help her state of mind. I doubt it, but it's worth a shot."

"You're inviting us to the *DiZzy Girl* set?" I asked.

"You'll be my personal guests," Durham replied. "But let me make something clear. You'll have an escort. You will not interfere with filming, and you will not fuck with Priya."

"We're not going to do anything to hurt Priya," I said.

"You're not listening to me," said Durham, his voice low and steady. "Priya Mistry is the Hope Diamond. She's the *Mona Lisa*. She's the goddamned Taj Mahal, understand? If you know what's good for you, *do not fuck with her.*"

SEVEN

We left the party and returned to the office. So much for remaining incognito; that thug with the syringe had forced me into the open. Anyway, we'd done our best to protect Priya; if anything happened to her now, it was out of our hands. At least Durham and his thugs knew we were suspicious of them.

I sat with an ice pack for a while and then went to bed. In the morning, I expected to head to the *DiZzy Girl* set, but I found Keane had other plans. He'd set up an interview with Jessica Díaz, the widow of the late Hugo Díaz. Keane seemed to think she might be able to tell us something useful about the missing sheep, but I couldn't imagine what. In any case, according to Priya's schedule, she wasn't due at the set until ten A.M., so we had some time. We took Keane's aircar to the quiet neighborhood in Pasadena where Jessica Díaz lived.

Jessica Díaz was a slim, slightly mousy-looking blond woman with excellent posture and a terse but cordial way of speaking. Her reserved demeanor could of course be explained by the recent loss of her husband, but I got the impression she was always like this. Reserved and aloof, as if her life were something she preferred to observe at a reasonable distance. If she was distraught, she hid it very well. Her house was tidy and spotless.

I'd begun by explaining there had been a theft at the lab where her husband had worked, and told her we'd talked to all the employees with access to the lab. In her husband's case that was obviously impossible, so protocol required we interview his next of kin. It was a reasonable-sounding fib. I also made sure to explain that the theft occurred after her husband's passing, so of course he wasn't a suspect.

"We just need to cover our bases," I said apologetically. The three of us sat around a coffee table in her living room. "You know how it is with these big corporations."

Jessica nodded sympathetically.

Keane kept silent as I ran through the basics (Sorry for your loss, had you noticed any changes in your husband's behavior, had he mentioned any problems at work, had you observed him having secretive conversations on his comm or in person, is there any possibility he left the house the night he died, etc., to which she gave the expected responses: thank you, no, no, and no), but he perked up at Jessica's response to my question about whether Hugo had seemed depressed lately.

"No," she said, "In fact, he seemed happier than usual. The happiest I'd seen him since before his accident."

"Accident?" I asked. Keane listened with interest.

"Four years ago, when he was working for Gendrome," Jessica said. "Hugo had an accident in the lab. A machine had been misprogrammed, and it nearly crushed his skull."

"Nearly?" asked Keane.

She shot him a quizzical look. "What do you mean?"

"I mean, I've never heard of someone's skull being *nearly* crushed," Keane said. "It's typically a binary thing. Either your skull is crushed or it isn't."

I glared at Keane, but he was oblivious.

"It crushed his shoulder," Jessica said, only a hint of irritation in her voice. "He had six surgeries. They put in a titanium joint."

"I see," said Keane. "And did anyone ever determine who programmed the machine incorrectly?"

"I don't believe so, no," said Jessica. "It was an honest mistake. Could have been anyone in the lab."

"Anyone including Hugo," said Keane.

"I suppose so," said Jessica.

"Did Hugo have a lot of friends?" Keane asked.

"He had a few," said Jessica.

"Did he hang out with people from the lab? Go to the bar for a few drinks, that sort of thing?"

"We don't drink," said Jessica.

"Did he ever mention anybody from work? Calvin? Jason? Susan? Mary?" I had no idea where Keane was going with this. The first two were the names of actual Esper employees. I didn't know of any Susan. Mary was, of course, the sheep.

"He may have mentioned Jason once?" said Jessica uncertainly. "I don't remember hearing about any of the others."

"What do you know about your husband's work?"

"He was a technician. He worked on lab equipment."

"For a genetics lab."

"Yes, that's right."

"Did you know he worked with animals?"

"He said there were animals around, yes."

"What kinds of animals?"

"Pigs, I think?" she said. "And sheep. I remember the sheep because he used to joke about getting me a cashmere sweater. 'Some assembly required,' he said." She smiled at this, and I gave her a sympathetic chuckle.

"Did your husband like animals?" Keane asked, ignoring the joke.

"We love animals," said Jessica. "We have two cats and a dog." None of this was in evidence, which I found a bit odd.

"Did your husband love animals?" Keane asked.

"I just said he did."

"No, you said 'we' love animals. What I'm asking is, did your husband *love* animals?"

"I don't know what you mean."

"I think you know exactly what I mean. Are you sure he never mentioned a sheep named Mary?"

"A sheep named Mary? I don't know why he'd have mentioned something like that."

"This is no ordinary sheep, Ms. Díaz. This is a very attractive sheep. The kind of sheep a man could develop feelings for."

Jessica looked to me for help. "Keane," I said, "I think this is probably not—"

"You knew, didn't you?" Keane said. "You knew about Hugo and the sheep."

"I don't . . . ," she started. "Mr. Keane, is it? I don't understand what you're asking."

A smile played at the corner of Keane's mouth. "Sure you do, Jessica. Your husband spends all day working with sheep, and then he tells you he's going to get you a wool sweater. Did he tell you what he was going to do to you while you wore the sweater? Did he say he was going to spank you and call you Mary?"

I was so blindsided by this sudden escalation that I couldn't think of a thing to say. Jessica stared, openmouthed, at Keane. "I think . . . ," she said faintly, "I think the children will be home soon. You should go."

"Sure thing," said Keane, springing to his feet. "We'll see ourselves out. Thank you for your time." He made a beeline to the front door. I wasn't sure how to apologize without making things worse, so I just sort of awkwardly waved and followed Keane outside. Jessica remained on the couch, in stunned silence.

"What the hell was *that* about?" I demanded as we made our way back to the car.

"Just having some fun," Keane said.

"Jesus Christ, Keane. Her husband just died."

"Yeah, she's real broken up about it, isn't she?"

"People grieve in different ways. . . ."

"*People* do, yes. But unfeeling harpies act like *that*." He jerked his thumb toward the house as he got into the car.

I got into the driver's seat. "You of all people have no right . . . ," I started.

"That woman is a sociopath," said Keane. "Did you see her house? Spotless. Smelled of Lysol and bleach. They have three children and, if Jessica is to be believed, two cats and a dog. There's no sign that anyone lives in that house other than Jessica Díaz. And did you notice her use of the pronoun *we* when referring to her husband? Appropriating his life, borrowing his emotions because she has none of her own. Can you imagine living with that? No friends, no life of your own, that creature living off your energy like a vampire. No wonder he tried to crush his skull in a vice."

"You think that was intentional?" I asked, still trying to process his comments about Jessica.

"No, I think somebody accidentally left the blender on the skull-crushing setting. Think about it, Fowler. Nobody at a corporation like Gendrome writes a line of code without documenting it. If a machine got reprogrammed, there would have been a record of it, unless somebody deliberately flouted protocol."

"That sounds like an argument for murder," I said. "Not suicide. If it were suicide, why would he care about covering it up? And Jesus, why would anyone commit suicide like *that*?"

"His family would get a nice compensation package from Gendrome for an on-the-job death," Keane said. "There probably aren't a lot of ways to kill yourself at a job like that, so Díaz got creative. Also, I was in a room with that woman for ten minutes, and I kind of wanted *my* skull crushed. My guess is that he flinched at the last minute, couldn't go through with it. Took him another five years to finally get out."

"Hang on," I said. "You're saying Hugo Díaz gave himself a heart attack to get away from his wife?" TAKO SUBO SYNDROME

"It would appear so," said Keane.

"Tell me how," I said, throwing up my hands. "How does it appear that way to you? What are you looking at that I'm not seeing?"

"It's sort of a general gestalt-type thing," said Keane with a frown. "Difficult to encapsulate in words. Are we going to go somewhere, or just sit in the car all night? Because while I like you, Fowler, I don't like you the way Hugo Díaz likes sheep."

"I do hope you're joking," I said, pulling away from the curb.

"No, I really don't have those sorts of feelings for you. I'm sorry to have to tell you like this."

"I meant joking about Hugo Díaz and the sheep."

"Oh," said Keane. "Yeah. Probably. I mean, you never know what people are into, but I suspect his tastes are more conventional. House cats and the like."

We headed toward the DZ. We were about halfway to the checkpoint when Keane got a call from Jason Banerjee from Esper. Keane put him on speaker.

"Mr. Keane," said Banerjee. "Jason Banerjee. Following up on your request for an autopsy of Hugo Díaz."

"Right," said Keane. "How's that coming along?"

"It's not," said Banerjee. "There isn't going to be any autopsy."

"Why not?"

"Because Hugo Díaz was cremated yesterday."

"Already?" Keane asked. "How is that possible?"

"His wife requested an expedited cremation," Banerjee said. "I'll message you the information for the funeral parlor, but I don't think they're going to be able to tell you much. I assume this isn't your only avenue of investigation, Mr. Keane?"

"You're breaking up, Banerjee," said Keane. "We're going through a tunnel." He ended the call.

"Was that a good idea?" I asked.

"He was getting on my nerves," said Keane. "Go through a tunnel if it makes you feel better."

"Jessica sure was in a hurry to get Hugo cremated," I said after a moment. "You think she's trying to hide something?"

"Maybe. Or somebody else is trying to hide something, and they persuaded Jessica to expedite things. What do you think they did with the shoulder?"

"The what?"

"Jessica told us Hugo Díaz had a titanium shoulder. That would be a strange thing to make up, so I'm going to assume she was telling the truth. A cremation incinerator burns at up to 1800 degrees Fahrenheit. The melting point of titanium is 3034 degrees Fahrenheit. So unless Díaz was cremated in the heart of a dying star, the funeral home has a titanium shoulder joint lying around somewhere."

"What would they normally do with such a thing?" I asked.

"Presumably they would wait for it to cool and then return it to the next of kin." He thought for a moment and then announced, "Change of plans. I'll drop you off at the *DiZzy Girl* set. I'm going to the funeral parlor."

"Why?" I asked.

He grinned at me. "To see if they'll give me the cold shoulder."

EIGHT

It was after noon by the time we got to the location where *DiZzy Girl* was shooting. There had been a backup at the checkpoint into the DZ; probably the police had gotten another tip about weapons smuggling. Priya had given us the address of the shoot, which was in a particularly run-down area of the DZ, the sort of neighborhood that directors loved because it had that authentic post-apocalyptic DZ look that made for good TV. We could have avoided the checkpoint and flown directly to the location, but flying into the DZ was risky. Keane had enough contacts in the DZ that kidnapping wasn't a big concern, but there was always a chance some paranoid gangbanger with a SAM would shoot us down before checking the car's radio signature. Going street side was no guarantee of safety either, but the biggest threat on the ground was carjackers, and they tended to be a little more careful about whom they targeted. Anyone who bothered to do an ID check of Keane's car would know they were better off leaving us alone. I don't pretend to understand the depth of Keane's connections in the criminal underworld, but I'd met enough of his "friends" to know he was virtually untouchable in the DZ.

The other problem with flying into the DZ was that it was

technically illegal. That wouldn't be a problem, except that eventually, unless you were really desperate, you had to *leave* the DZ—which meant either flying out or going through a checkpoint. If you went through a checkpoint, you'd have to explain why there was no record of your vehicle entering the DZ, and if you flew out, you might find yourself intercepted by the police and forced to the ground, where your car would be torn apart and searched for contraband. So we took the surface streets and suffered through the checkpoint. Once inside, we found ourselves in the urban wasteland known as the DZ. We made our way quickly to the area where *DiZzy Girl* was filming.

It wasn't difficult to find. An entire neighborhood had been blocked off by private security guards; they were only letting people through who could prove either that they lived there or that they belonged on the set. I wondered how the logistics of this worked. There were no civil authorities inside the DZ, per se, and no permits or police. Probably the production company, Flagship Media, struck some kind of deal with whatever gang ran this part of town to let them shoot in relative peace.

Keane let me off down the street from one of the barriers and drove away. A wave of humidity hit me as I left the air-conditioned car. Strange weather for this time of year; when the heat finally broke, it was going to rain like in the Bible.

I strode toward one of the men guarding the barriers and showed him my ID. The guy wore an ensemble somewhere between gang attire and corporate security uniform, which was probably an accurate summary of his professional affiliation. The outfit was dark-green and black, and I noticed a turtle tattoo on his neck: the signs of the Tortuga gang. Several similarly attired men loitered nearby. Last I'd heard, the Tortugas were working for Mag-Lev, one of the most powerful warlords in the DZ. If they were handling security for the set, Flagship must have made a deal with Mag-Lev. Selah Fiore, the ex-actress who now ran Flagship, had a reputation as a tough-as-nails negotiator; it wouldn't surprise me at all to learn she had personally met with Mag-Lev to arrange for *DiZzy Girl* to shoot in the DZ. Élan Durham was the creative genius behind the show, but Selah Fiore was the one with the money, connections, and resolve to get things done.

The guard looked at my ID, muttered something into his comm, and then said, "Wait over there." I obliged. A few minutes later a very large man wearing a turtleneck strolled down the street toward me. A Glock hung in a holster on his chest. He didn't look happy to see me. "I'm your escort," he said.

"Not really my type, Brian," I said, slipping between two Jersey barriers and brushing past him.

Brian turned to walk alongside me. "Yeah, well, I'm not exactly thrilled about it either," he said.

"That's what you get when you let someone disarm you," I said. "Babysitting detail."

"That was a lucky break," he said.

I laughed. "Luck? I grabbed your gun right out from under your nose."

"I had an itch," said Brian. "I was distracted. You just caught me at the wrong moment. Luck."

I shook my head. This was why Brian was never going to be more than hired muscle. He wasn't willing to learn from his mistakes. "Twenty bucks says I can do it again before the end of the day," I said.

It was his turn to laugh. "Take my gun? No way in hell. You're on."

"Candy from a baby," I said.

The street ended at a T, and looking to the left, I saw a flurry of activity. Along the street were parked a half dozen trailers, a dozen or so box trucks, and probably another two dozen other vehicles. A huddle of people was convened in the street, and several other technicians and workers were milling around. Camera drones buzzed lazily about, awaiting instruction. I headed that way, and Brian stuck by my side.

As we approached the epicenter of activity, I made a brief survey of the area. This was a particularly run-down region of the DZ. The streets were in bad shape, and nearly half of the buildings were boarded up or burned out. Graffiti covered much of the walls. The shop owners who remained had a harried, suspicious look about them, and nearly all of them openly carried guns. A few of them glared at us as we passed, and I wondered if this was because they assumed we were with the production and resented us taking over their neighborhood, or if they just always acted that way. Drunks, junkies, and other miscreants populated the streets—which struck me as odd, since such people could pose a threat to the cast and crew. Presumably someone had at least checked them for weapons.

We made our way down the street toward the trailers, passing an intersection that was cordoned off with police tape. Two security guards—not Tortugas but actual corporate security types—were checking IDs and letting people through. A sign hanging on a sawhorse read:

SHOOTING LOCATION ONE
AUTHORIZED PERSONNEL ONLY
QUIET PLEASE!!!

We continued past the cordoned-off area. To our right was an abandoned store whose plate-glass windows had several cracks running through them that had been repaired with black tape. Hanging crookedly inside the window facing us was a faded plywood sign that read EVERYTHING MUST GO. The rest of the street was lined by nondescript brick and stucco buildings. We followed the street a hundred feet or so past the Everything Must Go store, where large trailers were parked along either side of the street. Between these two rows, a few trailers down, were several canopies that had been erected to give shelter from the Southern California sun. Beneath these, card tables and folding chairs had been set up, and a number of crew members and extras sat, playing cards or eating. Along one edge of the shelter was a row of lawn chairs in which sat several actors I recognized, including Priya. She looked beautiful as always, her hair pulled back in the style of her character on *DiZzy Girl*. She wore a faded green T-shirt, blue jeans, and black leather boots.

"So, what are your instructions, Brian?" I asked, as I walked toward the shelter.

"I'm your shadow," said Brian. "Wherever you go, I go."

"Right, but what are you supposed to do, exactly?"

"Keep you out of trouble."

"In that case," I said, "it might help if you give me some idea what trouble you expect me to get into. That way I can avoid it preemptively and make your job that much easier."

Brian remained silent.

"Like, if there are any areas I'm not supposed to go, or particular people I'm not supposed to talk to."

He continued to ignore me. Oh well, it was worth a shot. I approached Priya, who was seated next to her bodyguard, All-Grown-Up Noogus, and several of her costars. I figured that since I was no longer incognito, I might as well say hi. Maybe I could make up for my behavior the previous night. But as I approached, Priya waved to someone behind me, got up, and hurried away. I turned, but couldn't tell who she had waved at. Possibly no one. Did she really want to avoid me that badly? She seemed to be headed toward the shooting location, the area blocked off with police tape.

Meanwhile, I stood there in the middle of the street like

a schmuck. I became aware that people were watching me, which shouldn't have bothered me, but it did. At this point I had to decide to acknowledge the fact that Priya had snubbed me, or pretend I hadn't wanted to talk to her in the first place. I did the latter. I kept on walking toward where Priya had been sitting, and plopped down in her chair, grinning broadly at All-Grown-Up Noogus. The giant Samoan, who had been engrossed in a book, turned to look at me.

"Shouldn't you be watching Priya?" I said.

"Who the hell are you?" asked All-Grown-Up Noogus. He turned to look up at Brian, who was now standing, his arms crossed, glaring at me. There weren't any other empty chairs. All-Grown-Up Noogus acknowledged Brian with a nod. "Hey, Brian," he said.

"Hey, Roy," said Brian.

"You know this guy?" asked All-Grown-Up Noogus, whose name was evidently Roy.

Down the street, Priya passed the Everything Must Go store, and one of the guards lifted the police tape to let her through. I think he might have even bowed a little. She disappeared around the corner.

"Durham's got me watching him," said Brian. "Some kind of private investigator."

"Blake Fowler," I said. "I'm looking into a possible threat against Priya."

Roy regarded me with confusion. "I didn't know anything about this. Why didn't . . ." Recognition dawned on his face. "Hey, you're the asshole who took Priya out the other night!" He looked seriously angry. He'd apparently been too preoccupied with TC Gemmel to notice I'd been at the party the previous night as well.

I held up my hands. "Hang on, chief," I said. "I was just *acting* like an asshole."

Brian shook his head. "Nah, he really is an asshole," he said.

"You're making it easy for me, leaving that snap undone," I said, glancing at Brian's holster. He checked it, of course. I almost felt bad for him. "Candy from a baby," I said. His face went red. Evidently tiring of my taunts, he walked away and began chatting up a cute young actress a few chairs down.

"Does Priya know about this?" asked Roy.

"Why don't you ask her?" I said.

"I will," said Roy. "Count on it."

"Why aren't you with her now? Aren't you her bodyguard?"

"I try to give her some space on the set," said Roy, relaxing a bit. "Between the Tortugas at the barricades and Flagship's security on the set, this place is pretty secure. She doesn't need me hovering over her every second. And she sure as hell doesn't need any private investigator harassing her."

"I'm here to keep Priya safe," I said. "Same as you."

"I was doing okay before you showed up."

This was tricky. I didn't want to imply that Roy couldn't be trusted, but I also didn't want to tell him too much about our ongoing investigation. Particularly since I knew so little about our ongoing investigation that I was a little embarrassed to talk about it.

"We've got information about a potential threat," I said. "I'm afraid I can't say much more than that right now."

"But you think it's for real?"

"We don't have a lot of solid information on the threat," I said. "My boss, Mr. Keane, is looking into it."

"Hold on," said Roy. "You work for Erasmus Keane?"

"I do," I said. "You know him?"

"By reputation," said Roy. "He's kind of a legend. I even interviewed for a job with him a few years ago, but I got beat out by some corporate security hack."

I smiled at him.

"Oh," he said, suddenly embarrassed. "I didn't mean—"

"Don't worry about it," I said. "I *was* a corporate hack. Before I sold out, though, I ran diplomatic security details all over the Arabian Peninsula. And did three tours in Saudi Arabia before that."

"Marines?"

"Ranger. Seventy-fifth regiment."

"Damn," he said. "Did you get stuck in that shitstorm in Jeddah?"

"I got there after the worst of it was over, but yeah, I saw enough action to last me awhile. You're a Marine?"

"Twenty-sixth expeditionary unit. We were the last ones out of Riyadh when the provisional government took over."

"Should have left you there a little longer."

"Wouldn't have made any difference. We never should have gotten involved after the Wahhabi coup in the first place. There was no way those guys were going to be able to hold things together after they killed Khalid. We should have waited for things to go to hell and then found some Saudi prince to back. Somebody who could restore order and get the oil flowing."

"The American way," I said.

"Damn straight," he said, with a laugh.

Brian had apparently been shot down in record time, because he was no longer talking to the actress. Whatever his instructions were regarding me, he apparently hadn't been told to eavesdrop on my conversations—at least not my conversations with Priya's bodyguard. He was sauntering down the street toward the security guards at the police tape barrier, looking bored. Every once in a while he would look back just to make sure I hadn't made a run for it or something.

Roy, meanwhile, was deep in thought. "So that's why Priya sneaked out the other night," he said at last. "Got it in her head to hire Erasmus Keane. Guess I should have paid more attention to what she was saying. It's hard to know how seriously to take her. But if Keane thinks there's something to it . . ."

"Did she mention some kind of threat to you?" I asked.

"Not in so many words." After a moment he leaned over and said quietly, "Between you and me, Priya hasn't been herself lately. She's been acting . . . strange."

"Strange how?" I asked.

"On edge," he said. "Even more than usual. And spacey, like she's not all there. She forgets things. Like yesterday she asked if I wanted to try the new pizza place on Figueroa. I thought she was joking, because we had just eaten there three days ago, and she hated it. Said it was the worst pizza she'd ever had. So I laughed, but she was serious. She didn't remember going there. She was so certain, I told her I must have remembered wrong, and we went there again. And she hated it again. Ordered the Hawaiian, just like last time. Said it was the worst pizza she'd ever had—again."

"And she never remembered she'd been there before?"

"Not that I could tell. I didn't push her, because she's already so anxious. Paranoid, even. She keeps saying things like 'You won't let anything happen to me, will you, Roy?' And I tell her, you know, that's my job. I'll do my best. And then she doesn't say anything. Sometimes she just cries."

"You tell her you'll do your best? Not exactly reassuring."

"I don't lie to Priya," Roy said. "Never. She's surrounded all day by people who tell her what she wants to hear, or what they think will get her to do what they want her to do. That isn't my job. My job is to protect her. And that means being straight with her. If she can't trust me when it counts, then I've failed."

"And does she trust you?"

He shrugged, and for a moment a pained expression showed on his face. "Obviously not completely, since she felt she had to sneak out to hire Keane. All I can do is be honest with her. It's tough, though, when she starts talking all paranoid. How do you talk someone out of paranoia? The more I try to reassure her that there's no vast conspiracy out to get her, the more I sound like part of the conspiracy. And to be honest, I don't know that there *isn't* a conspiracy. I haven't seen any evidence of one, but that doesn't mean it doesn't exist."

"Is that what she tells you? That there's a vast conspiracy out to get her?"

"Not in so many words. But she's on edge all the time. She doesn't trust anybody. Freaks out when she sees one of her own commercials on TV. Says that people on the street are watching her. Well, what am I going to say to that? She's Priya Mistry, for Pete's sake. Of *course* people on the street are watching her. So tell me, Mr. Fowler, *is* there a conspiracy?"

"If there is," I started, "Erasmus Keane is the man—"

I saw the blast a split second before I felt it: a hailstorm of broken glass propelled by a fireball, the promise that EVERYTHING MUST GO splintering into a million pieces. I instinctively shut my eyes and raised my hands before my face, and a hundredth of a second later the shock wave hit, knocking me to the ground. A rush of hot air and debris followed, and I lay there for a moment, waiting for a chunk of concrete to crack my skull open or a shard of glass to sever my jugular. It didn't happen.

I opened my eyes and looked around. My ears were ringing, and the air was thick with dust and debris. I pulled my shirt up over my nose so I could breathe. Roy, who was already getting to his feet, was doing the same. Glancing around, I took in the scene: chairs and folding tables lying scattered across the street, a dozen or so people sitting or lying, stunned, in the street. I didn't observe any serious injuries, though; we'd been too far away from the blast for it to do much damage. There were some skinned knees and elbows, but everyone was conscious and I didn't see any obvious broken limbs or profuse bleeding. Fortunately, we'd all been sitting down, so we hadn't had far to fall to the pavement. The air was too thick with dust and debris for me to be able to see to the corner, but I wasn't optimistic about the chances of the security guards manning the barrier to the set. Hopefully they had at least died quickly.

Roy tugged on my shirt and pointed through the haze at a pile of rubble about halfway between us and the store. I realized after a moment that it was Brian, lying facedown in the street, covered with dust and glass shards. He wasn't moving.

I got to my feet and followed Roy to Brian. The fire was still raging inside the store, and I had to use my hands to shield my face from the heat as we got close. We turned Brian over carefully, checking for any lacerations or signs of broken bones. We didn't find any.

"Is he breathing?" I yelled over the buzzing in my ears.

Roy felt Brian's neck for a pulse and put his ear to his nose. "Yeah," he said with a nod. "Probably just took a knock on the head when he fell. Let's get him out of here."

Easier said than done. Brian was a big guy, and while Roy probably could have moved him in a fireman's carry, we didn't want to aggravate any internal injuries by lifting him. That meant dragging him. But while I didn't particularly like Brian, I didn't necessarily think he deserved to be sliced to ribbons by being dragged across a street littered with glass shards. Roy ended up grabbing him under his arms, clasping his hands in front of Brian's chest, while I held his ankles. We moved fifty feet or so back the way we had come and sat him down up against the wall of a building across the street.

"Brian," I said, slapping his cheek lightly. He didn't move. "Brian!" I said, louder this time. I slapped him a little harder. This time he stirred. His eyes fluttered open. It took him a moment to focus on me. "What . . . happened?" he murmured.

I held his gun before his eyes. "Candy from a baby," I said. He tried to grab the gun, but I pulled it away. He groaned.

The actress he had been chatting up and a couple of the others had come over. "Is he okay?" the actress asked.

"He'll be fine," I said. "Get him some water and an ice pack. Keep him conscious. And don't let him have this." I handed her the gun. "It's real, and it's loaded," I told her, to prevent any misunderstandings. She held the gun in both hands, staring wide-eyed like I'd just handed her a live cobra.

I got up and saw that Roy was gone. He was running into the dust cloud. I followed.

NINE

I saw her boots first, protruding from a pile of concrete, stucco, and twisted rebar. My heart sank. If that was
Priya Mistry under all that, there was no way she was still
alive. By the time I got there, Roy was already tearing away
chunks of concrete with his bare hands. I moved in to help,
but Roy was three hundred pounds of frantic energy and
adrenaline, tossing hundred-pound slabs of concrete like
they were pieces of Styrofoam. It was like watching Lou Fer-
rigno breaking through a wall on that old *Incredible Hulk*
show from the 1970s. I had to keep reminding myself that
those were real cinder blocks he was hurling. I decided it
was best for everyone if I observed from a safe distance.
The fire in the store had settled to a steady blaze, but it was
still throwing off a hell of a lot of heat. I stood on the other
side of Roy, waiting for him to finish or collapse from exhaustion. A camera drone buzzed nearby, and I wonder if it
had caught anything of interest. I had a feeling that if it did,
I'd never be allowed to see the footage. For a moment I considered attempting to shoot the thing down, but that was no
good either: those things were programmed not to allow un-
authorized access to their onboard memory.

Eventually Roy stopped digging. He sank to his knees and

held a bloody hand over his mouth. I couldn't read the expression on his face.

I approached, looking into the depression in the pile Roy had dug. She was dead, there was no doubt about that: black hair smudged with blood obscured her face. I moved the hair away and then pulled off my jacket. I wiped her face with my jacket, trying to clear enough blood and dirt away to get a good look at her face. It almost had to be Priya, but it was hard to tell.

I became aware of sirens, and a man and a woman in paramedics' uniforms pushed us aside. Well, they pushed *me* aside. They sort of shoved impotently at Roy, and eventually he got the idea and stepped away from the body. He was panting and dripping with sweat.

More emergency personnel were moving in, and the Tortugas were escorting the uninjured away from the scene. Roy and I made our way through the rubble back to where the other actors were waiting. We were covered in dust, and Roy's hands were bleeding. He looked like he was on the verge of breaking down.

Taki Soma, who played Priya's mother on *DiZzy Girl*, ran up to us. "Is it true?" she asked. "Stacia Acardi was killed?"

"Who?" I asked.

"Priya's stunt double," Roy murmured. "They were doing an action scene today. She'd have been wearing the same clothes as Priya."

"Well, hell," I said. But if the girl in the rubble had been the stunt double, then where was Priya?

"We should check the shooting location," Roy said.

I nodded. We cut through an alley to skirt the bombing site.

"Does this happen a lot?" I asked.

"What?"

"Explosions on the set." I'd been struck by the lack of panic among the crew members, as if a corner store exploding was unexpected but not unheard of, like a freak thunder-storm.

"Not on the set," Roy said. "But we're used to explosions. We hear them, usually a few blocks away. The DZ is basically a war zone. Gangs competing for territory. Mag-Lev is supposed to provide us a safe haven for shooting, but I guess one of the other gangs decided not to cooperate this time."

"What do they want? The bombers?"

"Mag-Lev gets a lot of money from Flagship for letting them film here. If the other gangs can make it too danger-ous to shoot, Flagship will pull out of the DZ. That hurts Mag-Lev. Anything that hurts Mag-Lev helps the other war-lords."

Glancing down the street, I saw most of the other princi-pal actors, but Priya was nowhere to be found. Some distance away stood Élan Durham, who was barking animatedly into his comm. While Roy quizzed crew members on Priya's whereabouts, I sidled closer to Durham. Between the buzz-ing in my ears and the general commotion, I could only make out about half of what he was saying, but whatever he was yelling about, he was not happy.

"We're paying that son of a bitch . . . at least a week behind schedule . . . second fuckup in two days . . . made him, and we can sure as hell destroy him . . ." He was quiet for a mo-ment, then let out a long sigh. "Yeah, I know . . . I won't . . . know how hard you worked . . ." Then he saw me, muttered something into his comm, and ended the call.

"What the hell are you doing here?" he demanded. "Where's Brian?"

"Resting comfortably," I said. "He nearly got blown to pieces by the explosion. Roy and I dragged him to safety."

Durham nodded, registering the information as if I had told him craft services was out of capers.

"Do you know where Priya is?" I asked.

He shot me a puzzled look, as if he wasn't quite sure what I was asking him.

"Priya?" I said impatiently. "The star of your show?"

He shrugged. "She's around here somewhere. I can't have you wandering around the set without Brian. If he's out of commission, you'll have to leave."

"Yeah," I said. "I wouldn't want to disturb the equanimity of your set." I turned and walked back toward Roy, who was still questioning crew members. He shook his head as I approached.

My comm chimed in my ear. It was April. Not great timing, but if she had information on Priya, I didn't want to miss it.

"April, what's up?"

"Hey, Fowler," she said. "Your girl, Priya? She's nuts, all right. My friend at Ballard and Greene says she's got a contract to make ten commercials for Prima Facie. She's made four of them already. No sims."

"Hmm," I said, not sure how this new information fit with everything else that had happened recently.

"You must know this, though, right?" she asked.

"What do you mean?"

"Aren't you watching her?"

"Sure, but we just started yesterday."

"Well, she's down there right now," April said. "At a set in Culver City. Where are you?"

For a moment I couldn't think of anything to say.

"Fowler?"

"You're sure she's there right now?"

"Yes," April said. "My friend is over there, getting some signatures from some Marcus and Shea people. He's, like, the world's biggest *DiZzy Girl* fan. Keeps gushing about how she's even more gorgeous in person."

"Do you have an address?" I asked.

"Fowler, you need to leave that girl alone."

"April, I need the address. I don't have time to explain. Please."

She gave it to me.

"Thanks, April," I said. "I have to go." I didn't want to be rude, but I'd have to explain the situation to her some other time—preferably after I had a better grasp on it myself.

What in the hell was going on? Priya disappears from the *DiZzy Girl* set, and then ten minutes later she's filming a commercial across town? Even if she'd taken an aircar, she'd have been hard-pressed to get to Culver City from the DZ in ten minutes. Had I imagined seeing her a few minutes earlier? Had Roy and I both been taken in by her stunt double? It seemed impossible.

"No one has seen her since the explosion," Roy said worriedly. "A couple of people say they saw her walking this way just before, but Taki said she thinks it was Stacia."

For a moment, I considered telling Roy about Priya being spotted across town. But I figured it was better for him to stay on the set and try to find some answers here. Besides, telling him would just prompt a lot of questions I either couldn't or didn't want to answer, and I still wasn't entirely sure I could trust him. His concern for Priya certainly seemed genuine, but he was an X factor I just didn't have time for.

"She'll turn up," I said. "Any word on who set the bomb?"

"Nah," he said. "We'll never know unless one of the other gangs claims responsibility."

"Okay," I said. "Hey, I've got to go. I've got another case to check on." I wondered if that sounded as lame and ridiculous as I thought it did.

"Another case?" Roy asked incredulously. "Aren't you supposed to be looking into threats against Priya? She's *missing*, for Christ's sake. She could be buried under rubble!

Durham clearly doesn't give a shit, so I could really use your help."

"I'm sorry, Roy," I said. "I would stay if I could, but I *have* to leave." I tapped my comm and tossed my ID to him. "Call me if you hear anything."

Roy turned and walked away without a word. I sighed. Making friends and influencing people, that's me. I hit up Keane on my comm.

"Hey, Fowler," said Keane cheerfully. "How goes the glamorous life?"

"Not great," I said. "There's been an explosion on the set. Some kind of terrorist attack by a rival gang. And Priya is missing. Well, sort of."

"She's *sort of* missing?"

"That's the weird part," I said. "April says she's making a commercial on the Flagship lot. But she was just here, like, ten minutes ago. Keane, I don't know what the fuck is going on."

"All right," he said. "I'm on my way."

TEN

Keane picked me up at the DZ barrier. Not twenty minutes later we were at the address April had given me. The building wasn't part of the main Flagship studios complex; it was one of the old warehouses they had acquired and converted during their rapid expansion of the past few years. Circling the building from a safe distance, we determined that our best bet was to wait for Priya to leave, and then follow her, assuming she was actually inside. Other than the shipping bays, which were all closed, there were only two entrances: one at the front of the building and one at the rear. Armed guards were posted at each. There was also a guard stationed at a gate on the side street that led around to the back of the building. The front entrance didn't seem to be in use. While we watched, three people entered the building and two left, all through the rear door. The vehicles were stopped at the side gate, both coming and going.

An amber light blinked on the dash, indicating that we had dropped below the minimum altitude for this area. Ascent corridors were tightly regulated in most of the city, in part to prevent people from doing exactly what we were doing: flying at low altitudes to spy on someone. If we didn't start climbing pretty quickly, the light would go red, indicating that the LAPD had been notified. They'd pinpoint our transponder and send a couple of cruisers to intercept us. Once that happened, there was nothing to do but land and hope the cops weren't in the mood to strip-search us or impound the car.

"Keane," I said, as he made another circle around the building, and the frequency of the amber light increased.

"I got it," Keane said, craning his neck to keep an eye on the building. The amber light's frequency continued to increase.

"Seriously, Keane," I said after a moment. "This is a very bad idea."

The light had gone from insistent to frantic. Ordinarily, the car's safety override would have kicked in by now, telling the autopilot to climb to an acceptable altitude, but Keane had hacked the override. That was a felony. Another good reason not to let that little light go red.

"There!" Keane exclaimed.

"What?"

"Limo. Headed toward the guard tower."

I looked where he was pointing. There was indeed a limo pulling up to the gate.

"So?" I asked.

"Could be our girl's limo," said Keane.

"It could be anybody's limo!" I snapped.

"On an out-of-the-way set like this?" Keane said. "No. There aren't going to be a lot of bigwigs here. I'm surprised they even make Priya come down here. Are you sure April's intelligence is good?"

The light went red.

"Well, shit," I said. "When they arrest us, do you mind telling them I'm a hostage you were holding at gunpoint? I'll let you borrow my gun." I was slightly more than half serious.

Another warning flashed on the dash: ERROR! TRANSPONDER OFFLINE!

"Whoops," said Keane. "Our transponder seems to have malfunctioned. How will the LAPD ever find us?"

"Oh God," I moaned. "You hacked the transponder? Do you have any idea how much trouble you'll be in if they catch you?"

"The amount of trouble I'll be in is inversely proportional to the odds I'll get caught."

"That's not as reassuring as you probably think it is," I said. It wouldn't take the LAPD long to pinpoint our last known location and scramble up a couple of cruisers to find us. We needed to beat them, and quick. But Keane continued his slow bank to the right, around the back of the building, watching the limo pull up to the door. Red and blue lights flashed on the horizon.

"Keane," I said.

"I see them," he said. "We'll have to circle back."

A driver got out of the limo and opened the rear door facing the entrance to the studio.

"Looks like he expects someone pretty soon," I said. "We're going to lose him if we circle back."

"Good point," he said. "I'm going to need a spotter."

I nodded. I didn't like the idea, but on the plus side at least I wouldn't be in the car when Keane got pulled over.

Keane banked sharply to the right and then straightened out over the alley that ran alongside the studio building. He deployed the flaps, and the car's wings rotated just over a quarter turn, using the jet thrust to brake while slowing our descent. The wheels folded out of the undercarriage a breath before we hit. Then the wings flattened out, and the extensions folded up, making the car more maneuverable on the ground. Keane hit the thrust again, and we rocketed down the alley, now on wheels. He braked hard as we approached the street, and I threw my door open. "Good luck!" I yelled, and slammed the door shut. The car squealed around the corner to the right, merging between an SUV and a Porsche.

While Keane did his best to blend in with traffic, I raced on foot around the front of the building toward the guard station. When I was fifty feet or so away, I slowed to a walk. I was already sweaty from running around the *DiZzy Girl* set, and it hadn't cooled down any in the meantime. The air was muggy and still.

I got to the guard station and kept walking. Three police cruisers roared overhead. Hopefully Keane had gotten far enough away that they wouldn't spot him and match the description of his car to the vehicle whose transponder had suddenly stopped functioning nearby.

I spotted a bus stop on the other side of the street about half a block down from the guard station, so I walked to it and sat, doing my best to look inconspicuous. A few minutes later I saw the limo pulling away from the gate. It turned my direction.

"Got 'em," I said into my comm. "Heading southwest on Olympic." I sure hoped that was Priya's limo, or this was a lot of risk and running around for nothing. I also hoped the car stayed on the ground. It was an aircar, but it couldn't legally take off in this neighborhood. If they were only going a short distance, the driver probably would remain street side rather than drive out of his way to a takeoff point.

"Roger that," said Keane. "Can't risk going airborne right now, so it's going to take a minute to get to you. Try to keep them in sight."

"Yeah," I said as the limo passed the bus stop. I got up and started jogging on the sidewalk, following after the limo. It turned right again at the next intersection, and I cut through an alley to try to keep up. "Going right on Westwood," I said.

"Roger," said Keane. "ETA three minutes."

"Three minutes? You realize I'm on foot here, Keane?"

"Can't be helped," said Keane. "Try not to lose them."

Cursing, I sprinted down the alley and made a left. I came out on Westwood and glanced left, then right. Spotted the limo half a block down, and ran after it. I was losing ground. Traffic was amazingly light for the middle of the day, and the limo seemed to be getting one green light after another. Where was LA traffic when you needed it? I thought of hailing a cab, but I was worried that by the time I flagged one down and got in, I'd have lost the limo.

Finally a light turned red, and I saw the limo coasting to a stop a hundred yards or so ahead. I put on a burst of speed, thinking I might actually catch up to them before the light changed. But then I heard the bark of a siren behind me and realized I was being tailed by a police cruiser. I cursed again and darted down a side street. Nothing like a grown man running at top speed in street clothes to pique the attention of the LAPD.

The cruiser's siren blared, and the car shot down the street after me. Traffic was on my side here. A light ahead was red, and the cars were just creeping along. The cruiser was an aircar, but it didn't have room to safely get airborne here. I darted across the street, barely managing to avoid being hit, and ran down another alley. By the time the cop had cleared the traffic, I'd come out at the other end and turned back toward Westwood. Panting like a dog in heat, I stopped at the corner of Westwood and scanned for the limo again. For a moment I was sure I'd lost it, which was almost a relief under the circumstances, but then I spotted it stopped at another light a couple of blocks down. I groaned and took off running.

"Can't . . . keep . . . up . . ." I said, gasping into my comm. Keane didn't respond.

I followed for several more blocks, barely keeping the car in view. The limo made a right on Wilshire and disappeared around the corner.

"Lost . . . it . . ." I said, continuing to gasp, and slowed to a walk. Keane still didn't respond. "Keane," I said after a moment. "Hear me?"

"Palomar Hotel," said Keane. "Get here as soon as you can."

I cursed and hailed a cab. The Palomar was less than a mile away, but there was no way in hell I was walking the rest of the way.

"Palomar," I grunted at the driver, and he obliged. Five minutes later the cab pulled in front of the hotel. I was drenched with sweat and still shaking with adrenaline. I paid the cabbie and got out.

"You were supposed to pick me up," I growled at Keane, who was standing beside his car in the loading area of the hotel. "That's how this works."

Keane shrugged. "Figured Priya would be headed for a hotel. I got on Wilshire and followed the limo here."

As I watched, a limo pulled away from the curb. I was pretty sure it was the one I had been running after. "It's getting away," I said to Keane.

"She already got out," said Keane. "I'm not that interested in the limo per se."

"You saw her? Priya?"

"Either Priya or someone who looked an awful lot like her."

"Why didn't you stop her?"

"I tried. She acted like she didn't recognize me. Also, her bodyguard doesn't seem to like people yelling at her from across the parking lot. I decided that, in this case, discretion is the better part of valor."

"Damn it, Keane. That's why you have me around. If you had picked me up, I could have stopped them."

"If I had picked you up, I'd have missed them entirely."

"Maybe," I said. "But . . . hold on, what did her bodyguard look like?"

"Stocky Aryan type," Keane said.

"Hmm," I replied. Apparently, Priya had another bodyguard besides Roy. "So now what?"

"We send her a message," said Keane. "Come on." He handed the keys to his car to an attendant and walked to the door of the hotel. I followed as he strode across the lobby to the concierge desk. He grabbed a pen and paper, scribbled something on it I couldn't make out, folded it in half, wrote *Priya Mistry* on it, and then handed it to the young woman behind the desk, along with a hundred new-dollar note. "A message for one of your guests," he said with a smile. The woman nodded, took the note, and walked away.

"Let's get something to eat," said Keane. I didn't argue.

On the way to the hotel bar, Keane stopped in at the gift shop and bought a Dodgers T-shirt. He handed it to me. "Here," he said. "My way of apologizing for not picking you up."

"I hate the Dodgers," I said. "I'm a Cubs fan."

"Oh," he said. "They don't seem to have any of those. Their selection is rather limited."

"Whatever," I said. "Let's go get something to eat."

"Okay, tell me what you want and I'll order. You go change."

"Change?"

"You smell like a city bus," he said. "Go put on the T-shirt."

"You're paying," I said, grabbing the shirt. "Get me a turkey sandwich." I went to the bathroom and stripped off my shirt. Keane was right; I was getting pretty ripe. I washed my torso as best I could in the sink, dried off with paper towels, and put on the accursed Dodgers shirt. At least it was clean. I went to the bar and found Keane scarfing down a turkey sandwich.

"What's this?" I asked, looking at my plate.

"Ham sandwich," he said. "Isn't that what you wanted?"

"I said turkey."

"Oh," he said. "I guess I got our orders switched. Just eat it, you big baby."

I was hungry enough that I didn't particularly care what was on the sandwich. I was just popping the last bite into my mouth when a black-haired woman in a jogging outfit and a baseball cap appeared at our table. Even with the oversized sunglasses, there was no mistaking her.

"Priya," I said.

For a moment she didn't say anything. She just glared at me. Then she reached into her pocket and pulled out the scrap of paper with her name on it. She unfolded it and put it on the table. "What the hell is this supposed to mean?" she said. The note read:

Meet me in the bar.

Noogus :)

PS I'm wearing a Dodgers shirt and eating a ham sandwich

"God damn it, Keane," I said.

"Sorry," said Keane. "I needed a Noogus."

Priya looked at Keane and then back at me. "How do you know about that?" she demanded. "I never told anybody."

"You told me," I said. "Two days ago, in my office."

She shook her head. "No," she said faintly. Then she said it three more times, more like she was trying to ward off some unspeakable evil than simply responding to my statement.

"Here, why don't you sit down?" I said, grabbing a chair from the next table.

She was still shaking her head.

"Priya," I said firmly. "My name is Blake Fowler. This is my boss, Erasmus Keane. We're here to help you. Please, sit down."

She did. She tried to hide it, but her hands were shaking. If she remembered meeting us before, she showed no sign of it.

"You have no memory of us?" asked Keane, staring intently at her.

Priya shrugged, her lower lip quivering. She looked like she was going to break into tears.

"Would you like something to drink?" I asked.

She shook her head, but then said, "Water. Please." She looked at Keane again. "Are you really Erasmus Keane?" she asked. "The private investigator?"

Keane nodded. Apparently, even he didn't have the nerve to correct Priya in her current state. He flagged down a waiter and got Priya a glass of water.

"I thought about hiring you," she said, staring into her glass. "But it's hard to get away. Jamie is probably looking for me right now. I don't understand. . . . How did you know?"

"Jamie," I said. "Is that one of your bodyguards?"

"Jamie's my bodyguard, yes," she said.

I put my hand gently on hers. "Priya, we don't have a lot of time. Mr. Keane and I are trying to get to the bottom of this, but if we're going to help you, you have to trust us."

She looked at me and nodded. I saw desperation in her face.

"I need you to do something for me, Priya," I said. "Close your eyes and try to relax. Take deep breaths."

She did.

"Okay, now I want you to think about what you were doing two days ago."

"I was on the set for the Prima Facie commercial," she

said, without even taking a second to think. "We wrapped the fifth one today. Seems like all I ever do anymore is commercials."

I shot a glance at Keane. He shrugged, apparently as puzzled as I was.

"Where did you go after the shoot?" I asked.

"Here. The hotel. The Palomar."

"Did you go out at all?"

"No."

"I'm talking about this past Monday. Did you leave your hotel at all after the shoot?" GOT IT!

"No."

"And you went directly to the hotel from the set? You didn't stop anywhere?"

"No!" she cried, opening her eyes. "The set, the hotel, the set, the hotel. That's all I ever do. I'd remember if I went out. What the hell is going on? How did you know about Noogus? What is happening to me?"

Keane nudged me, and I glanced over to see a stocky blond man with a dour expression on his face enter the bar. Presumably, Priya's bodyguard, the one she had called Jamie.

"Listen to me, Priya," I said. "It's going to be okay. Mr. Keane and I are on the case. Just act normal, and we'll update you when we can."

She nodded, bewildered. The big blond man put a hand on her shoulder. "Not safe for you to be down here alone," said Jamie. "Who are these guys?"

"We're huge fans," gushed Keane. "When Ms. Mistry came in for a glass of water, I recognized her immediately. Can't fool me with a hat and some sunglasses!"

"Yes," said Priya distantly. "I just needed to get some water."

"There's bottled water in the room," said Jamie. His eyes fell to the paper on the table. I doubted he could read Keane's scribbled handwriting upside down, but I put my hand over the paper.

"Oh!" I exclaimed. "We were so excited to actually talk to Priya Mistry that we almost forgot to get her autograph! Ms. Mistry, would you mind?"

Keane produced a pen, and I carefully turned the paper over, refolding it to hide Priya's name. Priya scrawled, in big round letters:

Priya Mistry

"Come on, Priya," said Jamie. "Let's go."

"Wait," said Priya. She scribbled something else at the bottom of the paper. Then Jamie took Priya by the shoulder and escorted her out.

"I don't like him nearly as much as All-Grown-Up Noogus," I said after a moment.

"Hey?"

"Never mind. What did she write?"

Keane showed me the paper. Below Priya's signature was written:

12/25/34

"She got the date wrong," I mused.

"Given her mental state, we're lucky she got her name right," Keane remarked.

"I guess every day is Christmas when you're Priya Mistry," I said. "Keane, what the hell is going on?"

"That," he said, looking at his own comm screen, "is an excellent question. Don't lose that paper. We need to get to Sherman Oaks."

"Why?" I asked. "What's in Sherman Oaks?"

"Not what," said Keane. "Who."

"Fine," I said, growing impatient. "*Who* is in Sherman Oaks?"

Keane smiled. "Our sheep thief," he said. "Hugo Díaz, back from the great beyond."

ELEVEN

While I'd been at the *DiZzy Girl* set, Keane had been putting pieces together in the Case of the Lost Sheep. Whatever was going on with Priya, it was going to have to wait for a moment. Keane was back on the trail of the sheep, and there was no point in trying to redirect him.

The key, he said, was Hugo Díaz's titanium shoulder—or lack thereof. Keane related that the funeral home had no record of a prosthetic shoulder, which was enough to convince him that the body they had cremated wasn't Díaz's. That meant someone had produced a corpse that looked enough like Díaz to fool his wife. Keane didn't seem to have any definitive ideas on who did it or how, but one thing was certain: they couldn't have stolen the sheep and faked his death without Díaz's cooperation. And that meant Díaz had known about it in advance.

"So what?" I asked. "I don't see how that gets you to a house in Sherman Oaks."

"Think about it," said Keane. "Hugo Díaz is a sexually frustrated middle-aged man desperate to escape his humdrum existence. What do men normally do in such situations?"

"Buy a Camaro," I said. "Or . . ."

Keane smiled.

"So he had an affair," I said. "Probably with someone at work. But who?"

"You met most of the people he worked with. Any likely candidates spring to mind?"

One did, in fact. Stephanie Kemp, the plump brunette whom Keane had called "cooperative." I couldn't see her falling for Hugo Díaz, though. Unless . . .

"He told her," I said. It was all starting to make sense. "And you knew, didn't you? When we interviewed her."

Keane shook his head. "I only knew something was off with her. She was too helpful. But I didn't put it together until the funeral home couldn't find the shoulder."

Stephanie's excessive helpfulness, he explained, was a form of compensation—a combination of guilt about the theft and a sense of thrill of having gotten away with it. Keane was certain Stephanie didn't have the nerve or clout to be directly involved in the theft, but he suspected she knew the culprit. Stephanie's position afforded her only the lowest level of access to the lab, so assuming that the thief also worked there, no practical advantage could be obtained by informing her. So the question was: Why would someone spill the beans about a criminal plot to someone who couldn't possibly help them carry it out? And the answer was the oldest explanation of seemingly inexplicable human behavior there is: to get laid. Ordinarily, Stephanie wouldn't have given Hugo the time of day, but women like Stephanie (according to Keane) had a thing for bad boys. Stealing a genetically modified sheep from a research lab wasn't the typical path to bad boy status, but you work with what you have.

Keane hypothesized that if Hugo Díaz was dumb enough to tell Stephanie Kemp about the sheep plot, then he was presumably dumb enough to keep seeing her after his "death." When the funeral home couldn't find the titanium shoulder, Keane had instructed Pavel to watch Stephanie Kemp's apartment in Glendale, and tail her if she went anywhere after she got home from work. While we were talking to Priya at the hotel bar, Pavel had sent Keane a message telling him he'd followed Stephanie to a house in Sherman Oaks. Pavel had parked on the street and was waiting there now.

"And what makes you think Hugo Díaz is at the house?" I asked.

"It's owned by a real estate management company," said Keane. "Care to guess who the majority shareholder in that company is?"

"I haven't a clue," I said.

"Levi Magnusen," Keane replied. "Also known as Mag-Lev."

"The DZ warlord?" I said. "What does he have to do with this?"

"It would appear Mag-Lev masterminded the sheep theft," said Keane. "Although we won't know for sure until we verify Hugo Díaz is at the house."

"How would Hugo Díaz even get in contact with Mag-Lev? I wouldn't think they go to a lot of the same parties."

"Turns out, this isn't the first time something has gone missing from Esper," Keane said. "About a year ago, a large quantity of a synthetic opioid went missing from the same lab. Later some of it turned up in the DZ, being distributed by members of the Tortuga gang. The police never identified a suspect, but the timing of the theft corresponds with some financial difficulties Hugo Díaz was having. Apparently, one of Jessica Díaz's other endearing traits is a propensity for overspending on clothes and jewelry. They had over forty thousand in credit card debt. Over the next few months, after the police dropped the case, Hugo gradually paid off their debt."

"Even if Hugo stole the drugs, that still doesn't explain how he'd get in touch with Mag-Lev."

"The drug theft was probably a crime of opportunity.

Hugo saw a chance to take the drugs, and nabbed them. Then he probably started asking around, trying to figure out where he could unload them. Eventually he found one of Mag-Lev's people, or they found him. So when Mag-Lev decided he needed one of Esper's sheep, he had a man on the inside."

"What on Earth would a DZ warlord want with a genetically modified sheep anyway?" I asked.

"That," said Keane, "I have yet to determine."

We had arrived at the address Pavel had given Keane. It was a large Spanish colonial-style house with a lush green lawn, located in a wealthy area of Sherman Oaks. I parked a few houses down, behind Pavel's Suburban. Keane got out and had a brief conversation with Pavel. Pavel drove off a moment later, and Keane got back into the car. He filled me in while I drove to Sherman Oaks.

"Stephanie just left," said Keane. "Pavel says she was alone."

"You know," I said, "Anybody could be renting this house from that management company. How do we know Stephanie's not just watering a friend's plants?"

"Oh, she's watering his plants all right," said Keane.

"Congratulations," I said. "That's the worst euphemism for intercourse I've ever heard."

"No," said Keane. "*Intercourse* is the worst euphemism for intercourse you've ever heard. Normal people call it *fucking*."

We waited for some time in silence. It had gotten dark, and some lights went on inside the house—the only indication anybody was home. I was still trying to figure out the logistics of Hugo Díaz's illusory demise.

"So if Díaz faked his death," I said at last, "does that mean he didn't really have a heart attack?"

"*Somebody* had a heart attack," said Keane. "But I don't think it was Hugo Díaz."

"Who then?"

"Somebody who looks an awful lot like Hugo Díaz. Enough to fool his wife."

"Could it have been a twin brother?" I asked.

"Hey?"

"The corpse Jessica Díaz identified. Maybe someone swapped out her real husband with the twin?"

"A forty-eight-year-old twin would have developed enough physical differences that a spouse would notice the difference. But sure, it's possible."

"You already looked into whether Hugo Díaz had a twin, didn't you?"

"Yup."

"And?"

"Only child. And in answer to your next question, he was not adopted."

"Plastic surgery? They find someone who fits Hugo's rough appearance and modify him to match?"

"Who is 'they'?" Keane asked.

"Hell if I know," I replied. "Whoever is behind all this."

Keane shrugged. "Again, the wife would know. Even a self-obsessed, sexually repressed harpy like Jessica Díaz. And why go to the trouble, just to draw attention away from Hugo Díaz? It's an absurdly complicated plan if their goal is just to muddy the waters a bit. And after spending months, maybe years, carving him up to make him look exactly like Hugo Díaz, they forget to give him a titanium shoulder? Doesn't fit. Ah, here we go."

The garage door had opened, and a brand-new BMW pulled out. It was hard to tell in the dim light, but the driver looked quite a bit like Hugo Díaz. The BMW backed out of the driveway, turned, and then sped down the road to the east.

I followed at a safe distance in the aircar. Half an hour later, we found ourselves in a rundown industrial neighborhood in Inglewood, not far from the DZ. The BMW pulled into the parking lot of what looked like an abandoned auto body shop, and I cut the lights and parked down the street. The BMW was out of sight behind a fence.

I opened the dash and handed a spare nine-millimeter to Keane. "Just in case," I said. Keane generally didn't care for guns, but I didn't know what we were up against, and figured it was better to err on the safe side. He took it from me reluctantly, and the two of us crossed the street and made our way along the fence toward the body shop. As we neared the corner, I saw headlights turning onto the street a couple of blocks down. From the height of the lights, I surmised it was some kind of truck. "Back!" I whispered to Keane.

We shuffled along the fence and retreated into the next driveway. I peaked around the corner as the car moved toward us and then turned down into the body shop. Evidently, Hugo—or whoever had been driving the BMW—was meeting someone.

I ran along the fence again, stopped at the corner, and peered down the driveway just in time to see the truck's taillights disappear around the back of the building. I drew my gun and ran down the driveway to the corner. Keane followed. Peering around the corner, I saw a twenty-foot box truck parked maybe thirty feet from the back of the building, with two men standing in front of it. The feet of a third man were visible on the other side. I couldn't make out the license plate of the truck, but the side of the truck bore the logo for Nifty Truck Rental. In front of the truck was the BMW. Across the parking lot, a hundred or so yards away, was a long squat building, probably a strip mall. The lot was lit sporadically by streetlights, but the one nearest the body shop was out, so the only light in the vicinity was from the headlights of the truck. There was enough reflected light from the BMW to see that the two men on this side of the truck wore sidearms, and I assumed the third did as well. A fourth man, who may have been the driver of the BMW, was opening a door in the back of the building. The door closed, and he disappeared inside. The two men near me conversed in hushed tones.

Tactically speaking, the situation wasn't great. Ideally, I'd have sent Keane around behind the truck to cover the man on the far side while I dealt with the two closer to me. But for all his brilliance, Keane isn't particularly stealthy, and he's a terrible shot. I didn't like the idea of him having to face off against an armed man who might be a hell of a lot more comfortable with a gun than he was. I didn't know who these guys were, but I had to assume they were pros. So I stayed where I was while I assessed our options.

Our options diminished significantly a second later, when two halogen floodlights went on, bathing the whole area in white light. I heard a garage door going up, and a moment later something like a child crying. I glanced at Keane, and he shot me an impatient glare. We both knew what that sound was. I shook my head. If we were going to intervene, we needed to wait until the right moment.

I took another look and saw the fourth man walking the sheep toward the truck. I'd seen too many strange things over the past couple of days to say for certain it was him, but it sure looked like Hugo Díaz.

"Room for one more?" said the man I took to be Hugo. He laughed after he said it, like it was a joke.

"Fucking hilarious," said one of the two men.

"God damn," said the other man. "That's a big fuckin' sheep."

"It's like a fucking buffalo," said the first. "Braden, open the truck and get the ramp."

Braden? I thought. For some reason, I hadn't figured the sheep thieves would have a Braden among their ranks.

The man on the far side of the truck, whose name was

evidently Braden, came into view and opened the cargo door of the truck. This would have been a perfect moment to act, but now the men were too close to the sheep. If I drew on them and things went wrong, there was a pretty good chance Mary would end up taking a bullet. That was not an acceptable risk. Keane tapped impatiently on my shoulder, but I ignored him.

Hugo and Braden coaxed the sheep up the ramp into the truck while the others watched. I was starting to think we were just going to have to hold off, wait for the truck to leave, and follow it. The problem was that there was no telling which way the driver might go out of the parking lot. We could get back in the Nissan and take to the air, but the sheep thieves would see us for sure.

So: immobilize the truck. Decrease the number of variables, as Keane would say, and hope for the best. I stepped around the corner and took aim at the right rear tire. From inside the truck, I heard Díaz say, "Well, that's that. Signed, sealed, and delivered. Now where's the rest of my—" But his voice was cut off by the sound of two gunshots. For a sickening moment I thought Braden had shot the sheep, but then she gave a terrified bleat and bolted back down the ramp—and headed right at me.

I'd never have guessed it by looking at her, but that sheep could *move*. I suddenly had a three-hundred-pound farm animal coming at me at close to thirty miles an hour. I reflexively trained my gun on her, but couldn't bring myself to shoot. Maybe it was because Mary was a multimillion-dollar genetically engineered marvel of science, or maybe it was because she was just a big, dumb, scared animal trying to get out of a bad situation, and I felt sorry for her. I could have dived out of the way, but Keane was right behind me and had no idea what was coming. The only thing I could think to do was to raise my arms over my head and start yelling.

It worked. That is, it scared the shit out of Mary the sheep, causing her to skid to a stop close enough to me that I could have grabbed a handful of wool, and then took off running across the parking lot. It also attracted the attention of the three sheep thieves. All three pulled their guns and started shooting. This time I dove out of the way, retreating back around the corner. Bullets tore chunks out of the masonry in front of my face.

"Move!" I yelled to Keane. "Go!"

Keane ran back down the driveway toward the front of the building, and I followed. We dodged another rain of bullets as we rounded the corner of the fence. The shooting stopped, but we kept running until we got to the car, where we could take cover and see anybody coming out of the driveway. We strained to hear what the sheep thieves were saying.

"Who the fuck was that?" one of them asked.

"The fuck do I know?" replied another.

"Are they gone?"

"I think so. Where's that goddamned sheep?"

"The fuck did you shoot him inside the truck?"

The conversation continued, but it was mostly inaudible. After a moment all I could hear was a horrible screeching sound, like nails on a chalkboard.

"Stay here," I said to Keane. I ran across the street and peered around the fence down the driveway. There was no sign of anyone. I moved quickly down the driveway until I had a good view of the parking lot. The sheep was just a white patch of fuzz retreating in the distance. Two of the men were running after her, and the third was driving the truck. They'd left the ramp down, so it was dragging on the asphalt, making an unbearable screeching noise. Poor Mary had to be on the verge of cardiac arrest, from sheer terror if not from the physical strain. Finally the driver had the idea of making a wide right and then swinging around to the left, blocking Mary's egress while the two men cornered her from behind. The geniuses had their guns out, so they either didn't realize the value of the sheep or thought she could be coaxed with the threat of violence.

I think Mary finally gave in from exhaustion more than anything else. The men managed to corral her and lead her back into the truck. They put up the ramp, closed the door, and drove off. One thing was certain: these guys weren't pros.

TWELVE

I dreamt of the sheep again. I saw fear in her eyes, and I was trying to reassure her.

"Someone is trying to kill me," the sheep said.

"Mr. Keane and I will get to the bottom of this," I told her. "It's going to be all right." Then Keane showed up with his shears again. The sheep panicked and ran across a parking lot into a warehouse. I followed her, and found myself inside a fun house. When I looked in the mirror, the sheep was looking back at me.

"I don't want to do this anymore," the sheep told me. Everywhere I looked, there were sheep. Hundreds of them, all around me. I wanted to help the sheep escape the mirrors, but I didn't know how.

"Keane," I said. "Get in here. You have to help me."

"Sure," said Keane, coming up behind me. He raised a gun and fired. Everywhere, mirrors shattered, leaving only blackness in their place.

"Hell," I said. "I could have done that."

"Done what?" said Keane.

I opened my eyes to find him standing over my bed. "Never mind," I said. "You don't knock anymore?"

"I did," said Keane. "You told me to come in. Get up, we've got to get to the *DiZzy Girl* set."

An hour later we were inspecting the site of the explosion. Cleanup was already well under way; most of the rubble had been cleared, and there was no sign anyone had been killed. There was also no sign of Priya's body double. We asked around a bit, and nobody seemed to know where she was. Priya hadn't been seen on the set since the explosion either. Roy was beside himself. I was sorely tempted to tell him we had just seen Priya alive and well at a hotel a few miles away last night, but Keane insisted that was a bad idea until we knew exactly what was going on. Keane and I were debating what to do next when we saw Élan Durham walking our way.

"Do you think he knows what's going on with Priya?" I asked.

"I would guess we're about to find out," replied Keane.

But Élan didn't want to talk to us about Priya. In fact, Durham didn't particularly want to talk to us at all. "Somebody wants to see you," he said gruffly. "This way." He turned and started walking back the way he had come.

I looked at Keane, who shrugged. We followed Durham to his trailer. He opened the door and gestured for us to go inside.

As we entered, Keane and I both balked. Sitting on a burgundy leather couch inside the trailer was Selah Fiore, the legendary actress and current CEO of Flagship Media. Keane did a better job than I of hiding his surprise, but I think we were both a bit starstruck. Fiore smiled and got to her feet. After getting a scowl from Fiore, Élan did the same. "Mr. Keane," she said, shaking his hand. "Mr. Fowler." Élan nodded curtly to us, not saying a word. Clearly, this meeting was not his idea.

"It's an honor to meet you, Ms. Fiore," said Keane. I nodded. Now in her late sixties, Selah Fiore's beauty had begun to fade a bit, but she was still a head turner—not to mention one of the most powerful people in Los Angeles. "Please, gentlemen, sit down. Can I get you something to drink?" She held up a ceramic mug with the *DiZzy Girl* logo on it. "The coffee is excellent."

"I'm fine," said Keane.

"I'll take some coffee, Ms. Fiore," I heard myself saying.

"Please," she said. "Call me Selah." She turned to Durham. "Élan, get Fowler some coffee."

"Seriously?" asked Durham. Selah glared at him. Durham got up and poured me a cup of coffee.

"Cream, two sugars," I said with a smile. I hated cream and sugar in my coffee, but I wasn't going to pass up the opportunity to have Élan Durham wait on me. Durham grumbled but fixed the coffee and brought it to me.

"Thanks, Élan," I said with a smile. I took a sip. Even with the cream and sugar, I had to admit it was damn good coffee.

Durham turned toward Selah. "Anything else?" he asked, a tinge of irritation in his voice. "I've got a scene to shoot."

Selah gave him a dismissive wave, and he left, slamming the trailer door behind him. Selah laughed. "Talented guy," she said, "but a bit of a prima donna. Has to be reminded who signs the checks."

Keane and I nodded as if we understood.

"I'm surprised Mr. Durham is shooting today," I said. "After the explosion yesterday, I mean."

"We're on a very tight schedule," said Selah. "The explosion was a setback, but I'm dealing with it."

A setback, I thought. *That's how she thinks of an event that killed at least three people.*

"How is Priya this morning?" I asked.

Selah smiled at me. "Priya is taking the day off," she said. "She's a little shaken up, but she'll be fine."

"Uh-huh," I said, and took what I hoped was an ominous sip of coffee.

"I didn't ask you here to talk about Priya, though," said Selah. "I would like to talk to you about a completely unrelated matter."

Yeah, I thought. *Anything other than Priya Mistry, probably.*

"Really," said Keane. "And what might that be?"

"I understand, Mr. Keane," said Selah, "that you're the best private investigator in Los Angeles."

"Phenomenological inquisitor," said Keane. "But yes, I am."

"Good," said Selah. "I'd like to hire you."

"I'm rather booked up at present," said Keane.

"I'll pay double your normal rate."

"Hmm," said Keane. "And if your case happens to distract us from another investigation we're engaged in, that's purely incidental."

Selah sighed. "Feel free to follow Priya around the *DiZzy Girl* set if you like," she said. "She should be back tomorrow. But you're wasting your time. She's in no danger. Meanwhile, I have a very pressing matter I would like you to look into."

"I'm listening," said Keane.

"To be blunt," said Selah. "Something has been stolen from me. I want it back."

"I see," said Keane. "And this stolen item, what might it be, exactly?"

I took another sip of coffee.

"A sheep," said Selah.

I came very close to spitting out the coffee. Instead I swallowed hard and coughed violently for a while. Selah Fiore, world-famous film star and multibillionaire, couldn't possibly have just said what I thought she said. I had sheep on the brain. It was the only explanation. "I'm sorry," I croaked. "Went down the wrong pipe. I thought you said someone stole your *sheep*."

"You have to understand," Selah said, regarding me disapprovingly, "this is no ordinary sheep."

So I *had* heard her correctly. "Lot of that going around," I murmured.

"And you're the legal owner of this sheep?" Keane asked hurriedly, shooting me a disapproving glance.

Selah took a sip of her coffee. "Ownership is a tricky thing," she said.

"Not in my experience," I said. "Either you own something or you don't." I was starting to really dislike the vibe I was getting from Selah Fiore.

"It may help if I give you a little background," said Selah, studying her coffee cup. "A parable, if you will. The parable of the lost sheep."

I gave Keane a dubious look, but he just shrugged.

"Once upon a time . . . ," started Selah.

"Hold on," I said. "I thought this was a parable. Not a fairy tale. Parables don't start with *once upon a time*."

"This one does," said Selah, irritably. "Once upon a time," she said again, glaring at me as if challenging me to interrupt. I shrugged and took another sip of coffee. She continued, "There was a king of a very large and very powerful kingdom. This king became overconfident in his wealth and abilities, and overextended himself fighting wars against other kingdoms. His resources were spread so thin that eventually his own kingdom fell into anarchy. It took him five years to get control of the kingdom again. Now in this kingdom there were certain wizards, practitioners of what you might call black magic—a kind of sorcery that had been outlawed by the king. When the kingdom collapsed, these wizards seized up their chance to pursue their arcane work. But the work these wizards were doing was expensive. They needed gold to buy . . . let's say, materials."

"Eye of newt, toe of frog, wool of bat, and tongue of dog," said Keane.

"Right," said Selah. "That sort of thing. Now, a certain merchant gave a certain wizard a lot of gold to buy newt eyes and the like, with the understanding that the merchant would be given access to the fruit of the wizard's sorcery. But then the king reasserted control over his kingdom and threatened to imprison any wizards who had been practicing black magic. A few of them did get imprisoned, but most of them just destroyed the evidence and kept the results of their work to themselves."

"And our generous merchant got screwed."

"Precisely. The wizard claimed not to know anything about any black magic, so the merchant never got what she paid for. Now let's suppose the merchant became aware of some of the fruits of the wizard's work, and found an opportunity to avail herself of those fruits. Under those circumstances, Mr. Keane, wouldn't you say that the merchant would be justified in claiming the fruits for herself?"

"The scenario is too abstract for me to make any definitive judgment," Keane said. "Let's just say I can see the merchant's point of view. But whether or not the fruits belong to you, I'm not a thief. I'm not going to break into a lab and steal your fruits for you."

"Just so we're all on the same page here," I said, "you do both realize a sheep is not a variety of fruit?"

Selah glared at me.

"I'm just saying," I grumbled. "The story was supposed to be about a sheep."

"The sheep has already been removed from the lab," Selah said. "But it never got to me."

"You hired someone to steal the sheep, but they double-crossed you," said Keane.

"Something like that," replied Selah. "I'll give you the details once you've agreed to take the case."

I suspected we already knew quite a few of those details, but I kept my mouth shut.

Keane shook his head. "I'm sympathetic to your plight, but I'm afraid I have to decline. I have a conflicting engagement." Presumably, Keane was talking about the fact that he had already promised to return the sheep to the Esper Corporation. After all, it had to be the same sheep, didn't it? How many genetically modified sheep could be at large in Los Angeles at any given time? But of course Selah thought he meant he was busy on Priya's case.

"I'll triple your rate," said Selah. "No, quadruple it. Hell, Keane, name your price. I need this sheep found."

"Why do you even want this sheep?" I asked. "You're a movie star and a powerful executive. What possible use do you have for a genetically modified sheep?"

"That's my business," said Selah curtly. "I'll tell you anything that might help you find the sheep, but why I want it is none of your concern. What do you say, Mr. Keane?"

"I'm sorry," said Keane. "I just can't do it."

Selah sighed. "A man of principle, eh? So there's nothing I can offer you that will change your mind?"

"I'm afraid not," said Keane.

"In that case," said Selah, her jaw set firmly, "I have no more use for you."

THIRTEEN

We took the hint and got the hell out of Selah's office. I was doing my best not to read too much into her comment about having "no more use" for us—I'd heard stories about Selah Fiore's ruthlessness, and after witnessing her reaction to an explosion that killed three of her employees, I wasn't eager to see what she was capable of.

"Did you notice anything strange about that conversation?" Keane asked as we strolled down the street past the site of the explosion. We seemed to be headed back to the car.

"Well, there was the part where she asked us to locate a sheep for her," I said.

"I was referring to the way she ended it," said Keane.

"The comment about having no use for us?"

"No, she's right about that," said Keane. "She has no use for us. My point was that despite the fact that she has no use for us, she didn't kick us off the set. She wanted nothing more than to tell me to go to hell, but she didn't. She *wants* us here."

"Why?" I asked.

"Presumably, because there's nothing for us to find. And perhaps because she doesn't want us somewhere else."

"Like the Palomar," I said.

"Right," said Keane.

"So you don't think the sheep was a red herring?" The mixed metaphor didn't register until it had left my mouth.

"No," said Keane. "I think she's actually desperate to get her hands on that sheep."

It took me a moment to realize he wasn't being facetious. "Why?" I asked.

"I haven't the faintest idea."

"So it's just a coincidence that she asked us to find a sheep we're already looking for."

"A coincidence?" said Keane thoughtfully. "I'd call it a confluence of events."

"We do think it's the same sheep, right?"

He raised an eyebrow at me. "How many genetically engineered sheep do you think are at large in Los Angeles?"

I nodded. So we were in agreement on that one.

"I take it we're done here then," I said.

Keane nodded. "If Selah wants us here, this is the last place we need to be."

"Where to then?"

"Back to the office. I need to think."

"All right," I said. "I'll drop you off. I'm going to check out some of the Nifty Truck Rental locations and see if I can find any leads on the sheep thieves."

Keane nodded absently, deep in thought. I doubt he heard a word I said. But it didn't matter, because we never made it to the office.

"Erasmus Keane," said the cop at the DZ checkpoint, leaning over to see Keane in the passenger's seat. "I need you to follow that officer over there." He pointed to a sunglasses-wearing cop standing next to an aircar some fifty feet away. Officer Shades gave us a slight wave as we looked in his direction.

"This relationship isn't entirely about your needs," said Keane. "Am I being arrested?"

"Not if you do as you're told," said the cop. "Otherwise I might find I suspect you're transporting contraband and have to tear your car apart."

Keane gritted his teeth but said nothing. He knew when he was beat. You couldn't fight the LAPD.

"What's this about?" I asked.

"Orders," said the cop. "Get moving."

I glanced at Keane, who shrugged. I pulled up behind the aircar. Officer Shades got in and pulled away from the curb. When he got to a launching area down the street, he took off and arced toward Downtown. We followed. A few seconds later a second police car closed behind us.

"These guys aren't messing around," I said.

"It's for show," Keane said. "Somebody is trying to impress us."

He turned out to be exactly right. Five minutes later we were directed to land on the roof of the Esper building. We were met by the head of security for the Esper Corporation and escorted to the office of Jason Banerjee. He didn't offer us coffee. In fact, he didn't even get up from his desk.

"You could have just called," I said.

"It seems you've been a bit distracted of late," said Banerjee. "I wanted to get your attention. I assume my friends in the LAPD treated you well."

"Is that who those guys were?" said Keane. "I thought we had crashed some kind of fascist parade."

Banerjee smiled wanly. "Please, have a seat."

Keane and I took the chairs opposite him.

"So, gentlemen. Any progress in finding our missing sheep?"

"The investigation is ongoing," said Keane. "Your theatrics aren't going to make things move any more quickly."

"Nor is your feigned indignation," replied Banerjee.

Keane studied him for a moment. "We've identified an employee who was involved."

"The dead man, yes," said Banerjee. "I heard you harassed his widow."

"*Harassed* is a harsh term," said Keane. "I heckled her a bit."

"Mr. Keane's interrogative technique can be a bit brusque," I said. "We believed Jessica Díaz may have been withholding some critical—"

"Let me be clear," said Banerjee. "I don't give a damn about Jessica Díaz. You can tar and feather her if it gets results. What I want to know is, where the hell is my sheep?"

"We've connected Hugo Díaz to a criminal organization operating in the DZ," said Keane. "As the investigation is ongoing, I'd prefer not to say more at the moment."

"I see," said Banerjee. "And might this criminal organization have some connection to Selah Fiore?"

"Not that I know of," said Keane, without hesitation. "Why do you ask?"

I had to admire Keane's composure. Where the hell did Banerjee get the idea Selah Fiore was involved? Did he have somebody watching us?

"I've got a source in Selah's organization," said Banerjee. "Esper has done some business with her in the past, and I've found it worthwhile to keep an eye on her. Mr. Fowler was seen on the *DiZzy Girl* set yesterday, and you two were there again today. My source says Selah was there at the same time."

"We spoke to her regarding another case," said Keane. "You understand I can't give you details."

"I see," said Banerjee. "So Selah didn't ask you about the sheep?"

"Why would you think Selah Fiore has any interest in your sheep?" I asked. "Just what sort of business did you do with her anyway?"

"My past dealings with Selah Fiore aren't relevant to this case," said Banerjee. "Suffice it to say she has a bit of a grudge against Esper."

"You know," I said, "I'm getting really tired of people not telling me things because supposedly they aren't relevant. I have a crazy idea. How about we all tell each other what we know, and then we can all decide for ourselves what's relevant. I'll start. Selah Fiore thinks you owe her a sheep. Your turn."

Keane scowled at me. I ignored him.

Banerjee smiled. "Selah provided Esper with some capital for an off-the-books project we were working on a few years ago."

"During the Collapse," I said.

"Yes," said Banerjee. "Not illegal, but not commercially viable in the conventional sense. Selah wanted Flagship to be the sole beneficiary of the research."

"Which was what?"

Banerjee studied me for a moment. "That information isn't relevant to the discussion at hand—"

I groaned and pounded my fist against my head.

"But I'm willing to tell you as a show of good faith. Understand I'm putting Esper in a potentially compromising position by sharing this with you."

I nodded impatiently. Keane regarded Banerjee, a curious expression on his face.

"What is it, then?" I said. "What was Esper working on that Selah Fiore was so interested in?"

"Age reversal," said Banerjee.

I frowned. "What, Selah wants to relive her glory days?"

"No," Banerjee said. "That wasn't her stated motivation,

in any case. She wanted to—as she put it—maximize her investment."

"In what?"

"In people. Actors and actresses, primarily. Imagine how much a Clive Harrow or a TC Gemmel is worth."

"Or a Priya Mistry," I said.

"Exactly," said Banerjee. "Priya Mistry's actually a better example, because the shelf life of actresses is so short. Even Selah Fiore's career really only spanned a couple of decades. How much time do you think Priya Mistry has left? Flagship Media spends a lot of money developing programs, finding out which actresses have star potential. And then, a few years later, they have to start over with someone new. Imagine how much more money they could make if they could just extend the life of Priya Mistry's career by five or ten years."

"Hundreds of millions," I said.

Banerjee nodded. "At least."

"Did it work?" asked Keane.

"Animal trials showed some promise," said Banerjee. "But there's a societal barrier to the adoption of this technology."

"Which is?" I asked.

"Like many new technological advancements, it's prohibitively expensive for most people. Generally, the way technology companies get past such a barrier is by marketing the first-generation product to wealthy people who value the cachet of having the latest thing."

"The stupid rich," said Keane.

"To put it bluntly, yes," said Banerjee. "The stupid rich pay the cost of the initial R and D. Once the initial development is paid for, prices begin to come down, and the user base expands. As the volume produced increases, prices drop even more. The cycle is self-reinforcing, and prices ultimately bottom out somewhere just above the cost of the raw materials. So, for example, in 1980 a basic videocassette recorder cost over two thousand dollars. By 1990, you could get one for less than one hundred dollars."

"But eternal youth isn't a VCR," Keane said.

"Correct," said Banerjee. "Nobody in 1980 expected everyone in America to be able to afford a VCR. But you can't sell immortality at a hundred million dollars a pop to the obscenely wealthy with the promise that everyone else will be able to afford it in twenty years or so."

"It isn't a crime to sell things to rich people," I said.

"Not a crime, no," Banerjee said. "But it's bad PR to be viewed as catering solely to the elite, particularly if you're a company like Esper, which relies heavily on federal funding. Politicians like to be seen supporting companies believed to be promoting the general welfare. During the Collapse, when both the funding and the oversight were intermittent, Selah's scheme seemed like a potentially profitable one. Post-Collapse, it's too risky."

"Selah came to you?" I asked.

"It was a mutual arrangement," replied Banerjee. "We approached several potential investors regarding various . . . sensitive projects we were considering. Selah was very interested in the possibility of age reversal."

"So you promised her immortality and then welshed on the deal," I said. "No wonder she's pissed off at you."

Banerjee shrugged. "Esper promised her exclusive access to the results of our R and D for ten years. The program was shut down, so there were no results. We abided by the letter of the agreement. But I'm glad you brought up the importance of fulfilling one's contractual obligations." He opened a drawer in his desk and extracted a large brown envelope. He placed it on the desk in front of us. On the upper right-hand corner was a label on which was written a single word:

Maelstrom

"What's this?" I asked, picking up the envelope.

"Insurance," said Banerjee. "Against the possibility you'll be tempted to renege on your agreement with Esper or expose sensitive information about us."

"How is that?" I asked. "What is 'Maelstrom'?"

Banerjee smiled. "Why don't you ask Mr. Keane?" he asked.

I turned to Keane, who was studying Banerjee dispassionately.

"Go on, Mr. Keane," Banerjee said. "Mr. Fowler is your partner. Surely, you trust him."

Keane was silent a moment longer. At last he said, "Maelstrom was a project I worked on several years ago."

"What kind of project?" I asked.

"It's not important," said Keane. "It has nothing to do with this case."

I sighed. There it was again. Not relevant. Nothing to see here.

"No," said Banerjee. "But it has everything to do with *you*, Mr. Keane."

"How did you find out about Maelstrom?" Keane asked. He was clearly rattled, which I found extremely unsettling. I'd never seen Keane rattled before. "Nearly everyone involved is—"

"Dead?" said Banerjee. "*Nearly* everyone, yes," he said. "But not everyone. You, for instance. I'm a very careful man, Mr. Keane. I didn't make the decision to hire you lightly. Although, as you deduced, I didn't originally plan on you conducting a full investigation, I wouldn't have put you in a position to discover potentially compromising information about Esper if I didn't have some leverage over you. A few weeks before our sheep went missing, I happened to come into some information about Project Maelstrom, and

I held on to it in case I needed it." He smiled broadly at Keane. "So when our sheep went missing, I knew you were the perfect man for the job."

"Why didn't you just ask your friends in the LAPD to help you?" asked Keane.

Banerjee smiled. "I prefer to keep my relationship with the police simple," said Banerjee. "I help them, they help me. No need for them to get involved with the seamier side of my business."

"What's in here?" I asked, indicating the envelope. Keane continued to stare at Banerjee dispassionately.

"Everything I could find about Maelstrom," said Banerjee. "It's by no means a complete accounting of the project, but it will give you a general idea. Your boss doesn't come off too well, I'm afraid. You can keep that copy; I've got another."

I was sorely tempted to pick up the envelope and tear it open, but I was pretty sure that was exactly what Banerjee wanted me to do, so I hesitated.

"Not a big reader?" Banerjee said, smiling at me. "Let me give you the executive summary. Ten years ago Los Angeles was on the verge of imploding. Half the city was rioting. Fires everywhere. Anybody who had the means had gotten out, and the people who were left behind were just trying to survive. Nobody expected the city to last. But then, by some miracle, our notoriously ineffective city, state, and federal governments got together and came up with a plan to save Los Angeles: wall off the problem areas and focus on saving the more crucial parts of the city. You ever wonder how that happened, Mr. Fowler?"

I had to admit, I had been as surprised as anyone by the city's bold and decisive action during the crisis. At the time, the debate (to the extent there had been one) had centered on the ethics of essentially trying to quarantine the criminal element within the city. Only a few fringe conspiracy theorists had thought to ask how the city had come up with such an effective plan so quickly.

"You're saying Keane knew the Collapse was coming," I said. "That this Maelstrom project developed the plan to create the Disincorporated Zone in advance." No wonder Keane wanted to keep that secret: he had known the Collapse was coming and had done nothing to stop it. "Jesus, Keane," I said. "Why didn't you do something? Hundreds of thousands of people died during the Collapse. If you had warned the feds, maybe they could have done something."

Keane didn't reply.

"Don't be too hard on him," said Banerjee. "Maelstrom was much bigger than one person. There probably was nothing he could do to prevent the Collapse. Of course, it's doubtful the general public will see it that way. And the feds will probably want to prosecute him for conspiracy to commit mass murder or some damn thing. In any case, understand I'd prefer to keep this information secret. I really only brought it up because your meeting with Selah Fiore has me . . . concerned. Remember who you work for, and everything will work out just fine."

"I've never double-crossed a client," said Keane.

"Good," said Banerjee. "Deliver the sheep, and we won't have a problem."

"And if we fail?" I asked.

Banerjee returned Keane's glare. "Then the contents of that envelope will be delivered to my friends at the FBI."

FOURTEEN

Ten minutes after leaving Banerjee's office we were once again soaring over Los Angeles in the aircar. The envelope labeled MAELSTROM rested on the dash.

"Are you going to open it?" I asked.

"No," said Keane.

"Then may I?"

"It has no bearing on our present case," said Keane. "If you have some other pressing reason to review the contents, be my guest."

"No need," I said. "But to be clear, if he gives that information to the FBI . . ."

Keane stared straight ahead. "It will destroy me," he said.

We rode the rest of the way to the office in silence. I dropped Keane off and asked the car's nav system to bring up all the Nifty Truck Rental locations in Los Angeles. There were fourteen of them. I figured I'd start at the Inglewood location and move outward. Maybe one of them had a truck that had been returned with its innards smelling like a frightened sheep. On the way to Inglewood, I called April. I hadn't talked to her since I'd hung up on her the previous morning.

"Oh, hello," she said cheerfully. "I think I recognize this

number. You're some sort of appendage of that famous phenomenological inquisitor, Erasmus Keane, aren't you? Do you have his permission to be using the comm?"

"Sorry," I said. "Things have been just . . . well, crazy."

"You haven't found Priya yet?"

"No."

"Well, Tom will be thrilled you're still on the case," she said. "He's looking for any excuse to go down to the set and gawk at her. I think he's dummying up some fake legal documents right now."

It took a moment for me to register that Tom was her lawyer friend who had spotted Priya on the set of the Prima Facie commercial yesterday. "Tell Tom his sacrifice is appreciated," I said.

"So I should tell him to take his fake contracts down there?"

"Can't hurt to have another set of eyes looking out for Priya," I said.

"Are you working on her case now?" April asked.

"Actually, I'm back on the hunt for the missing sheep," I said.

"How's that going?"

"Not great. We had a lead on it the other night, but things went sideways and we lost her again. It seems our sheep is in high demand."

"Well, I don't think Tom can help you there."

"I suppose not," I said. "Hey, there's one more thing I wanted to ask you."

"Shoot."

"Does the word *maelstrom* mean anything to you?"

"You mean like a storm?"

"A very powerful whirlpool," I said. I had already done a Web search for the word and hadn't found much of interest beyond the dictionary definition.

"Sounds like you know more than I do," she said.

"So you've never heard of a Project Maelstrom?"

"Not that I can recall. What's this about?"

"Probably nothing," I said. "Thanks for your help, April."

"Anytime." She ended the call.

It was just after three o'clock, so I figured I had enough time to hit at least three or four Nifty Truck Rental locations before I needed to head downtown to meet April. I parked at the Inglewood location and sat for a moment, staring at the still-sealed envelope on the dash. If Keane really did have some dark, criminal past, didn't I deserve to know about it? I was his partner, after all. If he was involved in something illegal, it could come back on me. I'd never asked about his life before becoming Erasmus Keane, just as I had never formally asked him to look into Gwen's disappearance. In my mind, we had a sort of unspoken agreement that he would help me with the latter if I didn't bring up the former. After three years, though, this arrangement had produced no fruit, not a single lead on what had happened to Gwen, and I had begun to wonder if I wasn't imagining this agreement— or at least taking it much more seriously than Keane was. I'd exhausted most potential leads before I'd started working for Keane, but I kept working on her case in my spare time, tracking down classmates, ex-boyfriends, previous employers . . . anyone who might have had a clue what had happened to Gwen. I'd never really expected Keane to help with the mundane stuff, of course. In fact, part of my frustration with Keane was that it was virtually impossible to quantify his work. He had no process I could discern, so I couldn't say for certain he wasn't doing anything to help find Gwen. All I knew was that the flashes of insight we relied on to solve other cases were in extremely short supply when it came to locating my ex-girlfriend.

Whether or not an agreement was still in effect (or even

existed), though, what could be the harm in looking in the envelope? I could reseal the envelope, and Keane would never know. Would he?

I sighed and put the envelope in the glove compartment. Of course he would know. I don't know how, but he would know. He always knew.

I got out of the car and went to the Nifty Truck Rental office. The pimply-faced kid behind the counter wouldn't give me the time of day at first, but he got a lot more helpful after I slipped him a hundred new-dollar note.

Keane and I always used new dollars for bribes, because they got people's attention. The conversion rate for new dollars to greenbacks was pegged by the government at twenty to one, but the truth was that nobody really wanted those wrinkled, ugly old bills. I think it was a psychological barrier as much as any sort of economic principle at work: those who had held a lot of dollars didn't like to be reminded how much they had lost in the Collapse, and those who had dumped their dollars at the bottom of the market didn't like to be reminded of how much more they'd lost by not waiting it out. Greenbacks were just bad juju, and everyone felt it. New dollars held the promise of better days to come.

Anyway, the pimply-faced kid didn't recall renting a truck to anyone matching the descriptions of the three sheep thieves I gave him, but he let me sniff around the company's recently returned trucks and gave me a printout of the last few days of rental records. The rental trucks smelled like . . . well, rental trucks, and no names on the printouts jumped out at me. Not a lot of information for a hundred new dollars, but maybe I'd have better luck at the next Nifty location.

Sadly, I struck out there as well. This store, in the Torrance area, was staffed by a pretty young blond woman, and I might have charmed her into giving me the rental logs if her manager, a dour Middle Eastern gentleman, didn't keep peeking out of the office at me, throwing off my mojo. I had her show me a few trucks under the pretense of needing to move some furniture, but when I insisted on seeing (not to mention smelling) the interior of six different identical trucks, the manager decided he needed to take over. When I agreed to take one of the trucks, he handed me back to the blonde, and I slipped her a hundred for the rental records while he took a phone call, and then got the hell out of there.

I was on my way to the third closest location, northeast of Downtown, when my comm chirped. It was Dr. Takemago, the scientist Keane and I had talked to at the Esper Corporation.

"Hello, Doctor," I said. "What can I do for you? Another sheep gone missing?"

"Mr. Fowler?" I heard Takemago's voice say. "I tried to call Mr. Keane, but he didn't answer. Something very strange is happening."

"What is it, Dr. Takemago?"

"Mary's GPS tracker. It's back online."

"You mean it's transmitting?" I asked.

"Yes."

"So you have Mary's location?"

"Yes." My comm display lit up with coordinates. After a moment the comm identified the location.

"She's in Griffith Park," I said.

"It would appear so," said Dr. Takemago.

"Have you told anyone else this?"

"No," said Dr. Takemago.

"Doctor, this is important," I said. "You haven't told anyone at Esper. Not even Jason Banerjee?" I was fairly certain Banerjee didn't want the police involved in the case, but I wasn't sure what he might do if he knew the sheep had been located. He might try to cut Keane and me out of the deal entirely.

"I have told no one but you," she said. Then her voice got quiet. "I . . . don't trust Mr. Banerjee," she said.

"You and me both, sister," I said. "Don't say a word to anyone. I'll get ahold of Keane. Stay ready. When I get close to the park, I'll message you for updated coordinates. We'll get your sheep for you."

"Safely, please," said Dr. Takemago. "It is . . . imperative that the animal not be harmed."

"I'll do my best," I said, and ended the call. I put the car on a course to Griffith Park and called Keane. He didn't answer, so I left him a message. I couldn't imagine why the thieves would take Mary the sheep to a public park, or why they would have reactivated her tracking device, but there wasn't much to do but go there and find out.

When I got near the park, I messaged Takemago again, and she sent me another set of coordinates. The sheep had moved a few hundred yards to the northwest. The original coordinates Takemago had sent me were near the southeast entrance of the park, but now the sheep was a bit farther into the park—probably near the old merry-go-round. If I were Keane, I'd probably just have landed the aircar right in the middle of the park, but I didn't particularly want to get arrested—nor did I want to terrify Mary the sheep into running headlong into a ravine. I parked in the closest lot I could find and then took off on foot toward the coordinates. The parking lot was mostly empty, and only a few dozen people—mostly young couples and families with small children—meandered around the area.

I was nearing the carousel when another message, with a third set of coordinates, came in from Takemago. The sheep was moving more slowly now, north by northwest. It should be just on the other side of the merry-go-round. I walked clockwise around the perimeter, my hand on my gun, not knowing what to expect. The tracker coordinates were probably only accurate to within thirty feet or so, but I didn't think I'd have any trouble spotting a three-hundred pound sheep anywhere in the vicinity.

But I didn't see it. All I saw were families, couples . . . and one very shapely young woman with long black hair. I'm usually pretty good at staying on task when I'm working, but I couldn't help but admire this girl's figure. In fact, I was still looking when she turned around and found myself—after a momentary correction of attitude—staring straight into the eyes of a face that had become very familiar of late.

"Priya," I said. It was her. It had to be. The exact same woman I had met in Keane's office two days before.

Her eyes were wide with fear. "Do I . . . know you?" she asked.

I noticed, fifty or so yards away, a muscular man with dark spiky hair walking rapidly toward us.

"I work for Erasmus Keane," I said. "You know who that is?" There was no hint of recognition in her face. Priya had forgotten she'd ever met me. Again.

"The private investigator? But how—"

"Mr. Keane is . . . looking into your situation," I said. "I'm his partner. You can trust me."

"Um, okay," she said, looking around nervously. She didn't sound convinced. I didn't blame her. Spike had closed about half the distance between us.

"Do you have a GPS tracker on you?" I asked. "A small electronic device?"

She nodded and pulled something from her purse. It was a little plastic box, complete with a clip that could be used to attach it to a belt—or animal collar.

"Where did you get that?" I asked.

"I don't know if I should—"

"Priya!" called the muscular man, who was coming up behind her.

"Somebody told you to come here," I said. "Somebody wanted you to meet me here."

"I found a letter in my room at the Four Seasons this morning. It told me to go to Selah's office, find the tracker thing, and then go to the merry-go-round at Griffith Park."

"Let me guess," I said. "The letter was from your—"

"Priya," said Spike sternly, putting his hand on her shoulder. "You can't run off like that. It's not safe." He was regarding me suspiciously. Around us, people had begun to turn and stare at Priya. Priya's eyes darted from me to the gathering crowd. She looked like a frightened little girl.

"Who is this guy?" asked Spike. "You said you wanted to go for a walk in the park. You didn't say anything about meeting someone."

"I . . . don't know him," said Priya distantly.

"I'm a friend," I said. I saw Spike's eyes fall to my gun. "A concerned friend. Who are you?"

"This is Carlos," said Priya. "My bodyguard."

Another bodyguard. How many bodyguards did one woman need?

"Well, concerned friend," said Carlos. "Ms. Mistry needs to be going." He grabbed her upper arm lightly and began to coax her away.

"I'm *extremely* concerned," I said, my hand hovering over my gun. I didn't know what was going on here, but I had a pretty good idea that whoever had sent the letter that had prompted the original Priya to hire Erasmus Keane had also sent the letter that told this Priya to come to Griffith Park. Noogus must have figured out that Keane and I were looking for the sheep, and that the tracking device would lure us here. That meant he wanted Keane to meet Priya. But I didn't yet know why, and I wasn't about to lose her until I found out.

"Priya," said Carlos, putting himself between me and her,

"go to the car." His hand was on his own sidearm. Priya began moving uncertainly away from us.

"You don't want to do that," I said. "Carlos, you seem like a decent guy. I don't want to shoot you. But I can't let you take Priya."

"Fuck off," growled Carlos, drawing his gun. "I don't work for you."

I was having second thoughts about Carlos being a decent guy. There were now close to a hundred civilians in the immediate vicinity, and he was escalating the situation. Once again I found myself nostalgic for Roy, whom I still thought of as All-Grown-Up Noogus. Priya continued to walk away from us, the assembled gawkers parting in front of her like the Red Sea.

"That's right, Carlos," I said. "You don't work for me. In fact, you don't work for Priya Mistry, either, do you? If I'm not mistaken, Selah Fiore signs your checks."

"What's your point?" demanded Carlos. "Who the fuck are you?"

"My name is Blake Fowler. I'm a private investigator. I work for Erasmus Keane."

"Who?" Carlos grunted.

So much for name-dropping. I pressed on. "I'm looking into a threat against Priya. I have nothing against you, Carlos, but I have some reason to believe that Selah Fiore can't be trusted. Until I know more, I can't let you take Priya."

Carlos laughed and shook his head. "Whatever, man," he said. He must have decided I wasn't much of a threat, because he holstered his gun and turned to follow Priya.

"Carlos," I said. But he just kept walking. I sighed. Why did guys like Carlos always want to do things the hard way?

I drew my gun and took aim. A few of the bystanders screamed, but not in time to warn Carlos. I squeezed the trigger, and a flurry of turf erupted between his feet. Carlos fell to the ground, clutching his right foot. "God damn you!" he snarled. "You shot me!"

"I grazed your foot, you big pussy," I said. "Next one is going to hurt a lot more." I saw him reaching for his gun. "Bad idea, Carlos. I'm pretty sure I can shoot that gun right out of your hand, but it's not my wrist that's going to shatter if I'm a couple inches off."

Carlos raised his hand and swiveled on the ground to face me. The crowd was getting hysterical, so I reached into my back pocket and flipped open my wallet to reveal my badge. "Official business," I announced. "Please leave the area." This had the desired effect: it deescalated the mood and prompted most of the crowd to disperse. It's funny what a plastic badge and a meaningless phrase can do. The authority of the police is another mass delusion that can be useful at times. I hadn't even needed to claim I was a cop; all it took was a couple of simple cues to invoke the delusion.

"What the fuck do you want?" demanded Carlos.

That was actually an excellent question. What *did* I want? Ideally, I'd convince Priya to come with me so I could bring her to Keane, and we could sort this all out. But Priya was currently hunched over on the lawn about twenty yards past Carlos, her hands over her ears, shaking with fear. I didn't get the impression it would be particularly easy to get her to cooperate with my plan. She didn't know whom to trust, and I could sympathize. I didn't know whom to trust either.

"Call your boss," I said at last.

"Huh?" said Carlos, looking up from his bloody shoe.

"Call Selah Fiore," I said. There was a time for sneaking around, gathering clues, and piecing together puzzles, and there was a time for laying your cards on the table and demanding to know what the fuck was going on. In my estimation, we were well into the latter phase. I'd abandoned subtlety when I shot Carlos in the foot.

"I can't just c-call Selah Fiore," Carlos stammered. "I don't have a direct—"

I took a few steps toward him. "Call your boss," I said. "Call Flagship. Call whoever you want. Tell them whatever you like. But you get one call, and at the end of that call, either I'm going to be talking to Selah Fiore or you're going to be picking a lot of little pieces of your kneecap out of the grass."

Thirty seconds later he had Selah Fiore on his comm. He tossed the call to me.

"Mr. Fowler," she said. "You have my attention."

"We need to talk," I said. "About Priya Mistry."

"Yes, I understand you've interrupted Priya's day off."

"Funny thing about that," I said. "I ran into Priya here at the park, and she didn't recognize me."

"Priya is under a lot of stress," Selah said. "Please leave her alone. Let Carlos do his job."

"Stress can do some crazy things to a person, I guess. Maybe I'll take her back to the office so Keane and I can debrief her."

Selah was silent for a moment. "Perhaps we should talk about this in person. Come to the Flagship lot at five p.m. Make sure Mr. Keane is with you."

"I'll bring Priya as well," I said.

"No," replied Selah curtly. "You will let Carlos take Priya home. Her mental state is not going to be helped by being dragged into this. You have my word she is in no danger."

"Your word," I said. "And what is that worth, exactly?"

"Whether you trust me is of no consequence, Mr. Fowler. Let her go, or we have nothing to talk about."

I considered the matter. Priya was still cowering alone on

the grass, clearly terrified. I may have had a chance to get her to trust me, but I was pretty sure I'd blown that when I'd shot Carlos. I got the impression that the bodyguards—Carlos, Jamie, and Roy—were out of the loop regarding the great Priya Mistry conspiracy. Whatever was going on here, I was willing to bet they had been intentionally kept in the dark by Selah.

"Fine," I said. "Keane and I will be there at five." I ended the call.

Carlos had taken off his shoe and sock and had hobbled over to Priya. He was doing his best to console her. There was a fair amount of blood on the sock, which he had left strewn on the grass next to the ruined shoe, but the wound seemed to be superficial. That was good; I hadn't intended to cripple the guy just for doing his job.

"Carlos," I said. I had lowered my gun, but was still holding it at my side in case he got any ideas. "This is your lucky day. Take Priya and get out of here."

He didn't argue. He helped Priya to her feet, and they began to walk away, Carlos leaning slightly on Priya as he favored his right foot.

"Hey, Carlos," I said. He turned and looked at me. "Take good care of her."

He grunted and kept walking. Priya didn't even look back.

While I was trying to imagine what might be going on in her head, my comm chirped. It was Keane.

"Fowler," he said. "What's going on? Did you find the sheep?"

"Not exactly," I said.

"You said the GPS tracker was in Griffith Park."

"It was. Priya Mistry had it in her purse."

"Priya Mistry? What the hell was she doing in the park?"

"No idea," I said. "She didn't recognize me. Again."

"Fascinating."

"Yeah, fascinating," I said. "I had to make a few executive decisions in your absence."

"Like what?"

"I'll pick you up in twenty minutes," I said. "We're going to meet Selah Fiore."

FIFTEEN

"You're certain it was Priya Mistry?" Keane asked on the way to the Flagship Media lot.

"It sure as hell looked like her," I replied. "But she had no idea who I was. Just like when we met her at the Palomar. I'd say she's got some serious memory-retention issues, but that doesn't explain how she was on a set in Culver City ten minutes after she disappeared from the *DiZzy Girl* set. None of this makes any sense, Keane."

"You have a hypothesis, though," said Keane.

"No, I don't."

"Sure you do. The fact that you brought up the two key problems with Priya—her inconsistent memories and her ability to seemingly be in two places at the same time— indicates you've devised a way to resolve both of them. So what is it?"

I sighed. The fact was, I did have an idea, but it was crazy. I mean, seriously crazy. The kind of crazy that made a giant bioengineered sheep running loose in Los Angeles seem downright mundane. "I had a thought," I said, "but it's pretty ridiculous."

"Out with it," said Keane.

I had no doubt Keane would ridicule me for my idea mercilessly, but he clearly wasn't going to let me off the hook until I told him. "Okay," I said. "Well, I was thinking: if Hugo Díaz had a doppelganger, then maybe Priya Mistry does too. Maybe there are two of them."

"Two Priya Mistrys," said Keane.

"Well, yes."

"Why not three?" asked Keane.

"Hey, you asked," I said. "That was my idea. Make fun of me all you want."

"I'm serious," said Keane. "Wouldn't three make more sense? Otherwise, you still have to account for the fact that she didn't recognize you at the park, either."

"Um," I said, unsure if Keane really was considering the possibility or merely pointing out the idea's absurdity. "Sure, I suppose there could be three."

"Or more," said Keane. "Others we haven't met yet."

"Jesus, you really are serious," I said, turning to face him. "You think there are a bunch of Priya clones running around Los Angeles."

"I didn't say that," said Keane. "But the simplest explanation for what we've experienced is that there are multiple instances of a Priya-like entity in the area."

"Occam's razor," I said.

"That's right," said Keane. "It sounds crazy, but it's less crazy than any other explanation I've come up with."

"But then . . . ," I started.

"Yes?"

"Well, by that logic, our two cases are connected. If there are multiple Hugo Díazes and multiple Priya Mistrys, then it makes sense to conclude that both phenomena have the same explanation. Not to mention the fact that somehow Priya ended up with the sheep tracker."

Keane smiled. "Very good, Fowler. I'll make a detective out of you yet."

"Not a phenomenological inquisitor?"

"Don't flatter yourself."

"But what does it mean, Keane? What the hell is going on in this city?"

"That's what we're going to find out."

I nodded. I wasn't sure whether to feel reassured that Keane shared my suspicions or worried I was starting to think like him. I was supposed to be Keane's tether to reality. If I went nuts, there was nobody to pull me back from the edge.

At five o'clock we were sitting across from Selah Fiore in her office on the main Flagship Media lot. We were seven floors up, overlooking the bustling activity of Selah's sprawling media empire.

"Gentlemen," said Selah. "What can I do for you?"

"You asked us here so we could talk in person," I said. "So talk."

She smiled at me. "About anything in particular, dear?"

"Priya Mistry," I said impatiently.

"What would you like to know?"

"I'd like to know why the woman I met at the park today looked exactly like Priya Mistry but seemed to have no memory of ever meeting me." Keeping Keane's advice in mind, I didn't mention meeting Priya at the Palomar.

"As I mentioned, Priya is under a lot of pressure," said Selah. "She has occasional lapses."

Keane regarded her curiously, but said nothing.

"Are we really going to play this game?" I demanded. "You're really going to pretend nothing screwy is going on with Priya Mistry?"

"I'm not sure what you mean," said Selah. "There was an explosion on the set. Priya needed to take a few days off. You ran into her at the park while she was trying to relax. In fact, now that I think about it, she was probably just pretending not to know you because she wasn't up to dealing with your dramatics. Frankly, I'm getting a little tired of them myself."

Keane leaned forward and put his palms on Selah's desk. "What do you want?" he asked.

"I told you what I want," Selah said.

"The sheep again," I groaned. "Forget it. We're not getting your damned sheep. On the phone you indicated you were going to level with us about Priya."

"I did no such thing," Selah snapped. "I promised Priya would be kept safe, and I offered to meet with you to talk in person. I've done both."

I shook my head. I should have seen this coming. "Offering to meet us was a stall tactic," I said. "She just needed some time to cover her tracks, hide Priya, cover up what's really going on. Well, it's not going to work. We know the truth: there are two Priya Mistrys. At *least*." Maybe it was a mistake to reveal so much, but Selah was pissing me off. I wanted to rattle her a little.

Selah laughed. "Ridiculous," she said. "Two Priyas? And even if it were true, so what? Are you going to turn me in to the doppelganger police?"

"Priya Mistry hired us to investigate a potential threat on her life," I said. "We know you're hiding information about her. That makes you our prime suspect."

Selah sighed. "Again with the dramatics. There is no threat against Priya Mistry. And I'll share one other fact with you: Priya Mistry never hired you."

I snorted. What the hell was she talking about?

"I have a signed contract that indicates otherwise," said Keane.

"That contract is a fiction," said Selah. "Completely unenforceable."

"How's that?" I asked.

144 || ROBERT KROESE

"I'm sure you'll figure it out eventually," said Selah. "I could clear everything up for you right now, of course, but I would need something in return."

"The sheep," I said.

Selah smiled. "The sheep," she said.

I was about to tell her what she could do with her sheep when Keane spoke up. "All right," he said. "We'll do it."

"You will?" Selah asked.

"We will?" I asked.

"Sure," said Keane. "We'll get your sheep for you, on the condition you'll tell us everything we want to know about Priya Mistry."

I shot Keane a puzzled glance but said nothing. If he wanted to double-cross a guy who had the power to destroy him, that was up to him.

"Excellent," said Selah.

"Great," I exclaimed. "Now tell us what the hell is going on with Priya."

"It might be easier," said Selah, "if I showed you." She spoke into her comm. "Camille, patch my office display into the feed from Building G. Give me the waiting room first."

A few seconds later the window overlooking the lot darkened, and the wall opposite lit up with a high-resolution display. We were looking down from a high angle at a large room in which sat several dozen people who covered the gamut in race and seemed to range from about twenty-five to sixty in age. Most were male, but there were a few women. They seemed to have little in common, although in general they were exceptionally fit and good-looking.

"We're auditioning for a part in a new drama," said Selah. "These are the actors who have tried out. Mostly unknowns, looking for their big break. These are the second-round auditions; we've already eliminated close to three hundred candidates."

"What's the role?" asked Keane.

"DZ warlord," said Selah.

"Like Mag-Lev," I said.

"Yes," said Selah. "The role is partly modeled after him."

"Quite a range of candidates," I said, regarding the motley group.

"For this role, we wanted to cast a wide net," said Selah. "Sometimes it's easier to find the right person and modify the script around them than to try to find someone who perfectly fits a predefined role."

"What does this have to do with Priya Mistry?" I asked.

"Patience, Mr. Fowler," said Selah. She spoke into her comm. "Give me the audition room, Camille."

The view switched to that of a smaller room, in which two women and a man sitting at a table were watching an obviously nervous young man reading from a script.

"That guy as a DZ warlord?" I said. "I don't see it."

Selah nodded. "I agree, although we might find a place for him if he tests well enough."

"Tests?" asked Keane. "What sort of test are you talking about?"

"Excellent question," said Selah. She spoke into her comm again. "Camille, give me the testing room."

A moment later the view switched to another room. Two men sat across a table from each other. One man—obviously an actor—was tanned and muscular, with chiseled features and short-cropped blond hair. The other was older and pasty-faced, and wore a suit and tie. On the table between them was a small silver box from which protruded an articulated robotic arm. At the end of the arm was some sort of sensor that was tracking the actor's movements. The man in the suit was staring at an amplified view of the other man's face on a screen in front of him. Superimposed on the man's face, not quite large enough to be visible on the display on Selah's wall, was a variety of multicolored textual readouts.

"You're standing below a tree," the man in the suit was saying to the actor. "In the tree above you is a large feral cat. The cat is—"

"Feral?" asked the man. "What's that?"

"Wild," replied the man in the suit, obviously bored. "A wild cat."

"Got it," said the actor.

"The cat is stuck in the tree, and is obviously terrified. There is a ladder nearby. You could easily move the ladder under the tree and rescue the cat, but as you're thinking about this, you notice the cat has very long sharp claws. In its frightened state, it might very well scratch you if you try to rescue it. What do you do?"

"Does it have, like, rabies?" asked the actor.

"Not that you know of," said the suited man, in a monotone.

"I'd rescue the cat," said the actor. "But I'd keep him away from my face." He grinned, showing off perfectly aligned rows of unnaturally white teeth bracketed by a set of ridiculous dimples.

The suited man sighed and tapped a few keys.

"We call it the Feinberg-Webb test," said Selah. "We conduct it on all promising candidates as part of the casting process for any of Flagship's programs. It consists of a series of questions designed to provoke an emotional response. The answers the subject provides are secondary to their involuntary physical reaction to the questions. Quickened breathing, blushing, changes in the timbre of the voice, dilation of the iris, et cetera."

"And the point of this is?" I asked.

"Ever wonder what it takes to make a star?" Selah asked. "I suppose everyone has, to some extent. People look at some big-name actor and think, *Why her?* Or conversely, *Why not her?* But for me, it's not an idle question. Flagship bets billions of dollars every year on hot young actors who may or may not be the next big thing. Imagine what it would be worth if you could know, in advance, which bets would pay off. Which actors and actresses have what it takes to be an international superstar."

"Like Priya Mistry," I said.

"Exactly," said Selah. "Obviously Priya's looks help a lot. And she's a good actor. Not great, but good. But beyond those factors, she's got something else, what they used to call the it factor. Priya has *it*, whatever *it* is. *It* is what makes her a star, rather than just another supporting actress on some indie drama no one has heard of. Now imagine if you could test someone for *it*, the way you might test someone for mechanical aptitude or color blindness. What would a test like that be worth?"

"A lot?" I offered. I was growing impatient with Selah's show.

Selah smiled. She continued, "You've probably heard my success story. Aging actress-turned-producer makes billions by capitalizing on the entertainment value of the DZ. But that's only part of the story. I laid the foundations for my success years ago, before I even became the CEO of Flagship. When I was still producing low-budget action flicks, I bought a small research company call Empathix. I'm sure you've never heard of it; in any case, they've now been rolled into the Flagship empires. Empathix was a leader in what they called empathy metrics. Basically, quantifying the factors that allow one person to relate to the experiences of another. The researchers at Empathix claimed to have identified several measurable personality traits that mark a person as having *it*. The Empathix people call those who possess these traits sympaths."

"Sympath," I said. "What does that mean, exactly? That the person is easy to relate to?"

"That's part of it," said Selah. "Essentially, a sympath possesses four distinct characteristics: relatability, charisma, poignancy, and allure. The sympath serves as a proxy, an aspirational figure, an object of pity, and an object of desire. That is, the viewer simultaneously thinks of the sympath as a stand-in for oneself, wants to be more like her, feels sorry for her, and wants to—"

"Wants to fuck her," finished Keane coldly. "No need to mince words."

"Correct," said Selah, returning Keane's stare. "Of course, the dynamics are slightly different with males and females, and straights versus gays. And there's a great deal of variation in individual preferences. But a very strong sympath will appeal to just about everyone, in ways they can't quite define. These conflicting emotional responses can be confusing to some viewers; some mistake them for love, others for hate. That's why you get psychopaths stalking actresses or, conversely, people who claim to hate a charismatic actor like Clive Harrow, but nevertheless line up to see his movies."

I suppressed a grimace at the name Clive Harrow. The guy was the classic entitled Hollywood jerkwad. And in my opinion, he'd been coasting on the success of his first big hit, *December Rain*, for a few years now. His last three movies were mediocre at best.

"As part of the casting process for any of the shows I produced," Selah went on, "I had someone from Empathix administer a test to any promising candidates. I didn't put a lot of stock in it at first, but I had Empathix track the success of the subjects, whether or not I hired them for a role on one of my productions. Over the next two years it proved surprisingly accurate at predicting which actors and actresses would strike a chord with audiences. The Feinberg-Webb scale ranges from zero to ten, and it follows a bell curve distribution, meaning that the vast majority of the population ranges somewhere between three and seven. We found that candidates who scored in the eight plus range were much more likely to go on to star in hit shows. As a result, I instructed my casting directors to start considering the Feinberg-Webb results in their casting decisions. I didn't give them any definitive guidelines, but told them to look at the scores as one factor among many." She opened the folder she was holding and pulled out a sheet of paper. "The next day," she continued, "the woman I'd put in charge of casting a new drama I was producing gave me this picture."

Keane took the paper. It was a photograph of a girl who appeared to be in her late teens. She looked vaguely familiar, like a cousin of someone I knew.

"Who is this?" I asked.

"Her name is Bryn Jhaveri," Selah said. "Just one of the thousands of girls who came to Los Angeles in the years after the Collapse, looking for their big break. Not much to look at, is she? But then, looks aren't everything."

I studied the picture. The girl was cute, sure, but she was dreaming if she thought she was going to be a movie star. I guessed she was around eighteen.

"Okay, I'll bite," I said. "You're saying Bryn Jhaveri is one of these sympaths?"

"So you have some context," Selah said, "ninety-five percent of the population scores between three and seven on the Feinberg-Webb scale. Ninety-nine-point-nine percent fall between two and eight. Anyone scoring above an eight-point-six is considered a sympath, someone who emotes in such a way that it essentially scrambles the observer's ability to rationally process the input they're receiving. The mental barrier we construct between us and strangers evaporates. The viewer relates to the sympath on a purely emotional level."

"Logic Kryptonite," I murmured.

Selah smiled. "I like that. Logic Kryptonite. Genuine sympaths, people scoring a Feinberg-Webb of eight-point-six or higher, are literally one in a million. Most people never even meet one. Bryn Jhaveri scored a nine-point-four."

"How rare is that?" Keane asked.

"As I understand it," said Selah, "she's within the test's margin of error. The best guess Empathix could give me is that Bryn Jhaveri is one in a billion. We've only had one other subject test anywhere close to her."

"So she should be a superstar," I said. "How come I've never heard of her?"

"The Feinberg-Webb results are only one factor in determining potential stardom," Selah said. "The other two major factors are talent and appearance. Bryn was a reasonably talented actress, but as you can see, she's no Priya Mistry in the looks department."

Keane was nodding thoughtfully, as if he were processing some hidden subtext of Selah's monologue.

"So where is she now?" I asked. "Making Frappuccinos at Starbucks?"

Selah shook her head. "A nine-point-four on the Feinberg-Webb scale is too valuable to waste. You have to understand that appearance and talent are what you might call 'limiting factors' to stardom. Neither looks nor ability make a star, but their absence can limit a person's star potential. Bryn Jhaveri was a diamond in the rough. All we had to do was polish her a bit."

"Cut," said Keane.

"Sorry?" said Selah.

"You cut diamonds," said Keane. "The polishing comes after."

"Fair enough," said Selah.

"You gave her plastic surgery," I said, staring at the picture. The truth had finally dawned on me. "You made her into Priya Mistry."

SIXTEEN

Something still didn't fit. Bryn Jhaveri's head was rounder than Priya's. Her hair was dark brown, not black, and her eyes were a dull hazel. Priya's were blue.

"It required more than surgery," said Selah. "I had Empathix reverse engineer a physical form based on Bryn's Feinberg-Webb results. Basically, I asked them what Bryn Jhaveri *should* look like in an ideal world. Not just physical perfection, mind you, but the perfect match between appearance and personality. We wanted her not to be just beautiful, but beautiful in a way that precisely complemented her psyche. Form follows function."

"But how?" I asked, astounded.

"Surgery coupled with gene therapy. We essentially reprogrammed Bryn Jhaveri's DNA. Changed the shape of her head, corrected the curve in her spine, fixed her facial symmetry, changed her eye and hair color, et cetera. The process took several months."

I didn't know whether to be impressed or horrified. I ultimately decided a little of each was warranted. "How much did this cost?"

"Between us?" Selah said. "In the neighborhood of two

hundred million new dollars. An investment we've recouped ten times over with Priya."

I shook my head. "So you offer to pay for all these . . . enhancements, and in return Priya agrees to work for you indefinitely."

"Indefinite contracts aren't enforceable," said Selah. "That's tantamount to indentured servitude. We could have signed her to a long-term contract, but there are ways around that as well. As it turns out, Priya surpassed all our expectations, recouping our investment in less than two years, but at the time we assumed it would take ten years or more to turn a profit. There was only one way to guarantee Priya would work for us that long."

"You own Priya Mistry," said Keane.

"Exactly," said Selah, with a smile.

"Hold on," I said. "Indentured servitude is illegal, but slavery is totally okay?"

Keane shook his head. "They don't own the *person* Bryn Jhaveri. They own the *persona* Priya Mistry. Don't you see? They created a fictional character named Priya Mistry and then altered Bryn Jhaveri to look like her. They own Priya Mistry just as surely as Disney owns Mickey Mouse."

Selah gave Keane an impressed nod.

I was trying to wrap my head around this idea. "So the person who hired us," I said. "That was Bryn Jhaveri?"

"Correct," said Selah. "She may have represented herself as Priya Mistry, but she's not legally empowered to enter into a contract as Priya Mistry any more than Mickey Mouse can buy a Lamborghini. Her legal name is Bryn Jhaveri. She's contracted to play a character named Priya Mistry in public life. Part of her contract is also to play Priya Mistry playing Aria Velazquez on *DiZzy Girl*."

"What about the Prima Facie commercials?" I asked.

Selah smiled again. "This is where it gets complicated."

"Oh," I said. "Is this where that happens? Because I thought we passed complicated when you explained how it's okay for you to own a human being."

Selah continued, undeterred. "As I mentioned, Priya's success surpassed all our expectations. There are only so many hours in a day, and Bryn works a grueling schedule on *DiZzy Girl*. We decided it was in everybody's interest to . . . well, let's say, franchise Priya."

"You made copies," said Keane.

"Yes," said Selah. "Other actresses, who superficially resembled Priya, and who also scored well on the Feinberg-Webb test. We had them altered to be identical to the original Priya. We couldn't use the copies in a feature film; they don't have Priya's charisma, and some of the more observant fans would notice subtle differences in personality. But for a thirty-second commercial, the copies work just fine."

"So Priya doesn't remember making the commercials because she didn't make them," I said.

Selah shook her head. "Priya *did* make the commercials. Bryn Jhaveri doesn't remember making them, because she didn't. But Priya did."

"Unbelievable," I murmured. "So how many Priyas are there running around Los Angeles?"

"Currently, there are three, including Bryn. I have plans for more, but I prefer not to get more specific than that. Each of them travels with her own bodyguard and has her own set of handlers. Generally, no one on set is aware that the actress they are working with is not the 'real' Priya Mistry. Or, more precisely, that she is merely one instance of the real Priya Mistry."

I shook my head, trying to comprehend the logistics of all this.

"As you can imagine," Selah went on, "this all can get

rather confusing for Bryn. Playing a character twenty-four hours a day can do strange things to your head, and sympaths tend to be emotionally volatile in any case."

"Does she know about all this?" I asked. "The other Priyas?"

Selah nodded. "Yes. Well, she was informed at one point. It's hard to say what she 'knows' anymore. These days Bryn is so wrapped up in playing Priya that we try to shield her from the existence of the other Priyas. Whether we're helping or harming her, I honestly don't know. We have some of the best psychologists in the world consulting on her case, but obviously her specific circumstances are unprecedented. There's no consensus in the mental health community on how to maintain the sanity of a person whose whole existence is a fiction."

"So you just get as much use out of her as you can and then discard her," I said. "Chew her up and spit her out."

"First of all," said Selah, meeting my glare, "Bryn chose this life. She was informed of everything in advance. She was a consenting adult, certified as sane."

"By the same psychologists you've got salivating over her impending breakdown?" I said. "That worked out well for them, didn't it?"

"Second," Selah continued, "it's in my interest to keep Bryn sane and healthy for as long as possible. And if she ever does develop some type of serious psychosis, she'll have the best care on Earth."

"A padded cell with a silver lining," I said. "That's vastly reassuring."

"What would you have me do?" asked Selah. "Suppose I release Bryn into your hands and give you unlimited funds to care for her. Then what?"

"She's an adult," I said. "She doesn't need anybody to care for her." I looked to Keane for support, but he seemed lost in thought.

Selah laughed. "Bryn Jhaveri wouldn't survive a month in the real world. Her whole life for the past five years has been a fiction. She can barely keep it together with a full-time staff looking out for her."

"Because you made her into this thing, this creature!" I snapped. "She was just a kid, desperate to be famous, and you've made her into a monster. Taken over her life, destroyed any chance she has for a normal existence."

"I made her into a star!" Selah cried. "Gave her a life that most people can only dream of!"

"Your benevolence is overwhelming," I said.

"I gave her what she wanted," said Selah coldly. "What she begged for. And I gave billions of people what they wanted without even knowing they wanted it. Priya Mistry, a woman they can admire, pity, sympathize with, lust after. And yes, I got very, very rich in the process."

"And all it cost is one little girl's soul," I replied.

Selah sighed. "What you fail to understand is that while I created Priya Mistry, I didn't make Bryn Jhaveri a sympath. I didn't instill her with the need to be famous. I just made it possible. Would she have been better off as a frustrated actress, waiting tables in between tampon commercials? Maybe. But who am I to make that decision? Who am I to say to Bryn Jhaveri, *No, the risk is too great. Your dream will have to die.*"

I snorted at this. "Have you heard enough?" I asked Keane. "I'm ready to get the hell out of here."

"Wait," said Selah. "You haven't seen the best part."

"What's that?" I said. "The operating room?"

Selah smiled and spoke into her comm. "Camille, could you please send Bryn Jhaveri in?"

A woman who looked very much like Priya Mistry walked into Selah's office. She looked, I suppose, as much as it's possible for someone to look like Priya Mistry without actually *being* Priya Mistry. Nobody was Priya Mistry, I told myself. Priya Mistry was a fictional character, like Mickey Mouse. Keane and I stood to greet her.

"Hi," she said quietly as she approached Keane and me. "My name is Bryn. We sort of met the other night."

I shook her hand dumbly. She seemed calm but slightly embarrassed, like a coworker coming into work after a not-fully-remembered night of overindulgence.

"Hi, Bryn," I heard myself saying. "I'm Blake Fowler. This is Erasmus Keane." Keane was once again doing his duckwalk, trying to observe Bryn from all angles.

Bryn laughed shyly. "I know," she said. "I remember you."

"You do?" I asked.

"Yes," she said. "I came to your office. I was . . . distraught. I suppose you could say I was not myself. But I do remember it, like a dream."

"Why did you come to our office?" I asked.

"I thought . . . ," she started. "I was confused. Sometimes I get so wrapped up in being Priya that I forget I'm not her. But then things don't fit. There are still parts of my life where I'm not Priya, and there are the other Priyas, and people watching me. . . . It can get confusing. And the people around me, people like Roy, they don't know the whole story, so they start telling me I'm imagining things, which just makes it worse. Everybody around me insists I'm Priya, and I start thinking there's this conspiracy, that people are out to get me. I heard about Mr. Keane somewhere, I can't really remember where, but I started thinking he could help. So I sneaked away to find you."

"Have you seen us since that night?" asked Keane.

"I don't think so," she said. "But my memory is a little fuzzy. I'm sorry."

"It's okay," I said. "You've been through a lot." I figured that whatever else was true, that was a safe statement to make.

Evidently, she hadn't seen me on the set or at the party the night before. Either that, or she had forgotten about it.

"What about Noogus?" Keane asked.

"Sorry?" asked Bryn.

"What can you tell me about Noogus?"

Bryn blushed and looked for a moment at Selah, who was observing her dispassionately.

"Did I tell you about Noogus?" she said. "I don't remember. Noogus was my teddy bear. When I was very little."

Keane nodded approvingly.

"Just to be clear, Miss Jhaveri," I said, "you no longer believe there is any sort of conspiracy or plot against you?"

"No," she said. "I do not."

"And you don't wish to retain the services of Mr. Keane and myself to investigate any threat against your person?"

"No," she said. "That isn't necessary. I'll pay you for the time you've put in, of course. It's the least I can do."

"Don't worry about it," I said. "It was our mistake. We should have realized the condition you were in." I added, for good measure, "Mr. Keane would never take money from someone in a psychologically compromised state." That earned me a scowl from Keane.

"Thank you, Bryn," said Selah. "Sorry to drag you away from the set, but I thought it best if you cleared up this misunderstanding in person."

"No problem," said Bryn. "I'm sorry for all the trouble I caused." She gave a little smile and turned to leave.

"One more thing," said Keane. Bryn froze and turned to face him. She glanced at Selah, who continued to regard her with no identifiable emotion.

"Yes, Mr. Keane?" Bryn said. "What can I do for you?"

"If it's not too much trouble," Keane said, "I'd love to get your autograph. I mean, Priya's autograph."

"Oh, of course!" Bryn exclaimed. "No trouble at all." She walked to Selah's desk. "Do you mind . . . ?"

"Not at all," said Selah, handing her a pen. She pulled a sheet of paper from a drawer and put it on her desk. Bryn leaned over the desk and signed, in big round letters:

Priya Mistry

She handed the paper to Keane. "Thank you so much," Keane gushed.

"You're quite welcome," said Bryn, with a smile. She turned and walked out of the room, closing the door behind her.

SEVENTEEN

My comm was blinking as the aircar arced away from the Flagship lot. It was Priya's bodyguard Roy. Or one of her bodyguards, at least. I almost didn't answer it, but if he had learned something about Priya's disappearance, I needed to know.

"Hey, Roy," I said. "What's up?"

"Not much," he said. " Élan Durham is sticking to his story that it was Stacia who was killed in the blast. He's telling everyone Priya is taking a couple of days off. Any luck on your end?"

"Nothing conclusive," I said, which was certainly true. "I think Keane may have some ideas, but so far nothing has panned out."

"You'll tell me if you find her?"

"Of course," I said, feeling a little bad about the lie. Just a little, though. This was business, and Roy was smart enough to know I was lying. Priya was our client. For all we knew, he was involved in her disappearance. I wasn't going to tell him anything unless I thought it would help us find her. Still, there was something in Roy's utterly guileless nature that made me want to tell him the truth. Somehow I couldn't believe he'd ever do anything to harm Priya. "Seriously, Roy," I found myself saying, "I'll call you as soon as we know anything."

Out of the corner of my eye, I caught a quizzical glance from Keane, who was obviously wondering why I was making such a promise. I wasn't sure I knew myself.

"Thanks," said Roy uncertainly. "Same here. Although I'm not sure how much good I can do wandering around the set. I'm a bodyguard, not a detective."

A thought occurred to me. "Hey, Roy, one more thing," I said. "Do you know a guy named Carlos? Or Jamie?"

"I don't think so," said Roy. "You got last names? Who are they? Something to do with Priya?"

"Maybe," I said. "Don't know the last names. Just a couple of thugs I ran into recently. They could be related to this other case we're on." Again, technically true.

"If you tell me what they look like, I'll keep an eye out," said Roy.

They look like miniature versions of you, I thought. But I said, "I think it's unlikely you'll run into them." *Very* unlikely. In fact, it's almost as if you're intentionally being kept away from each other.

"Okay," said Roy, clearly not satisfied with this answer but not eager to press the issue.

"Gotta go," I said. "Good luck, Roy."

"Yeah," said Roy. "You too."

I ended the call, not sure why I felt like such a jerk brushing off Roy. It's not like I had shot him in the foot or something.

I turned my thoughts back to the conversation with Selah. "Are we really going to try to get the sheep for her?" I asked Keane. "We're already obligated to retrieve it for Esper."

"Our taking this case for Selah was preconditioned on her telling us the truth about Priya Mistry," Keane replied.

"You think she was lying."

"I do."

"Good," I said. "So do I."

He regarded me with bemusement. "Really?" he said. "About what?"

"Our meeting with Priya—or whoever that was—at the Palomar," I said. "If she wasn't Bryn Jhaveri, what was she so scared of? And how did she know about Noogus? Unless the story about Noogus is just part of the act. But why would anybody make up such a weirdly specific detail like that? It just doesn't hold together."

Keane nodded. "Selah seemed to be unaware we had spoken to Priya at the Palomar. She must have debriefed Carlos and concluded you hadn't had a chance to talk about anything substantive with Priya at Griffith Park. So she told us a story that was consistent with what she thought we knew."

"But then how do you explain the multiple Priya Mistrys? Who was the woman we just talked to in Selah's office?" I asked. "Was that the original Priya? The one who hired us? Or some kind of impostor?"

"I'm not sure any of them are the 'original' Priya," said Keane. "But no, I don't think she's the one who came to our office. Selah put her up to that. She's lying."

"Or acting," I said.

"Precisely," said Keane.

"So that whole story about Bryn Jhaveri, the sympaths, gene therapy . . . that was all bullshit?"

Keane thought for a moment. "It has the appearance of truth," he said. "Or it would, if we hadn't met the Palomar Priya. My guess is that most of the details of her story will check out. But she's definitely hiding something."

"Just like Takemago with the sheep," I said. "I'm getting tired of clients telling us most of the truth. It would make our job so much easier if they would just tell us everything up front."

"But so much less interesting," Keane said. "Do you still

have the note I sent up to the Palomar Priya? The one she autographed?"

I fished it out of my pocket and handed it to Keane. He pulled a sheet of paper from his own pocket, unfolded both of them, and then compared the signatures. "What do you think?" he asked.

"Looks like a match," I said. "But, assuming there are multiple Priyas, wouldn't Selah's people have trained them all to sign their name the same way?"

"Of course," said Keane, studying the two papers. "Signatures are tricky, though. It's a damn good match."

"How many do you think there are?" I asked. "Three? Four?"

"Priyas?" said Keane. "Impossible to know. Head toward Esper. We need to consult an expert."

"An expert on what?" I asked.

"Genetics."

It was a rare occasion that Erasmus Keane decided he needed to consult with any sort of expert, but he had researched Dr. Takemago's background, and he was convinced she was one of the very few people who could give us some meaningful advice about the Priya Mistry situation. Takemago had spent the better part of the past thirty years studying genetics and was considered a world-class authority on a wide variety of topics, including in vitro fertilization, cloning, and—of particular interest to Keane—biological mimicry. Just as important, Takemago had called us, and not Jason Banerjee, when the sheep's tracking device started transmitting. That meant she trusted us, and increased the odds that we could trust her.

We met Takemago in her office, which was cramped and sparsely furnished, but—she assured us—free of any cameras or listening devices. A wall display showed Mark the sheep amiably munching on cud in its pen. Occasionally the sheep would look up at the camera, as if wondering who was watching it. The effect was somewhat unnerving.

Keane gave her an abbreviated version of the story Selah had told us, and then handed the doctor the papers with the two signatures. She studied them with interest.

"They do appear to match," she said after some time. "And you met both of these women?"

"Yes," said Keane.

"Both of you?"

I nodded. "We spoke to each of them. They were no farther away from us than you are now. Keane wasn't there when I met the third one, in Griffith Park. But if I didn't know better, I'd have sworn they were all the same person."

"You concur, Mr. Keane?"

Keane nodded. "Regarding the two I met, yes."

Takemago shook her head. "Triplets," she said. "It has to be."

"It's possible," said Keane. "But if so, our client went through a lot of acrobatics to avoid a very simple explanation."

"Well," said Takemago, "in my professional opinion, the gene therapy story is nonsense. Even if the technology existed, and it's not clear it does, and even if somebody was crazy enough to actually try something like this, there's no way they could have fooled two reasonably observant individuals at close quarters."

Keane looked dubious.

"Consider this," said Takemago. "Human beings have evolved to be extremely good at identifying other individual humans. The race's survival depends on it. A guard lets the wrong person through the gate, and a whole settlement is wiped out. There are a million ways to tell two human beings apart. Not just appearance, either. Gait, odor, pheromones, speech patterns, dialect, nervous habits . . . even the way people breathe. Even parents of identical twins have little difficulty telling them apart, despite the fact that they are genetically identical and were raised in exactly the same environment, because of tiny differences in appearance and behavior that accrue as the result of differing experiences. The ability of one human to recognize another by appearance is especially acute when it comes to heterosexual males observing nubile females. There is nothing on Earth men pay more attention to than the appearance of sexually attractive young women."

I had to suppress a shudder while listening to Dr. Takemago clinically describe Keane's and my observation of Priya Mistry. Flashback to sex ed with the nuns at St. Stephen's.

"But if the impostors had been trained to act exactly the same as the original . . . ," I started. "Dress the same. Were given the same perfume to mask difference in odor. Given lessons in how to talk, how to walk . . ."

"Are you familiar with the uncanny valley?" asked Takemago.

"Sure," I said. I'd become pretty familiar with sim terminology while working at CSI. In fact, their name, Canny Simulations, Inc., was a play on the term. "The uncanny valley refers to the sense of revulsion that occurs in observers when a human simulation isn't quite right."

"Correct," said Takemago. "As a simulation's verisimilitude increases, it reaches a point where it's almost but not quite humanlike. The sense of dissonance, the is-it-human-or-not response, manifests itself as a feeling of revulsion in the viewer."

It occurred to me, as Takemago was talking, that this revulsion could be thought of as the diametric opposite of the overwhelming sympathy and attraction one felt about a sympath like Priya Mistry—that is, like Bryn Jhaveri. I didn't see what this had to do with the proliferation of Priyas though. "What's your point?" I asked.

"The point," said Takemago, "is that something like that also happens with two people who look very similar to each other. The more one person looks like another, the more the remaining differences are magnified. If one modifies person A to look like person B, no matter how hard one tries, one is going to end up with a person who is almost-but-not-quite-exactly like person B. What you are telling me is that you two men—two healthy, exceptionally observant heterosexual males in your thirties—met a woman whose affect and appearance were highly memorable, and you had a substantive conversation with her, interacting with her at a distance of less than five feet. Then, less than a day later, you met another woman in a hotel bar who was made up to look like the first woman, and you couldn't tell them apart? Unless they were monozygotic twins, it seems highly improbable. Even if they *were* twins, you probably would have noticed something was off if you were looking for it, and it sounds like you were."

"There are no other possibilities?" I asked.

Keane had gotten up from his chair and was staring, transfixed, at the docile beast happily chewing away in its cage.

"Clones," said Takemago. "I presume that's what you are implying. Also impossible, unfortunately."

"Why?" I asked.

"You said this woman is in her midtwenties. The technology to clone humans didn't exist twenty-five years ago. Even if it had, it was illegal. No reputable lab would have attempted it prior to the Collapse. And again, even if these women were clones, they would be no more similar than monozygotic twins. Unless they were raised under identical laboratory conditions, noticeable differences would have manifested by the time they reached their midtwenties."

"Let's assume they were grown in a lab, then," said Keane.

I raised an eyebrow at Keane, but Takemago just shrugged. "The technology to clone humans has existed for nearly a decade," she said. "That is, we've been able to make healthy, genetically identical copies of other mammals, and there's no reason the principle couldn't be applied to humans. But there is simply no way the clones could be in their twenties. Scientists couldn't reliably clone healthy pigs or monkeys twenty years ago."

"What if they only *appear* to be in their twenties?" Keane asked, still watching the wall display. "What if they are in fact much younger?"

"What are you talking about, Keane?" I asked. "Artificial aging?"

"Sure," said Keane. "Why not?"

"Because Priya Mistry is a human being, not a block of cheese," I said. "You can't put a person under ultraviolet light and make them age faster."

"Dr. Takemago," Keane said, ignoring me. "Are you familiar with the work Esper did a few years ago on age reversal?"

Takemago paused. "I . . . understood that was just a rumor."

I glanced at Keane, certain he had picked up on Takemago's hesitation. She was a terrible liar.

"Jason Banerjee indicated otherwise," said Keane, evidently deciding not to make an issue of it. "He implied that they were pretty close to cracking the problem of immortality when they were forced to pull the plug. If that's true, then Esper had probably identified the gene sequences responsible for aging, and determined, in theory, how to alter them to stall or even reverse that process. How much more difficult could it be to accelerate it?"

"Accelerated aging," said Takemago, nodding thoughtfully.

"It's possible, although it would likely give rise to a variety of health problems. Your hypothesis is that these clones were born some time in the recent past and then artificially aged to their current apparent age."

"Exactly," said Keane. "Let's suppose they were born six years ago and subjected to an artificial aging process to cause them to age at five times their natural rate, making them appear to be in their midtwenties."

I shook my head, thinking Keane's flight of fancy was getting pretty far removed from the empirical evidence. But Takemago took him seriously.

"The problem is," she said, "the accelerated aging would only affect their biology, not their mental development. In other words, they would have the mentality of six-year-olds."

I shuddered as I pondered the possibility that the Priya whose cleavage I'd admired was a kindergartner. But no, she didn't talk or act like a six-year-old or even a fifteen-year-old. She may have been a bit unstable, but she had the mind of a full-grown woman.

"Also, it doesn't explain Noogus," I said.

"Noogus?" asked Takemago.

Keane nodded. "Our subjects appear to share not only the same personality," he explained, turning to face Takemago, "but the same memories. They seem to have had the same childhood. And I don't mean they were sisters living in the same house. I mean, they both had exactly the same childhood."

Takemago nodded, deep in thought. "Well," she said after some time, "it's possible . . ."

"What?" I asked, as she trailed off, seemingly lost in her ruminations.

"Understand that this is purely hypothetical," she said. "I'm merely conjecturing, based on what you've told me."

"Got it," I said. "What are you getting at?"

"Suppose the subjects are clones, conceived sometime in the past decade, but artificially accelerated to an apparent age of twenty-seven. It's virtually unimaginable that anyone would devote the resources required for such a project, but so far this scenario is within the plausible realm of current technology. There are a number of practical problems with accelerated aging, the chief one being that once the process is started, it would be hard to stop. The subjects would continue to age at several times the normal rate, developing problems like osteoporosis, arthritis, and dementia at an extremely young age. Not to mention various forms of cancer, which would almost certainly develop as a result of the accelerated cell growth. But we're observing the subjects only over a very short period of time, so we'll ignore those problems for now. That leaves the matter of intellectual and emotional development."

"Memories and personality," I said.

"Correct," said Takemago. "The tendency is to think of the brain as hardware, and memories as software. In this model, the brain is just a big hard drive that stores memories for future use. But the reality is more complicated. A better analogy would be firmware, in which the physical form of a computer system is dictated in part by the programming the system has retrieved. In other words, you can't simply copy one person's memories into another person's brain and expect the subject to act exactly like the original, the way you can move your data and operating system from one system to another. You'd need to rewire the target's brain to function the same as the original."

"A firmware update," said Keane.

"Exactly," said Takemago.

"Is such a thing possible?" I asked. "A firmware update on the human brain?"

Takemago shrugged almost imperceptibly. "This goes well beyond my area of expertise. A few years ago I would have said no."

"But something happened to change your mind," said Keane.

"Nearly three years ago, a scientist at MIT, Dr. Henry Allebach, published a paper about the possibility of transferring memories from one person to another. The arguments he gave were fairly convincing."

"So Allebach thinks it's possible?"

"That was his theory," said Takemago. "But his paper was met with a great deal of criticism, and to my knowledge he hasn't responded."

"What sort of criticism?" I asked.

"Practical objections, mainly. But also ethical concerns. The concept of overwriting one person's memories and personality with another's is . . . morally problematic."

"I would imagine so," I said. Takemago had a way with understatement.

"It should be noted that this is all theoretical," Takemago said. "The idea that somebody would actually go to the trouble of doing all this, and be able to get away with it . . ."

"We understand, Doc," I said. "The whole thing is pretty ridiculous." *On the other hand,* I thought, *so was chasing a giant sheep all over Los Angeles.*

"Now," said Takemago, "what does this have to do with Mary?"

Keane had prefaced his account of the multiple Priyas with assurances that the information Takemago provided could help us find the missing sheep.

"To be honest," said Keane, "we're not entirely certain. But we have reason to believe the two cases are connected."

"Because the woman in the park had Mary's tracker," said Takemago.

"That's part of it," said Keane. "There have been other . . . confluences."

"Selah Fiore wants the sheep," I said. "If we knew why, it might help us figure out what's going on with Priya. And get Mary back."

"I can't imagine why someone like that would want Mary," said Takemago. "As I said before, Mary is a research subject. She has no practical value."

"Unless there's something you're not telling us," said Keane.

Dr. Takemago bit her lip.

"You lied when you said you didn't know about the age-reversal research," said Keane.

Takemago fidgeted nervously but said nothing.

"Banerjee instructed you not to talk about it, didn't he?" said Keane. "Probably threatened your job."

"You told me you don't trust Banerjee," I said. "Why?"

Takemago was silent for a moment. Then she said, "He doesn't care about these sheep. If he thinks the truth is going to get out, he'll have them killed. All of them."

"The truth?" asked Keane. "What truth? What haven't you told us about the sheep?"

"They . . . aren't sheep," said Takemago.

"What do you mean, they aren't sheep?" I said. "What does that mean? Of course they're sheep."

"No," said Takemago. "Not entirely."

"You told us that," I said. "They have human organs. Heart, lungs, liver, et cetera. So?"

Takemago looked from me to Keane and then to Mark the sheep, who we noticed was staring expectantly out of the wall display at us. If I didn't know better, I'd have said he could see us. In fact, if I were prone to wild flights of fancy, I might have said he was *judging* us.

"My God," said Keane. He was staring into the sheep's

eyes, and the sheep was staring back. "I thought I sensed something when I first encountered the sheep, but I dismissed it. I should have known better than to question my instincts."

"What?" I asked. "You mean when you were playing with its fleece? Or when you looked into its eyes and said you were taking measure of the sheep's . . . oh." It suddenly occurred to me what was so strange about these sheep. What Take-mago meant when she said they weren't sheep.

"They're human," I murmured. "Jesus Christ. Their brains. They're *human*."

EIGHTEEN

Mary the sheep, and all the others in the Esper lab, had been genetically engineered with human brains. That was why Esper had chosen such a large breed. Sheep brains were proportionately much smaller, but there was plenty of room in that big skull for a human brain. As Takemago explained it, the cerebellum and brain stem—the more rudimentary parts of the brain, which controlled bodily functions and basic motor activity—were mostly built from sheep DNA. But the cerebral cortex was almost entirely human. The result was essentially a human being who inhabited the body of a sheep. Their instincts—eating, sleeping, reproducing—were sheeplike, but their thoughts were presumably human.

The sheep were all less than five years old—Mary was the oldest, at four and a half—and had been raised in a lab with minimal intellectual stimulation, so it was hard to say how much they really understood about what was going on. Then again, that could be said of any human being. I had been raised by nuns in Rancho Cucamonga, and I was starting to think I didn't really have any idea what the fuck was going on either.

Takemago was a little vague on the rationale for giving the sheep human brains; evidently the original idea had been to breed hosts to provide brain tissue that could be transplanted into patients who had had parts of their brains removed because of tumors or other damage. How Esper thought they were going to get away with raising human-sheep hybrids was beyond me. The project only began to bear fruit shortly after the Collapse, and Banerjee must have figured he had a few years before anyone noticed anything was wrong with the sheep. Maybe he thought he could re-coup some of his investment by conducting experiments on the sheep during that time, or maybe he was simply betting on another regulatory holiday—another Collapse.

As far as Takemago knew, only she and Banerjee were privy to the strange truth about Esper's sheep. Another scientist, a Michael Guryev, had been involved in their design, but he had left Esper several months earlier to work at a research institute in Belgium. Takemago was worried it was only a matter of time before someone else figured it out, though: already the sheep were exhibiting behavior that was uncharacteristic of lab animals—behavior that some-times made technicians think the sheep understood what they were saying. As the sheep grew older, their brains would continue to mature, even with minimal stimulation. Merci-fully, Takemago informed us that this breed of sheep only lived for seven or eight years, so the poor creatures wouldn't have to live a full human lifetime in sheep bodies. Not that that would be allowed to happen anyway. If the sheep started showing clear signs of sentience, Banerjee would have them exterminated before Esper's crimes could become public.

After our meeting with Dr. Takemago, Keane dropped me off downtown near April's office. We had planned to meet for dinner so April could give me whatever she'd been able to find on Priya Mistry. She thought she'd be able to dig up a contract—I didn't ask how—but she came up empty.

"Maybe Priya Mistry isn't her real name?" I offered. I'd completely forgotten to tell April about Bryn Jhaveri.

"Should have been cross-referenced," April said. "If it were there, Tom would have found it."

I began to wonder what kind of relationship April had with Tom that made him so willing to risk his neck for her, no questions asked. April didn't talk much about her personal life. Best not to ask.

"Unless someone made a deliberate effort to keep it buried," I said.

April shrugged. "You're watching out for the woman, right? You're not going to let Keane screw up her life."

I sighed. "You wouldn't know it to look at her, but her life is already about as screwed up as it's possible to be," I said.

"All that glitters, huh?"

"It's not her fault. She's in a bad situation. Several bad situations, from the look of things."

"But you're going to straighten it out, right? Be her knight in shining armor?"

"It's not like that," I said. "I mean, okay, I'll admit I was a little starstruck at first. But at this point I just want to try to help her as best as I can. Anyway, she's too young for me. And not my type."

"You mean you're still hung up on Gwen."

"That too," I said wearily. There was no point in lying to April. She knew better than anyone how the specter of Gwen hung over all my relationships. We had both assumed I'd get over her in time, but it had been three years. What the hell was my problem? Why couldn't I just let her go? For a while it seemed like it was getting better, but lately I'd started obsessing about her again. And somehow the Priya Mistry case had only made it worse. It didn't make any sense.

"What about your other case?" April asked, apparently picking up on my self-destructive spiral. "The sheep thing?"

I sighed again. "The sheep is actually even more screwed up than Priya."

"What kind of problems can a sheep have?"

"Right?" I said. "It should be all bleating and chewing cud. Maybe a good shearing every now and then. But I don't envy this sheep one bit."

Concern came over her face. "Just be careful, okay?" she said. "A sheep isn't worth risking your life over, no matter how valuable it is."

"I know," I said.

"Although if it comes down to Keane or the sheep," said April, "that's another matter."

"Understood."

Just then her comm chirped, and she glanced at the display on her wrist. "Hang on," she said. "It's Tom." She stepped outside and spoke on her comm for a moment. When she came back inside, she had a troubled expression on her face.

"Tom says Priya was scheduled for a shoot this afternoon, but she never showed up. Nobody can get ahold of her."

I had to think for a moment. Assuming there really were multiple Priyas, this would be Palomar Priya. The one who'd sneaked down to the bar to talk to Keane and me. She'd been terrified.

"Have you seen Priya today?" asked April. "Is she okay?"

I didn't know what to say to that. "I should check on her," I said. "She's staying at the Palomar, on Wilshire."

"All right," April said. "Let's go."

"I didn't mean—"

"You don't have a car, remember? Mine is in the garage just down the block. Let's go."

We went. It took us over half an hour to get there. April pulled up to the curb, and I ran inside and went to the front desk.

"I need you to check on one of your guests for me," I said

to the young woman behind the counter. "Priya Mistry. She may be staying under another name."

The woman regarded me doubtfully.

"I'm a private investigator," I said. "I'm looking into a threat against Ms. Mistry. All I need you to do is call her room and make sure she's okay."

"Sir, I can't confirm whether a Priya Mistry is staying with us."

I gave a little involuntary laugh at the way she'd phrased this, as if there were several different Priyas, any one of whom might be staying at the hotel. Which of course there were. I don't think my reaction helped my case.

"Can you get a message to her?" I asked, remembering Keane's note.

"You can give me a message. If there is a guest with that name staying with us, I will get it to her."

"Fantastic," I said without enthusiasm. I could get a note to her asking her to come down to the lobby again. But if she wasn't here, or if she were incapacitated or under guard, she wouldn't be able to come down, which somewhat defeated the purpose of contacting her in the first place. If only she had given us her room number instead of writing the date, not to mention getting it wrong. . . . And then it dawned on me.

I ran to the elevator and pressed number twelve. Priya— or whatever her name was—may have been a basket case, but she was smarter than I'd given her credit for. She'd managed to give us her room number right under Jamie's nose.

I got out on the twelfth floor and ran down the hall toward room 1225. I was only halfway down the hall when I heard a muffled scream. I drew my gun and approached the door. I listened closely, but everything had gone quiet. I thought the scream had come from 1225, but there was no way to be certain. I debated for a moment whether I should wait, knock on the door, or kick the door in. The matter was settled when the door opened and I found myself face-to-face with a man with long red hair pulled into a ponytail. I'd seen him before. He was one of the guys who had "helped" Priya at the party the other night.

Red went for his gun, but the sight of my SIG Sauer in his face made him rethink his options. I put my finger to my lips and gestured for him to go back inside. I followed, closing the door behind us. We walked through a narrow hall into a good-sized sitting area. Somewhere to our left I heard scuffling, followed by a man saying, "Is it clear? We need to get this bitch downstairs." There was some more scuffling, and another scream. "Damn it, get in here!" the man yelled. A second later Priya burst from the hallway into the room in between Red and me. She wore only a bra and underwear and had a crazy, addled look in her eyes.

Red threw his arm around Priya's neck, his gun pressed up against her temple. The other man—the Filipino from the party—stumbled into the room and stood, agape, for a moment, taking in the situation. He pulled a gun from a shoulder holster.

"Easy," I said to Red. "She's your meal ticket. Anything happens to her, you're out of a job."

Red laughed. "This one? She's all used up. We're just taking her down to the trash."

A sickening sensation washed over me as I realized he wasn't joking. Maybe he was just being hyperbolic to make me think he'd really shoot her if it came down to it, but somehow I didn't think so. If they could make two copies of Priya, there was no reason they couldn't make four, five, or a dozen. Any particular instance was replaceable, disposable. Priya Mistry wasn't a person; she was a product. How many Priyas were there? How many had they already killed because they'd outlived their usefulness? It was impossible to know, but one thing was clear: if I didn't get this woman out of here, she was going to die.

As it turned out, though, this particular model had some pluck left in her. She ducked beneath Red's gun barrel and drove her elbow into his solar plexus, causing him to double over and stagger backward. Priya evidently had been in enough action scenes to know what happened next, because she dove to the floor. I shot Red right between his eyes.

While Red was still falling, the Filipino fired twice at me, but his aim was wide. I put three rounds into his chest for good measure. He hit the carpet a couple of seconds after Red.

"Is that it?" I said to Priya, watching the hall. "Is there anybody else?"

She didn't answer. She was trying to pull herself to her feet, using the back of a couch as support.

"Stay down," I said. I made a quick survey of the suite, but it seemed to be empty. I was a bit relieved Jamie the bodyguard wasn't around. I had no qualms about putting down a couple of Selah's henchmen, but as far as I could tell, the bodyguards weren't involved in the plot.

I came back and helped Priya to her feet. She was pretty unsteady, and her eyes were dilated. "Can you walk?" I asked. She nodded. "All right," I said. "We need to get out of here."

Somebody would have heard all those shots for sure. I wasn't too worried about hotel security, but LAPD could be a problem. Those guys weren't known for their restraint. A strange man dragging a famous actress through a hotel lobby could easily get a couple of extra holes put in him before he had a chance to explain anything. And I wasn't sure explaining would help matters much either.

"Wait here a sec," I said, and Priya braced herself on the couch while I went to the door. I opened it and looked down the hall. It was empty in both directions. "Okay, let's go," I said. But when I turned, I saw Priya was still hanging on to the couch. She looked like she was about to fall over. I don't know what those guys gave her, but it was working.

I went to her side and wrapped her arm around my neck, dragging her away from the couch. Her eyes began rolling into her head, and I gave her a light slap on the cheek to keep her conscious. "Priya!" I said. "Stay awake. We need to walk to the elevator." She groaned.

I made my way down the hall, half dragging Priya while holding my gun in my other hand. We got to the elevator without incident, and I mashed the down button with the butt of my gun. The elevator door opened. Empty. So far, so good. We got in, and I hit the button for the lobby.

"April," I said into my comm.

"What's happening, Blake?" April's voice answered. "Did you find Priya?"

"Yeah," I said. "We had a little trouble. Are you still parked up front?"

"I'm waiting down the street. I'll be in front by the time you get there."

"Okay, be ready to leave in a hurry."

"Got it."

Priya was leaning against the back of the elevator, and her eyes were rolling again. Her knees buckled and she began sliding to the floor, despite my best efforts to keep her upright. "Priya!" I yelled. "Stay awake! Just a few seconds more." She stirred and blinked. As her eyes focused on me, I saw no recognition in them.

"Blake!" said April's voice in my ear.

"Yeah," I said.

"The cops are here. Just one cruiser so far. Two men entering the lobby."

"Shit!" I snapped. "Roger that. Be ready for us. But if you hear gunfire, get out of there."

"But—"

I cut her off and gave Priya a hard slap across her face. She yelped and then backed away from me.

"Priya," I said. "Do you know who I am?"

"F-Fowler," she said after a moment.

"Right, I'm Blake Fowler. Keane's partner. I'm here to help you. Do you believe me?"

She nodded uncertainly.

"All right," I said. "In about three seconds, that door is going to open and things are going to get very scary. You're going to be okay, but you have to trust me. Can you do that?"

She nodded again. The elevator chimed.

I slid behind Priya, putting my arm around her throat and holding my gun to her temple. The elevator doors slid open, and I saw two cops with guns pointed at me. A clerk cringed behind the front desk, and an elderly couple cowered in a corner, but the lobby was otherwise clear.

"Don't anybody fucking move," I screamed, "or I swear to God I will put a bullet in this bitch's brain!"

Priya squeaked in fear and struggled vainly against my grip. I couldn't tell if she was acting or if she really was trying to get away, but I was a lot stronger than she was, and the sedative had taken most of the fight out of her. I moved slowly through the lobby, making sure to keep Priya in front of me as much as possible. "And don't fucking follow me," I hollered as we approached the front door, "or I'll shoot her in the head and throw her body out the window!"

We made it through the front door, and I shoved Priya outside. April's car was nowhere to be seen. I double-checked in both directions, but it wasn't there. Had the police gotten to her? Seconds were ticking away. The cops wouldn't wait forever. I needed to make a decision, and fast. So: ditch Priya and make a run for it? Hope the police would protect her? I didn't like it, but it was looking like my only option.

"Fowler!" I heard a woman's voice cry. April. She was getting out of the front seat of a cab, parked just down the street.

"Let's go," I urged Priya, grabbing her arm. I holstered my gun as we ran to the cab. April opened the door and we slid inside. April slammed the door behind us and got in the front. "Go!" she yelled to the driver, an elderly Middle Eastern man.

I looked behind us and saw that the cops still hadn't followed. I must have been pretty convincing with my threats. "What's up with the cab?" I said. "You scared the shit out of me."

"Figured it was safer," said April.

She was right. The hotel would have cameras covering the front. If they got April's license plate, they'd be on to us damn quick. A cab was practically invisible. As the hotel receded in the distance, I saw the cops pouring onto the street.

"Clear?" April said.

I turned around to face her. I shook my head.

April put two crisp twenty new dollar notes on the dash. "Faster," she said.

The driver nodded, and the cab leaped forward. Glancing back, I saw flashers in the distance, but I doubted they knew which car we were in. By the time they thought to check the monitors, we'd be long gone.

The cab weaved through traffic, passing cars left and right. "Go right here," April said, and the driver complied. After some time, she had him make another right, and then another. Soon we weren't far from where we had started. She told the driver to pull over. "Stay here," she said, handing the driver another twenty. She took off down the street.

A few minutes later April pulled up behind us in her car. She helped me transfer Priya to her backseat, and then we took off, leaving the cab behind. She turned right on Wilshire, and I ducked as we drove past the hotel. Several police cars were now parked out front.

"Drive slow," I said. "We don't want to attract any attention."

"I've got this, chief," said April, with a smile.

Half an hour later we were back at the office. April parked in front and helped me carry the semiconscious Priya into the building. I was tempted just to put her in the guest bedroom on the first floor and let her sleep off the sedative, but I thought Keane would want to see her. I grabbed a blanket and put it around her shoulders, and then we got into the elevator and took it up to the third floor. I banged a couple of times on the door to his study and then threw it open. "Look what I found," I said. Priya had one arm around my neck and the other around April's, and her head lolled from one side to the other, like a drunk in an old movie.

And then I saw Keane wasn't alone. Sitting in a chair facing him was a woman with long black hair. When she turned, my knees almost buckled. It was Priya Mistry.

NINETEEN

The two Priyas stared at each other for a moment in shock.

"Well," said Keane. "This is awkward."

"Who . . . is that?" asked the Priya hanging on to my shoulder.

"Just a bad dream," I said. "We're going to take you downstairs so you can get some rest." April gave me a wide-eyed glance but was smart enough not to say anything. We escorted Priya back downstairs and carried her to the guest bedroom. I went back upstairs while April tucked her in.

"So it's true," said the Priya in Keane's office. "They made copies of me." She was stunned but not hysterical.

I took the chair next to her and looked at Keane. He shot me a pained look. We were going to have to tell her the truth.

"Not exactly," I said. "We believe the woman downstairs is genetically identical to you."

"Like a twin," said Priya. "A perfect copy."

"More or less," I said.

She looked from me to Keane, a puzzled expression on her face. "What?" she asked. "What aren't you telling me?"

I sighed. There wasn't any easy way to break it to her.

"She's not a copy of you," I said. "That is . . . we're not certain you're the original."

Priya laughed. "Of course I'm the original," she said. "I wasn't raised in a lab. I grew up in Tucson."

"What is your real name?" asked Keane.

"I was born Bryn Jhaveri. But everyone knows me as Priya."

"And the stuff about the copies?"

"Selah put me up to that. She said someone pretending to be me had hired you, and that the only way to get you to leave me alone was to tell you that story."

"You didn't think that was strange?" I asked.

"I thought it was ridiculous," said Priya. "But Selah is the reason I'm a star. I owe her everything. So when she asks me to do something, I do it."

"But something changed your mind," Keane said. "Something brought you here."

She bit her lip. "Noogus," she said. "How the hell did you know about Noogus?"

"You told us," I said. "Or someone who looked exactly like you did."

She shook her head. "I've never mentioned that to anybody. Not since I was four years old. When you mentioned Noogus in Selah's office, I was . . . shocked. I almost broke down. But I've been acting so long, I guess my instincts just took over. I finished the scene and exited the stage."

"So you see the problem," said Keane. "Someone who looks exactly like you came to our office two days ago and told us about Noogus. She hired us to look into a threat against her life."

"That woman downstairs," said Priya.

I shook my head. "No. We don't know what happened to the original. That is, the first Priya we encountered. I suspect she was killed in that explosion on the set."

"I was there," Priya said. "When the bomb went off."

"You were?" I asked. How was that possible? How could there have been two Priyas on the set without anyone noticing?

She nodded. "My memory is a little fuzzy," she said. "But I remember the explosion."

"So you saw the car explode?" asked Keane. I shot him a puzzled glance.

"I think so?" said Priya. "Like I said, my memory is fuzzy."

"But you were definitely on the set at the time of the explosion."

"Yes."

"So you saw the burnt-out wreckage of the car after the bomb went off."

She nodded.

"Did anything strike you as strange about the wreckage? The way the car was parked facing the wrong way on the side of the street, for instance?"

She nodded again. "That was . . . a little weird, I guess."

"Or the fact that the car seemed to be made entirely out of mozzarella?"

"Uh . . . what?" Priya asked.

"There was no car bomb," said Keane. "A store exploded. You didn't see any blast. You were implanted with artificial memories. The other Priya, the one who hired us, was killed, and you were brought in to replace her."

"I'm not lying!" cried Priya. "I was there!"

"We don't think you're lying," I said, glaring at Keane. "We think you've been tricked into thinking you were there."

Keane continued, "Your memory is fuzzy because you were only given the bare details of what happened. You're trying to fill in the gaps, but you can't, because you weren't there. What's the last vivid memory you have from before the explosion?"

"I was on the set," she said. "Doing a scene. With Taki, I think."

"No," said Keane. "If you have to think about it, it didn't happen. Your brain is constructing false memories based on the coaching you received. Close your eyes. Where were you before the explosion?"

"The hotel?" Priya offered.

"No!" snapped Keane. "Don't think about it. Don't try to put things into sequence, or make sense of events. Just tell me the last thing you clearly remember before the explosion. Quickly!"

"I don't know!" she cried. "Everything is fuzzy. All I see is black."

"It doesn't have to be visual," Keane said. "A sound, a taste, a smell . . . anything that—"

"Licorice," she said.

"You tasted licorice?" Keane asked.

She shook her head and opened her eyes. "No, I smelled it."

"Anything else?" Keane asked. "An image or sound that goes along with the smell? Do you know where you were when you smelled it?"

"I'm not sure," she said. "I remember a place, but I'm not sure if it was a dream."

"What place?" Keane said. "Where were you?"

Priya sat for a moment, her eyes closed. Her head swayed slightly as if she were drifting with her thoughts. "I was . . . on a cliff overlooking the ocean," she said after some time. "It was very peaceful. I wanted to stay there, but then someone made me go inside a building. It was white, like a hospital. That's where I smelled the licorice. It was a . . . bad place."

"Who made you go inside the building?" Keane asked.

She shook her head. "I'm sorry. I don't remember."

"Do you remember anything that happened there?"

"No."

"And after the bad place?" Keane asked.

"I'm not sure if it even happened," said Priya. "I . . . went back to the hotel, I think? It all gets fuzzy after that. I think it was some time ago. A few months, maybe, but it's hard to be sure. I work such long hours on *DiZzy Girl* that everything starts to run together. What does it mean?"

Keane was silent for a moment, lost in thought.

"To be honest," I said, "we aren't entirely sure."

"You're a clone," said Keane, apparently having concluded his ruminations. "You and the woman downstairs. Copies of the original Priya, who may be an actual person, but could be some sort of fictional construct. It's possible you're the original, but the odds are against it. There are at least three of you, and probably more."

"But why?" Priya asked, horrified. "Why would somebody do this?"

"Partly because the demand for Priya Mistry is too high to be met by a single person. They needed more of you. But I suspect there's another reason as well. A somewhat more troubling reason."

I wasn't entirely certain I wanted to hear a rationale more troubling than cloning a human being to meet the demands of a populace desperate for more Priya Mistry, not to mention the insatiable greed of Selah Fiore and Flagship Media.

"What is it, Mr. Keane?" Priya asked. "Please, I have to know."

"The first Priya we met," said Keane. "Let's call her Priya One."

"Ritz-Carlton Priya," I interjected. I didn't want to have to deal with the Priyas fighting over who got to be number one. "You aren't staying at the Ritz, are you?" I asked the Priya next to me.

She shook her head. "The Peninsula Beverly Hills."

"Okay, then you're Peninsula Priya," I said. "Sorry. We need some way of keeping everybody straight."

She nodded glumly.

"Ritz-Carlton Priya," Keane continued, "was considerably more agitated than you are at the possibility of some sort of conspiracy surrounding her. She was convinced somebody was trying to kill her."

"So?" asked Priya.

"Fowler," said Keane. "What is your assessment of the mental state of the Priya downstairs? Let's call her—"

"Palomar Priya," I said. "She's been drugged, but I don't think she's doing well. She was on the verge of losing it at the hotel bar last night—assuming that was the same Priya—and she didn't show up for work today. I think they gave her a sedative because she was getting hysterical."

"Does she think people are out to kill her?" Keane asked.

"Well, yes," I said. I figured to err on the side of tact by not pointing out that people *were* trying to kill her.

Keane nodded. "What we're seeing is a progression," he said. "Each clone has a different incept date. Ritz-Carlton Priya was born first, for lack of a better term. She also went nuts first. Palomar Priya is a little behind her on the crazy scale, but she's gaining fast. And then there's you, Peninsula Priya. You were brought in to replace Ritz, probably only yesterday."

"What about the one I met in Griffith Park?" I asked. "Four Seasons Priya."

"Not enough information to say," said Keane. "Probably somewhere in the middle."

Priya stared at him in horror. "So all my memories before today—"

"Somebody else's," said Keane. "Well, your memories before

your visit to the bad place are somebody else's. The ones after that are probably artificial implants. The fuzzy memories start at the point the original Priya's memories leave off. Priya Zero. Sorry, we don't have a hotel to name the original after."

"Priya Zero," Priya murmured. "But if that's true . . . what happened to her? Where is she?"

"No idea," said Keane. "But she may be the one who sent that letter. The one from Noogus."

"Letter?" asked Priya.

"Sorry," said Keane. "I forgot you don't know. Ritz Carlton Priya showed us a letter warning about a threat on her life. That's when she told us about Noogus."

"But, Keane," I said. "The conspiracy is real. You can't blame her—them—for being paranoid."

"Paranoia is a form of psychosis," said Keane. "Whether or not it's borne out by the facts."

I frowned. "You're saying the woman downstairs is crazy for thinking there are people out to get her, despite the fact that there actually are people out to get her."

"The ability to correlate one's condition with external circumstances doesn't preclude the possibility of a pathological response," Keane said. "It's perfectly natural to be paranoid if people are out to get you. It's also perfectly natural to hemorrhage internally when exposed to the Ebola virus. Neither condition, however, is optimal."

"So the healthy response would be to remain ignorant, or delusional."

"Depends how you define *healthy*. She'd certainly be happier."

"Until she winds up dead."

"That's true for everybody," said Keane, with a shrug.

Priya listened to this exchange in silent horror. Finally she spoke: "You're saying I'm doomed to go insane."

"There's a possibility that if we were to put a stop to Selah's plans and eliminate the other Priyas, you might live a relatively normal life," Keane offered.

"What kind of possibility?" Priya asked.

"Fifty-fifty?" said Keane. "This isn't an exact science."

Priya started to cry.

We got Peninsula Priya calmed down at about the time Palomar Priya woke up. Palomar seemed somewhat recovered from her ordeal and kept asking about the "woman who looked just like me." We weren't going to be able to keep them apart for long inside our building, and there wasn't any other safe place where we could easily keep an eye on them, so we decided to bite the bullet and introduce them to each other. After the initial moment of shock, they both handled it pretty well.

"You know what the hardest part is?" said Peninsula to her double.

"Having somebody tell you that you're one in a billion," replied Palomar. "Only to find out it's not true."

"I'd give anything to go back to that life," said Peninsula. "Just to be another face in the crowd, to forget all this."

"A nobody," said Palomar. "In a sea of nobodies."

A *sheep*, I thought, but I didn't say it.

An hour later they were watching TV together in the sitting room we had set up just behind the lobby. They had the same taste in shows, so that helped.

"Clones," April murmured, watching the two of them sitting on the couch, eating popcorn together. "I wouldn't have believed it if I didn't see it with my own eyes. And they each think they're the original?"

"They did until today," I said. "Neither one of them knew about the existence of any of the others. They each have a complete set of Priya's memories. The death of her parents, being adopted, growing up in Arizona, coming to Los Angeles,

auditioning for a bit part on one of Flagship's shows, becoming an international superstar. For all practical purposes, they are both Priya Mistry."

"What are you going to do with them?" she asked.

"I haven't a clue," I said. Keane had gone back upstairs to
think, and we hadn't discussed our next steps. As far as we
knew, neither of the women on our couch, watching bad sitcoms from the late twenties, was the one who had hired us,
so technically we had no contractual obligation to either of
them. Still, as much as I liked the idea of two identical, drop-
dead gorgeous actresses lounging around the place indefinitely, eventually Selah's people were going to track them
down. I couldn't even imagine what that showdown was
going to look like, but I didn't see it ending well for anybody,
except maybe Selah.

"I love this part," said Palomar, enraptured by the program.

"Me too," said Peninsula.

I shuddered. The whole thing was just too fucking weird.

On the TV, an actor spoke some inane pseudo-witticism,
and the Priyas burst into laughter in time with the studio
audience.

"Your girlfriends have terrible taste in shows," muttered
April.

"Shh!" I said. A chill ran down my spine as something registered in the back of my mind. "Rewind that part," I said.

"Huh?" said the Priyas in unison.

"What that guy just said. Rewind it."

Palomar shrugged and grabbed the remote, blipping thirty
seconds back. I watched as a door opened, and the actor
walked in. I didn't know his name; he was just some average-
looking overweight comedian who had landed one big role
on a short-lived sitcom and then was never heard from

again. His claim to fame, such as it was, was a catchphrase that had briefly entered the national lexicon for a few months. *"Room for one more?"* he said. The audience went wild.

"Pause it!" I yelled. Palomar paused the program just as the show cut to a shot of three men sitting on a couch. "Jesus Christ," I said. I had seen those guys before. "Keane," I said into my comm. "Get down here. You need to see something."

A few minutes later Keane irritably entered the room. Peninsula and Palomar weren't exactly pleased either. April was just plain confused. "What is it?" Keane demanded.

"Look at the screen," I said. "Recognize anybody?"

He shrugged. "I think maybe that guy on the left has been in some muffler commercials. What do I win?"

"I guess you didn't get a good look at them," I said. "We met those guys in a parking lot last night. The muffler guy shot Hugo Díaz. His name is Braden."

"Oh yeah," said the Priyas in unison. "Braden Warner."

"And that guy next to him is Kevin . . . something," said Palomar.

Peninsula nodded. "And I think the third guy's name is Corey."

"No, Cody," said Palomar.

Peninsula nodded. "That's right, Cody."

"How do you know those guys?" asked Keane.

"I did a guest spot on this show," said both of the Priyas. Then they stopped and stared at each other. "Three episodes," they both added.

"When was this?" Keane asked.

"Four years ago or so," said Peninsula.

"It was . . . before," said Palomar. They shared a knowing glance. She meant she had been on the show back when she was still Bryn Jhaveri, before Selah made her into Priya Mistry.

"What clinched it was the catchphrase," I said. I rewound the program so Keane could hear it.

"*Room for one more?*" the guy said again. The audience burst into laughter once more.

"Hugo was making a joke," Keane murmured. "He recognized them."

"They didn't appreciate his sense of humor, apparently," I said.

"Why the hell would Mag-Lev hire those guys to steal the sheep?"

"Beats me," I said. "They probably work cheap."

"What about the fourth guy?" Keane asked. "The one speaking the line?"

The Priyas shrugged.

"Don't know about him," I said. "There were only three guys at the scene, besides Hugo."

"All right," said Keane. "Good work. See if you can find an address."

April cleared her throat. "Are you guys going to tell me what's going on?"

"It's complicated," I said. "But I think we just found our sheep thieves."

"Good," said April. "You can return the sheep to Esper and then focus on what to do about the Priya problem."

Keane and I exchanged glances.

"What?" asked April. "What am I missing?"

"Keane sort of agreed to deliver the sheep to Selah Fiore," I said.

"I thought you were supposed to return it to Esper," said April.

"That too," I said. "We've overbooked our sheep. So what'll it be, Keane? Who are we working for, Esper or Selah?"

Keane thought for a moment. "I don't particularly like being a pawn," he said. "We're going to hold on to Mary until somebody levels with us about why everybody in Los Angeles seems to want this damn sheep."

TWENTY

I found an address for the three actors; they were all living together in a small house in Culver City. Keane, Peninsula, and I headed over there in the aircar while April kept an eye on Palomar back at the office. I didn't want to leave April with both Priyas, so I called Roy and asked him to meet us down the street from the address. I still wasn't completely certain I could trust him, but we didn't have a lot of options. Peninsula seemed to know who Roy was, although it wasn't clear to me whether she had actually met him or had been brainwashed to think she had. It was all very confusing. I also called Pavel, mostly because he was the only person I knew who had a vehicle big enough to transport a three-hundred-pound sheep. What can I say? I'm an optimist.

The sitcom the three sheep thieves had starred in was called, imaginatively, *Room for One More*. It had aired for a single season six years ago, and seemed to be the death knell of the careers for everyone involved in it—with one exception: Bryn Jhaveri, aka Priya Mistry.

Room for One More was one of the first shows produced by Selah Fiore's fledgling company, Flagship Media, and it was Bryn's first regular acting gig. She played the girlfriend of Braden's character, the best friend of the fourth guy, who found at least one opportunity every week to speak the show's insipid catchphrase. The fourth guy's name was Giles Marbury, and he seemed to have fallen off the face of the Earth after *Room for One More* went off the air. He didn't live with the other three actors and hadn't done any more acting gigs—at least not under the name Giles Marbury. Priya—that is, Peninsula Priya, and presumably the others—had no idea what had become of him. I got the impression from her that Giles had had a bit of a crush on her, but she didn't share his feelings. I supposed that characterized most of Priya's relationships with men though, even before she was made into a goddess.

"Are we really going to get a sheep?" asked Peninsula on the way to Culver City.

"That's the plan," I said.

"Sometimes I dream about sheep," she said.

"Me too," I said. Keane raised an eyebrow at me, but I just shrugged. What the hell? It wasn't like I telling her about the dreams I used to have about Sister Olivia at St. Stephen's.

"In the dreams, I'm the sheep," said Peninsula.

"That sounds . . . disturbing," I said.

"No," she said quietly. "It's comforting. Nobody expects anything of a sheep. There's no running from one set to another, no autographs, no smiling when you don't feel like smiling, no strange hotels. It feels like . . . home."

I didn't know what to say to that. Being a TV star must really not be what it's cracked up to be if the life of a sheep seems preferable.

It was dark by the time we got to the house. Pavel was waiting in his Suburban when Keane, Peninsula, and I arrived. Roy showed up a few minutes later, while I was peering through the window of the garage. I saw Mary the sheep inside, contentedly munching on straw. I didn't dare get too close to the house, but I saw some movement inside, so presumably the sheep thieves were home. The Nifty truck was parked on the street in front. I ran back to Pavel's Suburban, where everyone else was waiting.

When I got there, Roy was hugging Peninsula and weeping. Peninsula was bearing the giant man's affection with good grace. "I still can't believe it," Roy was saying. "I had given up hope. I was sure you were dead."

Priya smiled weakly at him. Roy didn't seem to notice she was a little foggy on who he was.

"Hey, Roy," I said, slapping him on the arm.

Roy reluctantly released Peninsula and turned to face me. "What's going on?" he asked, suddenly all business again. "What are we doing here?"

"Nothing you need to worry about," I said. "You just get Peninsula somewhere safe."

"Peninsula?" he asked.

"Sorry," I said, glancing at her. "I meant Priya. Long story."

"Whose house is that?" asked Roy.

"Just some guys Keane and I need to deal with. They stole something we need to get back."

Roy looked from me to Keane, who was busily inspecting the bark of a nearby sycamore tree.

"How many guys?" asked Roy.

"Three that we know of."

"Armed?"

"Most likely."

"Is he going to help?" Roy asked, indicating Pavel, who was tapping the steering wheel of the Suburban and singing along to the Pet Shop Boys' "West End Girls."

I shook my head. "Pavel doesn't do guns."

"So it's just you and Keane? Against at least three armed guys?"

"Looks that way."

"What did they steal?"

"Believe it or not," I said, "a sheep."

"They have a sheep in their house?"

"It's in the garage."

"This must be a pretty valuable sheep," Roy said.

"Extremely."

"Can you just take the sheep and leave?"

"It's a really big sheep," I said. "And we can't risk her getting hurt. We're going to have to neutralize the threat in the house first."

Roy nodded. "All right," he said. "I'll take the front door. You and Keane go around back." He looked at Keane, who seemed to be chewing on a piece of bark. "In fact, leave Keane here."

"You don't need to do that, Roy," I said. "I really just called you here to get Priya to safety."

"She'll be fine for a few minutes. Keane can watch her."

"Hey?" said Keane.

I sighed. Roy was right: Keane wasn't going to be much help under the circumstances. I didn't like it, but I needed Roy's help. "Sheep's in the garage," I said. "Roy is going to help me get her. You stay here with Pen—Priya." I handed him the backup gun. "Keep her safe."

"Sure," said Keane. "No problem."

"Good luck," said Peninsula.

I turned to Roy. "You think you can kick that front door in?"

He shot me a pained look.

"Yeah, okay," I said. Dumb question. "I'll message you when I'm in position. Wait ten seconds and then go in."

Roy nodded, and I went around the back of the Suburban and crossed the street. Then I made my way around to the back of the house. When I was safely ensconced behind a post in view of the back door, I messaged Roy. I counted to seven and then ran to the door and tried the latch. It was unlocked. I opened the door and stepped inside, my gun drawn. As I did, I heard a loud crash from the front of the house.

"On the floor!" I heard Roy yell. There was some more yelling and scuffling as I went through a small pantry and the kitchen. I threw open the door to the living room to find three men lying on the floor, Roy standing over them. The house was a mess, fast-food containers, beer cans, and other trash scattered over every flat surface. In the center of the room was a coffee table that had been cleared off to make room for several stacks of cash and a large ziplock bag filled with what looked like orange pills. So that's how our out-of-work actors supported themselves when they weren't stealing sheep.

"I'll watch these guys while you get the sheep," said Roy.

"Give me a minute to check the rest of the house," I said. Once I knew the house was clear, I'd call Pavel and have him back his Suburban up to the garage door.

"Roger that," said Roy. "These guys aren't going anywhere."

But before I could even start down the hall to the bedrooms, another man, in black jeans and a black T-shirt, came through the front door behind Roy. He had a gun.

"Roy!" I shouted, training my gun on the newcomer. But then I felt cold steel on the back of my neck. The gunman wasn't alone. Our situation had taken a sudden, and seemingly inexplicable, turn for the worse. Who the hell were these guys?

"We'll take it from here," said the man behind me, with a slight Russian accent. And there was something else: the smell of licorice.

"We were managing okay," I said. I noticed one of the guys on the floor—the guy called Braden—was taking advantage of this new complication by pulling himself across the floor toward an end table on which was resting a .357 revolver. I hadn't noticed it before because it was partly hidden by all the garbage. Sloppy.

"Hey, Muffler Guy!" I snapped, pointing my gun at him. "Don't get any ideas."

"Put down your guns," said the man behind me.

"I think there's been a misunderstanding," I said to Licorice. "We both work for the same person. You're just making our job more complicated."

Licorice laughed. "There's been no misunderstanding," he said. "Selah has decided to cut out the middleman. *All* of the middlemen."

I had a bad feeling about that last part. It was a little too easy to imagine a news report about a drug deal gone bad and resulting in the deaths of five men in a small house in Culver City. Whether Roy and I got out of there alive depended on how concerned Selah was with tying up loose ends, and she struck me as rather thorough.

Braden crept closer to the end table. "Hey!" I yelled. "I realize you're an actor, not a writer, so let me help you out here, Braden. There is no variation of this story in which you grab that gun and get out of here alive. Leave the gunplay to the adults, all right?"

"Last chance," said Licorice. "Put down your guns." The barrel ground into the hollow of my neck.

"Fine," I said. "But in case you didn't notice, Muffler Guy over there is itching to play hero, so I highly recommend either putting a bullet in his head or letting me move that gun to a shelf he can't reach."

"Muffler Guy?" asked Licorice.

"Are you dragging in the morning?" said Braden, suddenly falling into character. "Come see the Muffler Guy!"

Licorice was quiet for a moment. "Go," he said, nudging me in the back of the head with the barrel.

I began walking toward the end table, my gun still trained on Braden.

"Slowly!" said Licorice from behind me. "Pick up the gun by the barrel and then walk backward toward me."

I was two paces from the gun when I heard another man's voice behind me. "Are you guys just about done in here?" he asked. I groaned as I recognized the voice. Risking a glance behind me, I saw Keane, standing, unarmed, in the middle of the room. He had simply strolled in through the front door, past Roy and the other man, and was just standing there expectantly, like someone waiting for a train. "Sorry I'm late," he said. "Had to see a man about a sheep."

Licorice and the other man didn't seem to know what to do. Keane clearly wasn't a threat, but he'd upset the equilibrium of the situation. I wasn't terribly happy about his appearance either, because now I had to worry about his safety on top of everything else.

"Keane," I growled, "what the hell are you doing?"

"Oh, you know," he said. "Passing time, creating a diversion, that sort of thing."

Sensing something in the mood of the room had changed, I moved to the edge, where I could see what was going on while keeping my gun trained on Braden. Standing behind Licorice, with a gun pointed at his head, was Priya Mistry.

I took a deep breath. The odds had shifted—slightly—in our favor, but there was an ungodly number of variables to account for: me with my gun on Braden; Roy with his gun on the other two actors; the Man in Black with his gun on Roy; Licorice with his gun on me; Peninsula Priya with a gun on Licorice; and Keane, the ultimate X factor, standing in the middle of the room like a man with a death wish.

"Priya," said Licorice, with a smile. He looked over his shoulder at her.

It took a few seconds for it to hit her. "You," she said, and gasped.

"You remember?" said Licorice.

"You . . . did something to me," Priya said, the gun quavering in her hand.

"I . . . tried to help you," said Licorice.

"No," Priya said, shaking her head. "You hurt me."

"Never," said Licorice. "I would never hurt you, Priya. You're special."

"No," Priya said. "I'm a copy. A clone."

Licorice turned his head to face me again and looked me in the eye. A smile played at the corners of his mouth. "Who told you that?" he asked. "Erasmus Keane? He's a liar, Priya. Why, he and his partner are double-crossing Selah Fiore right now."

Priya glanced at me and then at Keane, who was listening with apparent interest.

"He's playing with your head, Priya," I said. "Don't listen to him. You saw the other Priya. You know what Keane told you is the truth."

"The truth," said Licorice, "is that there are several clones of Priya Mistry. But you're not a clone, Priya. You're the original. You are the real Priya."

Priya looked searchingly at me. I could see the pain in her eyes. She didn't know where to turn, whom to trust.

"I feel like me," she said. "I feel like Priya. But how can I know?" There was desperation in her voice. "How can I know I'm the real one?"

"Surely, you can feel it," said Licorice. "Your memories are real. We couldn't fake something like that. The others, they went crazy because they could feel that their memories were false. But you . . . you know they are real."

"Sometimes I'm not sure," Priya murmured. The gun was

still in her hand, but she seemed to be losing awareness of her surroundings. "What did you do to me . . . at that place?"

"You underwent a procedure," said Licorice. "We copied your memories for the clones. You experienced some memory loss as a result. Nothing serious, but some of your recent memories may seem a little fuzzy. It will pass, with proper care. I can help you, Priya, but not if you give in to these delusions about being a clone. Not if you insist on running around with people like Erasmus Keane, playing private investigator."

Priya nodded slowly. She began to lower the gun.

"Priya," I said. "Don't do this. You know what he did to you. To the others like you."

"There are no others like you," said Licorice. "I promise you that, Priya. You're one in a billion."

That was when she shot him.

Her aim was a bit off, so the bullet just grazed the side of his head. He staggered forward and then spun around, swinging his gun in Priya's direction. I shot him twice in the back and then turned my attention to Braden, who had gotten his hands on the .357. At that point the whole room seemed to erupt in gunfire. Braden fired at me three times, waving the gun wildly in my direction and missing me completely. I put two rounds in his chest, and with a sigh, he collapsed on the carpet. The other two actors remained prone, frozen in fear. I turned my attention to the other side of the room.

The man who'd been guarding Roy was lying in a heap near the front door. Licorice was lying facedown near the kitchen. Next to him, Roy was bending over Priya. Keane remained standing, unscathed, in the center of the room.

I ran to Priya and crouched down next to Roy. He was cradling her in his arms. A bloodstain grew on her blouse. Licorice must have gotten a shot off before he died.

"Priya, stay with me!" Roy cried. "Somebody, call an ambulance!"

But I could see already there was no point. She'd been hit in the heart.

"I don't . . . want to do this anymore," she whispered, and then her head fell to the side. Priya Mistry was dead.

TWENTY-ONE

"Roy!" I yelled. "Pull yourself together. We've got to get the hell out of here. Keane, help me get the sheep into the Suburban."

"Pavel and I can do it," said Keane. "You should go."

"Look," I said. "You feel guilty for fucking this thing up, getting Peninsula killed. We can deal with that later. Right now—"

"It's not that," said Keane. "You need to get back to the office."

"The office?" I asked. "Why?"

"Selah's people knew we were going to be here," Keane said. "Somebody told them."

I hadn't had time to process the situation, but now it became clear to me. "The other Priya," I murmured. "Oh shit. April." Selah's people must have gone to the office and found April and Palomar there. Palomar had talked. And Selah's people probably had April.

I ran out the front door to the aircar.

When I got there, the building was empty. There was no sign of a struggle, or that anyone had been there. But then, if Selah's people had guns, there was no reason there would be. I called Keane and told him the situation.

"Okay," he said. "I'm sending you coordinates. Meet us there as soon as you can."

"All right," I said, and ended the call.

The coordinates turned out to be a remote trailhead in the Hollywood Hills. When I got there, I saw Keane standing in the dark next to Pavel's Suburban. I parked next to it and got out.

"What are we doing here?" I asked. "We need to find April."

"You got any idea where they're holding her?" asked Keane.

I shook my head.

"Neither do I," said Keane. "We needed a place to let Mary walk around a bit. And bury Peninsula."

"You're going to bury her *here*?" I asked.

"Roy's taking care of it," he said. "Look, we couldn't very well leave her at the house. We don't need that kind of heat." He had a point. Famous actresses turning up dead had a way of attracting a lot of the wrong kind of attention.

"What did you tell the actors?" I asked.

"I told them that if they didn't mention the names Priya Mistry or Erasmus Keane to the police, they might get their cash and drugs back. I may have also mentioned that if they talked, Roy would come back and break their arms."

"Carrot and stick," I said. "Let's hope it works. So, where are Roy and Pavel now?"

"This way," he said, flicking on a small flashlight and starting toward the trail. I followed him.

We walked about half a mile down the trail and then veered off into a shallow ravine. A few hundred yards later we came upon Roy and Pavel. Priya's body was lying under a tarp, next to which Roy was using a small camp shovel to furiously dig a hole. Pavel stood nearby, feeding Mary the sheep dried apricots out of a plastic bag. Dried tears stained Roy's face.

"Has Roy said anything about the clones?" I asked Keane quietly.

"He hasn't said much of anything," Keane replied.

"Lucky for you," I said. "He's in too much shock to realize she's dead because of you."

"The hell she is," said Keane. "Your genius plan to retrieve the sheep didn't account for Selah's people showing up. If I hadn't improvised, you and Roy would be dead too."

"We'd have been fine," I said not very convincingly. I regarded Roy, who had managed to dig about eight inches into the rocky ground. "Should we tell him?"

"Tell him what?" said Keane. "That the Priya he's burying is just one of God knows how many, all of which are either also dead, locked up in a secret lab somewhere, or slowly going crazy?"

"Hmm," I replied. I had been thinking Roy had a right to know, but now I wasn't sure if telling him would just make things worse. He was already pretty broken up, and we didn't need him going to pieces on us. Besides which, Keane and I still didn't fully understand what was going on, so telling Roy about the clones now was probably pointless. I was still pondering the matter when Keane's comm chirped. He put it on speaker and answered.

"Mr. Keane," said a woman's voice.

"Selah," said Keane.

"I believe you have something of mine," she said. "And I have something of yours."

"I don't know what you're talking about," said Keane.

"I think you do," said Selah. "Say hello, dear."

April's voice broke in: "I'm sorry, Fowler. I tried to get her out of there, but—"

Her voice cut off.

"I propose a trade," said Selah. "April for the sheep."

"Why?" said Keane. "What possible use do you have for a three-hundred-pound genetically modified sheep?"

"What use do you have for a one-hundred-and-forty-pound intellectual property lawyer?" Selah asked. "Life is full of little mysteries. Be at the La Brea Tar Pits at midnight. Bring the sheep. If you're not there, you won't see April again."

The line went dead.

I checked the time. It was nearly eleven, and it could easily take us an hour to get the sheep back to Pavel's Suburban and down to central Los Angeles.

"We'd better get going," I said.

Keane stood for a moment, rubbing his chin and watching Mary chew apricots.

"Keane," I said. "This isn't negotiable. We're making the trade. It's our fault April got tangled up in all this, and she's more valuable than any sheep." I tried not to think about the fact that the sheep had a human brain, which meant we'd essentially be handing Selah a young child. My only consolation was that the sheep wouldn't live much longer anyway.

He nodded. "Yeah, okay. Let's go."

I told Pavel we were borrowing his car and asked him to stay with Roy. At the rate Roy was going, it was going to take most of the night for him to dig a reasonably sized grave. I told Pavel we'd try to be back in a couple of hours. He gave me the rest of the dried apricots, and I led Mary back up to the trail, Keane walking a few feet ahead with the flashlight. We had a hell of a time getting Mary back into the Suburban; evidently, Roy had practically lifted her into the rear of the vehicle last time, but this time we had to rely almost completely on the attractive power of dried apricots. She barely fit into the rear of the vehicle, and I got the impression she wasn't looking forward to reliving the experience of riding in a cramped Suburban through the Hollywood hills. I wondered how much she understood about what was happening to her. Probably about as much as I did, which was to say: not much. By the time I'd gotten the tailgate closed, I was sweaty and exhausted, and we had a scant ten minutes to get to the La Brea Tar Pits.

I drove as fast as I dared down the winding, hilly road, Mary the sheep bleating in terror the whole time. At midnight Keane's comm chirped again. It was Selah sending the coordinates to a park not far from the tar pits. I pulled into the dark parking lot at 12:05 A.M. There were no other cars around. Keane and I got out and looked around, but there was no sign of Selah or her henchmen. His comm chirped again, and he showed me the display. It read:

NORTHEAST SOCCER FIELD

We opened the tailgate and coaxed Mary back out of the vehicle. It didn't take much; I think she'd had enough of Pavel's Suburban for a lifetime. I prayed this was the last stop for Mary, because I don't think there was any way in hell we'd get her back in that car—especially since I was out of apricots.

We led the sheep down a sidewalk in the general area of the soccer fields, as near as we could tell in the dim light. The moon was just a sliver, so the only appreciable light was the glow of the city on the horizon. Keane had his flashlight, but it didn't help much under the circumstances. Mary seemed relieved to be back on her feet; she barely bleated as we made our way through the park. We crossed a long swathe of grass, heading toward what I took to be soccer goalposts in the distance, practically dragging Mary to keep her from lying down. She had to be exhausted. I knew the feeling.

In the distance, headlights went on, aimed in our direction. They looked like they belonged to a pretty big truck. We headed that direction. When we were about fifty feet away, I heard a woman's voice. I thought it was Selah's, but I couldn't see anything with the headlights in my eyes. "That's far enough," she said.

"Where's April?" I said.

"Fowler?" I heard April say.

"I'm here," I said.

Selah spoke again. "Back away from the sheep, and I'll send April to you."

Keane and I took a few steps away from the sheep, and I drew my gun.

"Put the gun away, Fowler," said Selah.

I pointed the gun at Mary. "I'll put it away when April is safe," I said. I didn't want to shoot Mary, but threatening to kill her was the only leverage we had.

"Fowler?" I heard April say again. "Where are you?"

I saw someone silhouetted against the headlights, walking haltingly in my direction. She seemed to be blindfolded and her hands were tied, but I could tell by the way she walked that it was April.

"Over here, April," I said.

April continued to move in my direction. Behind her, I saw two more figures coming toward Mary. The sheep looked back at me uncertainly. I couldn't see her eyes, but I imagined there was fear in her face.

"It's okay, girl," I said. "These people will take good care of you."

She bleated an accusation at me.

"Yeah," I muttered. "I don't really believe it either."

The two figures got ahold of Mary and began escorting her to the truck. I embraced April with my left arm while keeping my gun trained on the sheep. I pulled off her blindfold and gave her a kiss on the cheek. "Let's go, Keane," I said.

We started walking back to the Suburban. I watched over

my shoulder for a while, but I don't really know why. Selah had what she wanted, and we had given it to her.

"Do they have Palomar?" I asked April as the three of us walked across the damp grass in the dark.

"She went with them willingly," said April. "I think she was actually relieved when they showed up."

"Her psychosis is fairly advanced," Keane said. "Her whole existence at this point revolves around her paranoia. She's just been waiting for them to come and get her. It's probably a relief for her to have it over with."

"Yeah," said April. "You know, Keane, I owe you an apology."

"You do?" asked Keane. "What for?"

"I thought Priya was just paranoid. I never considered there might actually be some sort of sinister plot centered on her." We had arrived at the Suburban, and I'd found a box cutter in the glove compartment to cut April's bonds.

Keane shrugged. "It's a common mistake," he said. "Even hypochondriacs get sick sometimes."

"Well, I'm sorry," said April, rubbing her wrists. "You were right and I was wrong. She really was in danger, and you were the only one who saw it."

Keane nodded, accepting her assessment with aplomb.

"By the way," April said. "How is your Priya? Peninsula?"

"She's dead," I said. "Keane's fault."

TWENTY-TWO

We dropped April off at home, and then Keane and I returned to the Hollywood Hills in time to catch Roy's impromptu funeral for Peninsula. At some point I dozed off and awoke to him soldiering through an off-key rendition of "Amazing Grace" in between sobs. The service probably would have gone on until dawn, but Keane and Pavel finally managed to coax him into a closing benediction. We climbed back to the trail and drove off.

I finally got into bed a couple of hours before sunrise. I awoke a few hours later to the sound of my comm chirping. It was Dr. Takemago. I groaned, but forced myself to answer the call.

"Mr. Fowler?" she said.

"Ugh," I replied.

"Mr. Fowler, I may have found another clue as to why Selah Fiore wants Mary."

I sat up in bed. "What is it?"

"Your mention of Esper's age-reversal research prompted some investigation on my part. I was not personally involved in that work, but I was aware of it. To my knowledge, all the animal subjects were destroyed shortly after the Collapse. But I was mistaken."

"You found a living subject?"

"Five of them," she said. "Six, if one includes Mary. I tested the DNA of three of the sheep here in the lab, and they all tested positive for a gene sequence that Esper developed as part of its age-reversal process."

"Hold on," I said, rubbing my groggy head and trying to make sense of what Takemago was saying. "You're telling me that the sheep not only have human brains, but they're going to live longer than normal sheep?" So much for them dying a merciful death.

"That is correct."

"How much longer?"

"Impossible to say," said Takemago. "All the other animal subjects were destroyed before we could evaluate the results of the gene therapy. The intent of the gene sequence was to block the aging process entirely once the animal reached adulthood."

A sickening feeling took hold in my gut. "You're saying . . ."

"The sheep may be immortal."

I shook my head. This couldn't be happening. Science had finally beaten death, and the end product was eternally youthful *sheep*?

"Why?" I said. "Why would they do this?"

"It's difficult to say with certainty. It may have been an attempt to increase the usable life of the sheep as research subjects."

"And since Selah Fiore provided the money, she undoubtedly knows about this feature. But why on Earth would she want an immortal sheep?"

"I can offer no hypothesis on that," said Takemago.

"Yeah," I said. "Keane and I will figure it out. Thanks for the info."

I ended the call, got dressed, and went upstairs to talk to

Keane. He was already (still?) up, researching something on-line. I told him what Takemago told me, and he just nodded.

"What?" I said. "You expected this?"

He shrugged. "It doesn't surprise me, given what we know about Selah's history with Esper."

"So you know why she wants an immortal sheep with a human brain?"

"That part I'm still working on," he said. "Look at this." He tapped a key and brought up his display on the wall screen behind him. It showed the website for an organization called the Tannhauser Institute.

"Tannhauser Institute?" I asked. "What's that?"

"Privately funded genetics research institute in Belgium," Keane said. He tapped his screen, and a page with the heading *Research Staff* appeared. Maybe thirty names were listed on the page. "See anybody you recognize?"

I scanned the list. "Henry Allebach, Ph.D.," I read. "Wasn't that the MIT scientist Takemago said wrote the paper on memory transfer?"

"The very same. And look at the top of the second column."

"Michael Guryev, Ph.D.," I read. "I know that name too," I said.

"He used to work at Esper," Keane said. "Takemago said he was involved in the design of their sheep."

"And now they're both working for this place in Belgium?"

"Supposedly," replied Keane. "But take a look at this." He brought up another window, showing a bio of Guryev, including a picture. I recognized him.

"It's Mr. Licorice," I said. "He flew from Belgium to get Selah's sheep?"

"Unlikely," said Keane. "I don't think he was ever in Belgium. I've been researching the Tannhauser Institute all morning, and I can't find any record of any work they've done.

No white papers, no lectures, no patents, nothing. They've been in existence for four years, and they haven't produced anything."

"Four years isn't that long," I said. "Maybe they're working on some big secret project."

"I think that's a safe bet," said Keane. "But I don't think they're doing it in Belgium. The address on their website is in a tiny town called Kaprijke. There's nothing there. I mean, the building exists, but it's in the middle of nowhere."

"Are you saying it's a dummy organization?" I asked. "Like a shell company?"

"Belgium recently loosened its restrictions on genetic engineering in the hopes of attracting more investment capital," said Keane. "I think whoever is running Tannhauser is using the Belgium location as a cover. The actual work is being done elsewhere."

"Where?"

"Here," said Keane. "Southern California."

"Because Guryev is here?"

"I checked the domain registration of the Tannhauser website," Keane said. "It's owned by the same company that owns the domain for the Solana Resort and Spa in Malibu."

"That's . . . odd," I said.

"The resort is located on top of a cliff overlooking the ocean," said Keane.

"Like Priya's dream," I said. "The bad place."

Keane nodded. "Except I don't think it's a dream. I think that's where the Priyas are born. Whoever is creating them does their best to suppress the clones' memory of the place, but it's their first real memory, so some of it sticks. They're probably also brought back occasionally for additional conditioning."

I thought for a moment. "It was pretty sloppy of them to register both domains under the same name, if the associa-

tion between Tannhauser and Solana is supposed to be secret."

"Yes," Keane replied. "And the domain registration for
Tannhauser was just updated yesterday. Before that, it was
registered to a completely different company."

"It's like somebody is trying to tell us something."

"Exactly."

"But who? Not Takemago. She's been pretty up-front, as
near as I can tell. Maybe the same person who sent the Noogus
letters?"

"Maybe," said Keane. "The other likely possibility is that
it's someone working for Selah Fiore."

"You think it's a trap? Selah trying to lure us to the
Solana?"

"Could be. Only one way to—"

His words were cut off by the sound of a deafening boom
somewhere above us. One of Keane's windows cracked, and
plaster dust fell from the ceiling.

"What in the hell?" I yelled, using my shirt to shield my
face from the dust cloud. I drew my gun and ran to the
stairs. Keane followed close behind. I bounded up the stairs
and threw the door to the roof open. The source of the noise
was immediately apparent: the aircar was in flames, a plume
of black smoke rising to the clouds. Shattered glass and
chunks of torn metal lay strewn around the gravel surface
of the roof.

I crept onto the roof, my gun raised before me. Making a
full-circle survey of the roof, I determined it was deserted.
I checked behind the vents and air-conditioning units just
in case. Other than Keane, myself, and the remains of the
aircar, the roof was empty.

"Any ideas?" I said to Keane.

"Yes," he said, surveying the wreckage. "We should get
off the—"

At that moment a man in combat gear clambered over the edge of the roof in front of us. An automatic rifle was slung over his back.

"Hold it!" I yelled, pointing my gun at the man. Then I saw another man, on the north side of the building. Then one on the south, and another on the east. I turned to see three more climbing over behind me. Maybe if I'd started shooting as soon as I'd seen the first guy, I could have taken them out, but now it was too late. Three of them already had their guns pointed my direction. I could get one, maybe two of them before Keane and I were both gunned down.

"Drop the gun," said the man right in front of me. I had no choice but to comply.

"Who the hell are you?" I demanded. The men wore masks concealing their faces.

"Who we are isn't important," said the man. "Our boss wants to talk to you."

I became aware of a large, armored aircar descending from the clouds behind me. It bore no markings that I could see.

"And who might your boss be?" said Keane.

"You'll find out soon enough," said the man. "But I think it's safe to say you've pissed him off."

TWENTY-THREE

The car landed, and we were forced inside. Three of the men boarded with us, keeping their guns trained on us the whole time. The aircar lifted off again and headed into the heart of the DZ. This was a flagrant violation of FAA and LAPD regulations; legally, they were required to pass through one of the checkpoints. Evidently, whomever these guys worked for didn't feel the need to play by the rules.

The car landed on a five-story building just north of Compton. Keane and I were prodded out of the car and down a set of stairs. We found ourselves in a luxuriously appointed office that contrasted starkly with its location in a dilapidated old building in the worst part of the city. Two armed men stood against the walls, watching us. Behind a large desk was a man whose face I had seen on the news: Mag-Lev, the most powerful warlord in the DZ. Mag-Lev was an ugly, mean-looking man whose silk shirt and clean-shaven head couldn't conceal the brutality of his nature. He sat, his elbows on the desk, his chin resting on his fists, studying us impassively like a wolf regarding its prey. The left side of his face was disfigured by a horrible burn scar, and his left eyelid drooped over a dead, bloodshot eye.

I'd heard a lot of theories about who Mag-Lev was and

where he had come from, but none of his would-be biographers seemed to be able to produce any solid evidence. He had simply appeared on the scene just over two years ago, and had begun ruthlessly eliminating other warlords and seizing control of territory. It took him less than a year to become the most feared man in the DZ, and he seemed to be well on his way to uniting all the DZ under his rule. A lot of important people were justifiably worried about that possibility: a disorganized, impoverished DZ, splintered into warring factions fighting over territory, could be managed and ultimately controlled. A unified DZ with a powerful leader posed a threat to the delicate equilibrium of Los Angeles.

As ugly as he was, I had to admit he had an unnerving sort of charisma. It came through on the brief snippets I had seen on TV, and I could feel it even stronger now, even though he hadn't yet said a word. It wasn't hard to imagine a man like that becoming the sole, unquestioned authority in the DZ.

"Keane and Fowler," Mag-Lev said in a low, gravelly tone. "I expect you know who I am."

"I'm hoping you're the guy from Triple A," said Keane. "Because I've got a serious problem with my car."

"That was just to get your attention," he said, with a grim smile. "A small taste of payback for destroying something I loved."

"The sheep?" I said. "We didn't kill the sheep. And to be honest, if your feelings for a farm animal are that strong, you've got problems that aren't going to be fixed by blowing up cars."

"The sheep was just business," growled Mag-Lev. "I was speaking of Priya Mistry. You should never have involved her in this. It's your fault she's dead, and you are going to pay."

"Uh . . ." I said, not sure which part of this to respond to. "You're in love with Priya Mistry?" I heard myself say.

"Suffice it to say I am deeply aggrieved by her death, and that is not good news for you. For her death, you will pay a thousand times over."

Keane started laughing. At first it was just a chuckle, but it soon turned into a chortle, and then a guffaw. He was bent over, gasping for breath.

Mag-Lev glared at Keane. "You find this amusing, Mr. Keane?" he growled.

"She . . . doesn't even . . . remember you," Keane said, gasping. "She could name every actor on that show . . . except for you."

Mag-Lev motioned to one of the guards, who took a couple of steps forward and jabbed his rifle butt into Keane's gut. Keane fell to his knees, still laughing.

"Priya and I have a connection you would never understand," snarled Mag-Lev. He was struggling to maintain his cool demeanor.

"Oh, I'm sure," Keane said between gasps, tears running down his cheeks. "It's the stuff of poetry. Two young sympaths in love, on the set of a shitty sitcom."

"You know nothing!" Mag-Lev snarled. "I loved her before she was famous, when she was still Bryn Jhaveri. And you will pay for her death!"

It finally dawned on me what Keane found so funny. He'd determined what had happened to the fourth actor, the one who'd spoken the catchphrase. Selah had told us there had only been one actor whose Feinberg-Webb score was anywhere near Priya's, and we'd found him. But instead of becoming a TV star like Priya, he had taken a different career path. Some combination of time, steroids, surgery, and maybe even gene therapy had transformed Giles Marbury, sitcom actor, into Levi Magnuson, aka Mag-Lev, DZ Warlord. I could only assume Selah Fiore had something to do with that transformation. But deep inside he was still just an insecure actor with a crush on his one-time costar Priya Mistry. Whatever special bond he thought he had with Priya existed only in his imagination: the Priyas we knew thought of him only as some guy they had worked with briefly years ago. I wondered what else having to do with Mag-Lev was illusory. Was he even a real warlord? Virtually everything I knew about him I had learned on the news, and the news could be manipulated.

"Leave us," said Mag-Lev to the guards, who were eyeing him curiously. Presumably, they didn't know about his secret past, and he wanted to keep it that way. When they balked, he growled, "Get out! I can handle these two." He pulled a gun from a holster. They complied.

"So how does it work?" Keane asked. "Selah Fiore is going through old Feinberg-Webb scores, finds your name near the top of the list, and gives you a call? You're out of work after *Room for One More* gets canceled, so you're desperate for a job. She tells you she's got the role of a lifetime. All you have to do is become an entirely different person."

"Who I was isn't your concern," said Mag-Lev. "It's who I am right now that you need to worry about." He leveled the gun at Keane. "And right now I'm the guy who's going to put a bullet in your head."

"You're not going to shoot me," said Keane, who had mostly recovered from his laughing fit. He was rubbing his belly where the guard had struck him.

Mag-Lev laughed. "Oh yeah? And why not?"

"For one thing, your beloved Priya isn't dead."

"Bullshit," growled Mag-Lev. "Cody and Kevin told me what happened. You guys showed up to nab the sheep, but Selah's people interfered. Priya got caught in the crossfire."

"That wasn't Priya," I said. "It was a clone."

He pointed the gun at me. "Don't you fucking lie to me," he said.

"He isn't," said Keane. "We've been working on her case for three days now, and we've encountered at least three different Priyas. We don't believe any of them are the real one."

"This is seriously the best story you could come up with?" Mag-Lev snarled. "Clones? Let me guess, the real Priya was abducted by aliens from Venus?"

"You of all people should understand what Selah Fiore is capable of," said Keane. "She transformed you from a sitcom actor into a DZ warlord. Made Giles Marbury disappear, altered your appearance, set you up in the DZ, got her media outlets to cover your remarkable ascendance to power. She created the myth of Mag-Lev, and the myth became reality. You think she's not capable of making copies of a popular actress in order to cash in on her success? Oh, and by the way, if you're looking for someone to blame for Priya's death, you might consider the fact that the clone that originally hired us was buried under a mountain of rubble on the *DiZzy Girl* set when a bomb went off. You wouldn't happen to know anything about that, would you, *Giles*?"

Mag-Lev shook his head. "That was her stunt double, Stacia Acardi."

"That's what they said on the news, anyway," said Keane. "And we know how reliable the news is. If it makes you feel better, Stacia Acardi probably is dead now, as it would have been awkward for Selah if Stacia showed up on the set after her supposed death. I could add that the Priya who got shot would never have been at that house in Culver City if you hadn't double-crossed Selah. You're to blame for her death as well. You killed Priya, Giles. You killed her *twice*."

"If you value your life, you'll stop calling me that," snarled Mag-Lev. "And stop talking about Priya. You don't know anything about her."

"I know that Priya Mistry is an illusion," said Keane. "Just like Mag-Lev, almighty warlord of the DZ. The good news is that we have reason to believe that the original Priya Mistry, the woman you knew as Bryn Jhaveri, is still alive. And if you let me and my partner go, we might still be able to save her."

"Not a chance," said Mag-Lev. "You're lying. You're making this all up."

Keane sighed. "These accusations, from a man whose entire life is a lie, are getting a bit tiresome. You want a demonstration of my veracity? Here's a story for you. Selah Fiore asked you to steal a sheep for her. She wouldn't tell you why she wanted it, but you used your criminal connections to get the sheep. Then you and Selah had a falling-out. Probably she's afraid of the monster she created becoming too powerful for her to control. That's what that bombing was about: you trying to show her who's boss. But Selah isn't going to back down that easily. Did you know she's auditioning for your replacement right now?"

Mag-Lev regarded him skeptically, but I could tell he sensed the truth in Keane's words. I knew it too, as he said it: the actors Selah had showed us weren't trying out for a TV show; they were—unknowingly, no doubt—auditioning for a role as a real-life DZ warlord. But if that was true, then Selah Fiore was even more powerful than I had thought.

"You double-crossed Selah," Keane continued. "You had Hugo Díaz deliver the sheep to three friends of yours, out-of-work actors who aren't part of your formal criminal empire, probably because you know Selah has spies all throughout your organization. You wanted to make sure you could hold on to the sheep without Selah finding out where it was. But we ruined that plan when we led Selah's people to the house in Culver City."

"Yes," said Mag-Lev coldly, "you did."

"That was completely unintentional, for what it's worth," Keane said. "But now that she has the sheep, you have no leverage over Selah. As soon as she finds an adequate replacement, you're toast."

"I won't be that easy to destroy," said Mag-Lev.

Keane laughed. "Do you really believe that? Selah created you by spreading your propaganda all over the news. How hard do you think it will be for her to destroy you the same way? All she has to do is sow the idea that your hold over the DZ is slipping, make the other warlords think you've become weak. Once the idea takes hold, they'll do her work for her. The DZ will devolve into chaos, and a powerful new leader will appear to take the reins. Second verse, same as the first."

"What does any of this have to do with Priya?" Mag-Lev demanded.

"To be honest," said Keane, "I'm not entirely certain. But I know Selah Fiore has the sheep, and I believe she is also holding the original Priya Mistry. She's planning something that involves both of them, and knowing Selah Fiore, it's nothing good. Fowler and I are the only ones who can stop her. We can rescue Priya and get your sheep back."

I shot Keane a dubious glance. Having already promised the sheep to Banerjee and Selah, he was now promising it to Mag-Lev as well. And I was fairly certain every single one of those people had the will and the means to ruin, if not kill, us. I was all for getting us out of this jam, but at some point that bill was going to have to be paid.

"Priya Mistry a clone," Mag-Lev murmured, shaking his head. He set his eyes on Keane. "Why should I trust you?"

"Have you heard anything on the news about Priya's death?"

"No."

"And you won't, either. Check with your Tortugas on the *DiZzy Girl* set. My bet is that she's back to work today, without a scratch on her."

Mag-Lev looked dubious, but he muttered something into his comm. A few seconds later an expression somewhere between bafflement and relief came over his face. "She showed up twenty minutes ago," he said. "But how . . . ?"

"Another clone," said Keane. "God knows how many they have. They seem to keep three or four of them active at any given time. If something happens to one, they have a replacement ready."

Mag-Lev sat down again. He seemed overwhelmed. I knew the feeling. "How do you know they still have the original?" he asked.

"Some of the clones have received messages I believe originated with the real Priya," said Keane.

"Where is she?"

Keane shook his head. "If I tell you that, you'll send a bunch of thugs in there with guns blazing, and probably get Priya killed. The sheep, too, most likely. And not incidentally, you'll then have no more reason to keep us alive. No, you're going to let us go, and we're going to rescue Priya and retrieve the sheep."

"If you think you can force my hand," said Mag-Lev, "you don't know me very well."

"I'm not forcing anything," said Keane. "Fowler and I are the only ones who can rescue Priya and get your sheep, and you know it. Wasting time, trying to get me to tell you Priya's location isn't going to help Priya, and it isn't going to help you. All it does is give Selah more time to execute whatever diabolical plan she's devised."

Mag-Lev studied Keane for some time. "Selah is a fool to think she can control me," he said at last. "She comes to me when she wants some dirty work done, but then she treats me as if I'm still just some unknown actor begging for her approval. Yes, Selah gave me this role, but *I'm* the one who created Mag-Lev. I *am* Mag-Lev, and I'm not going to roll over for some withered old crone who made her fortune off my people, my culture, my territory. The DZ is mine, and Selah Fiore will soon know it!"

"That's why you double-crossed her on the sheep?" I said.

He snorted. "I thought Selah could be reasoned with. I thought if I showed her how powerful I really am, she'd come to her senses. Stop lowballing me on protection payments for *DiZzy Girl* and the other shows, stop playing the other warlords against me, treat me with the respect I deserve. But I see now I was mistaken. Selah is never going to think of me as anything but a pawn of her creation. Right up to the second I destroy her."

"Um," I said. "Destroy her?"

He smiled coldly at me. "These bombings in the DZ," he said. "Ultimately they only hurt the DZ, and that hurts me. I'm taking the battle to Selah Fiore. At midnight tonight the Flagship building is going up in flames. The DZ has provided the rest of the world with entertainment long enough. Now it's time for us to sit back and watch the carnage."

"That's insane," I said. "If you destroy Flagship, you'll shut down production on *DiZzy Girl* and all the other shows shooting in the DZ. You'll lose all that income. How does that help you?"

"It's a short-term sacrifice," said Mag-Lev. "What Selah wants to do to the DZ, I'm going to do to the entertainment industry. A rebalancing of power. Selah Fiore and Flagship Media will be out; someone else will be in. I spent most of yesterday in meetings with other companies very eager to work with me." He grinned. "You might say I've been auditioning Selah's replacement. So you see, I don't need the sheep anymore."

"You've lost your mind," I said. "You're not even a real warlord! You're just an actor playing a role! This isn't a pretend war you're starting. Real people are going to be killed!"

"Not a real warlord?" Mag-Lev roared, pounding his fists on the desk. "Who do you think is really in control of this city? The mayor? Don't make me laugh. Nobody's cared who the mayor of Los Angeles is since the Collapse. In Los Angeles the appearance of power *is* power. Hell, even before the Collapse, California had two governors who were movie stars. You think that's an accident? You say I'm not a 'real warlord.' So tell me, Keane, what do I have to do to be 'real'? Make a movie with a chimp? Marry a Kennedy?"

"Well, I'd definitely recommend that option over making a movie with a Kennedy and marrying a chimp," said Keane.

"Very funny, Mr. Keane," said Mag-Lev. "Let me remind you who is holding the gun. And remember, when Selah wanted that sheep stolen from Esper, she came to *me*. Because I'm the one with the connections to get things done. I may have started out as a man playing a role, but now I *am* Mag-Lev."

"You're so full of shit," said Keane.

"Excuse me?" said Mag-Lev.

"You claimed to have brought us here because you care about Priya," said Keane, "but all you care about is showing Selah Fiore how big your dick is. You think it will make Mommy proud when you blow up her building? It's not going to change anything, Giles. If you think destroying Selah Fiore is going to give you the freedom you need to take control of the DZ, you're kidding yourself. Without Selah, you're nothing."

"You son of a bitch," snarled Mag-Lev, waving the gun at Keane.

Keane sighed. "Use your head, Mag-Lev. Three years ago you were just an unemployed actor. However thoroughly you've embraced the role of warlord, you wake up every morning with one thought in your head: *How much longer can I keep fooling everybody?* And you know what the answer is, Giles? Not very fucking long. The other warlords are uniting against you. You've overplayed your hand, fallen for your own hype. The only hope you have is to negotiate a compromise with Selah."

"It's too late for that," Mag-Lev growled. "We're at war."

"Everything you've done so far could be interpreted by Selah as negotiating tactics," I said. "But if you blow up her building, there's no going back. Then you *will* be at war."

"And trust me," said Keane. "You don't want to go to war with Selah Fiore."

"I have no other options," said Mag-Lev.

"Negotiate," said Keane.

"Clearly, you've never tried negotiating with Selah Fiore," said Mag-Lev.

"Actually," said Keane. "I have."

"And how did that go?"

"I'll let you know," said Keane.

Mag-Lev sighed. "Even if I wanted to keep negotiating, I have no leverage. All I had was the sheep."

"We're going to get the sheep back," said Keane. "And rescue Priya while we're at it. You said you're blowing up the Flagship building at midnight. If we can rescue Priya and get the sheep to you before that, will you call off the attack?"

Mag-Lev seemed unconvinced.

"What do you have to lose?" I asked. "Give us until midnight. If we fail, you can go ahead with your idiotic war."

Mag-Lev glared at me, but he said, "Fine. You have until midnight. Cross me, Keane, and you'll find out just how much power I have in this city."

TWENTY-FOUR

Mag-Lev had his people drop us off back at the office. The fire had gone out, and Keane's car was now a barely recognizable lump of twisted, blackened metal. Debris lay scattered all over the roof. Apparently oblivious, Keane strode past the wreckage and went downstairs to his office. I followed.

At this point I had no idea what he actually planned to do. There seemed to be no winning move: even if we somehow managed to get the sheep back from Selah, there was no way we could deliver it to both Jason Banerjee and Mag-Lev. If it were up to me, I'd deliver the sheep to Mag-Lev, because whatever deep, dark secrets were contained in the Maelstrom file, at least Banerjee hadn't promised to kill us. And maybe it was time for the truth about Erasmus Keane to come out. Frankly, I was getting sick of being completely in the dark about Keane's past. If the Maelstrom file hadn't burned up with Keane's car, I'd have been sorely tempted to open it.

Keane went into his office and closed the door, presumably to "think." I continued downstairs to my apartment. I thought about calling April, but decided that telling her about the morning's adventure would only make her worry.

I sat in my office for a while, trying to think of a way out of this mess, but came up with nothing. Both of the cases we had taken on had come to miserable ends. The sheep was in the hands of Selah Fiore, who was planning to do God knows what with it, and Priya, the woman who had hired us to protect her, was dead, twice over. I hadn't even imagined, when we took her case, that it would be possible for us to fail this badly. Adding insult to injury, we weren't likely to get paid for any of this. Maybe April was right. Maybe I was wasting my life, working for Erasmus Keane. I certainly wasn't getting any closer to resolving Gwen's disappearance.

After an hour of staring at the wall, getting no closer to a solution, I heated up some leftovers for lunch and then went back to bed. I'd only gotten about three hours of sleep, and that wasn't helping either my mood or my abstract problem-solving abilities. Maybe I'd see things in a different light in a few hours.

Less than an hour later, I was awoken by a banging on the door. My first groggy thought was that it was Priya Mistry. Then I remembered Priya Mistry was dead. Then I remembered an indeterminate number of Priya Mistrys were still alive, and any one of them could be at the door. Maybe, in fact, all the extant Priyas had gotten together and formed a union to protest their mistreatment. I went to answer the door.

It wasn't any of the Priyas. It was Peninsula's bodyguard, Roy.

"What the hell is going on, Fowler?" he demanded.

"Come in, Roy," I said. "I'll make some coffee." We went to my office, and I put the coffee on. Roy and I sat down. "Now," I said, "what's got you all worked up?"

"I got a call from somebody at Flagship this morning," Roy said. "Telling me my services were no longer required. I was kind of expecting it, because of . . . what happened to Priya.

But then Taki called me, asked where I was. She said Priya had a new bodyguard. I thought Taki had lost her mind. Because, well, Priya is dead. Why would she need a body-guard? But then I remembered that weird conversation Priya had with that guy at the house, about them making copies of her. So I'm going to ask you again: What the hell is going on?"

I sighed. There wasn't any way to halfway explain some-thing like this. I either needed to stonewall Roy or tell him everything. At this point, I didn't see the harm in leveling with him.

"The woman you buried," I said, "wasn't Priya Mistry. She was a clone."

Roy nodded. "I figured," he said.

"Really?" I asked, surprised at his blasé reaction.

"Yeah," he said. "I was up most of the night, thinking. That's why she acted so weirdly toward me at the house that night. The real Priya died in that explosion on the set, didn't she?"

I shook my head. "That wasn't the original either. Another clone."

"*Another* clone? How many are there?"

"Living and dead? We don't know. At least three, probably more. The one you were watching was probably replaced at least once before. Keane thinks they all go crazy after a while, so they have to be replaced."

"That's why she didn't remember the pizza place," mur-mured Roy. "She had never been there."

"Right," I said.

"So she's not dead," Roy said. "The real Priya."

"We think Selah is holding the original," I said.

"Where?"

I paused. "Roy, you need to understand . . . we're not sure what condition Priya is in, if there even *is* a real Priya. We don't know what Selah has done to her, what she's been subjected to. And, Roy, she isn't going to know you. In all likelihood, you've never even met her. All you've ever met is copies."

Roy thought for a moment. "I understand," he said. "I don't care. I love her."

"Did you hear what I just said, Roy? You don't even know her."

"I knew Priya before I even met her," said Roy quietly. "I've always loved her. And I always will. It doesn't matter what she's been through. I don't expect you to understand."

I sighed. The fact was, I did understand. That's exactly how I had felt about Gwen. How I still felt, if I were being honest. Once somebody got into your soul that way, you weren't ever the same.

"In that case," I said, pushing my thoughts of Gwen away, "the best thing for you to do is to talk to Flagship about getting your job back. Watch over the clone they've got working on *DiZzy Girl* now. She's as real as any of them."

"No," said Roy. "Even if I wanted to do that, Selah is never going to let me near Priya again. I think she suspects I know about Priya's death. If I show up at that set again, I'm going to be the next casualty of Selah Fiore's insanity. I don't even dare to go home."

"So what do you want?" I asked.

"I need to find her," said Roy. "The real Priya. She's in danger, I know it. She needs me."

"Look, Roy," I said. "Keane and I are working on it. If and when we find Priya, you'll be the first to know."

"No," said Roy firmly. "I'm going with you."

"Roy," I said, "I appreciate all your help, but Keane isn't going to—"

At that moment Keane walked in. "Keane isn't going to what?" he asked.

"Roy wants to go with us to rescue Priya," I said.

"Okay," replied Keane, regarding Roy thoughtfully.

"Okay?" I said. "Just like that?"

Keane shrugged. "We may need his help with the sheep."

Evidently, Keane had finished whatever he was doing in his office, and we were now going to try to rescue Priya and the sheep. I didn't like our odds, but at this point I was committed.

Keane called Pavel, who swung by in his Suburban. Two hours later Keane, Roy, and I were looking down on the Solana Spa and Resort in Malibu. Keane instructed Pavel to remain in the Suburban, parked just down the road, and to be ready to meet us at the resort entrance.

The place was a green oasis perched on top of a cliff that fell away steeply to the Pacific. A tall chain-link fence topped with razor wire encircled the resort, with a cluster of mission-style buildings, a swimming pool, and tennis courts taking up about half of the fenced-in area. We were two hundred yards or so from the entrance, lying on a rocky bluff across the winding highway that ran up the coast. Keane held up a pair of binoculars he'd brought along, surveying the resort, but there wasn't much to see. Except for a single security guard walking the perimeter, the place seemed to be deserted.

"What now?" I asked.

"Now we wait," replied Keane.

"Do we even know Priya is in there?" asked Roy.

"No," said Keane. "Nor do we know the sheep is in there. We're acting on pure conjecture. If you've got any better information, feel free to share with the group."

Nobody had anything further to offer, so we sat there, roasting in the sun. We had been there for nearly two hours before we saw any activity. People began emerging from bungalows and making their way toward one of the larger buildings. Mercifully, by this time a breeze had picked up. The temperature dropped, and clouds were moving in off the Pacific. I hoped that Biblical rain held off for a bit. We weren't equipped for a flood.

"Looks like the afternoon shift is starting," I said.

"Yes," said Keane. "But nobody is leaving. I think there is only one shift. They're on Belgian time."

Sure, I thought. *Why not? If you're going to pretend to be running a research institute in Belgium, you might as well go all out.*

We continued to watch for some time, but couldn't see much of interest from our vantage point. After another hour, we sent Roy to get some food. He returned a while later with sandwiches and drinks, and we had a brief picnic on the bluff, taking turns with the binoculars. By the time we had finished, the sun was nearing the horizon. All the staff— we had counted about two dozen people—had gone inside.

But then, just before the sun began to set, we saw some movement. I couldn't make out anything but silhouettes against the glare, but three figures seemed to be moving toward the cliff's edge.

"What's going on, Keane?" I asked. He was peering through the binoculars.

"Looks like two men and a woman," said Keane.

"Priya?" asked Roy anxiously.

"Hard to say," said Keane.

"Give me those," said Roy. Keane shrugged and handed him the binoculars. Roy watched the figures for a few seconds. "It's her," he said. "It has to be. They're going to throw her off the cliff!"

"Don't be ridiculous, Roy," said Keane. "They're not going to hurt Priya. At least not like that."

I took the binoculars from Roy.

"What are they doing?" he asked.

"If I had to guess," I replied, "I'd say watching the sunset."

The two men had escorted Priya—I was fairly certain it was her, or one of the clones—to a vantage point where she could see the sun setting over the Pacific. It was the kind of thing you'd do for someone who was sentenced to death.

Roy grabbed the binoculars back. "We have to rescue her," he said. "Now is our chance!" He started to get to his feet, and Keane and I both immediately leaped onto his back. It was all we could do to keep him down.

"We'll never get near her, you idiot," Keane snapped. "If we're going to have any chance to rescue Priya, we need to wait until it's dark."

"That could be too late!" Roy cried, still straining to lift himself against our weight. "They're going to kill her! Or worse!"

I wasn't sure what Roy was imagining, but I didn't have any trouble believing Selah Fiore was capable of devising a fate for Priya that was worse than death.

"Roy," I said. "Keane is right. If we go down there now, they'll see us coming. We'll never even get through that fence, and Priya will be no better off." I didn't add that going after Priya now would also ruin our chances to retrieve the sheep.

Roy struggled for a little longer, but his heart wasn't in it. Finally he lay down on the ground, and Keane and I got off him. We watched as the sun set, and the men escorted Priya back inside. There was nothing we could do now but wait for it to get dark.

Half an hour later, we crept down the bluff and crossed the street. The resort complex was dark except for the light cast by a few halogen bulbs on the buildings. The single security guard meandered slowly around the perimeter. The wind was blowing hard now, and we were being pelted with big sporadic raindrops.

"I've seen department stores with tighter security," I whispered to Keane as we crept along the southern fence.

"Presumably, Selah was counting on secrecy to protect her operation," said Keane.

I nodded, but couldn't help thinking that Selah's reliance on secrecy hadn't prevented us from finding this place. Either somebody had screwed up, or this was a trap.

We made our way along the fence toward the cliff. The western edge of the resort was open to the cliff side, but the fence extended far enough down the rocky face to make it very difficult, if not impossible, to approach from that direction. If we had rock-climbing gear, we could have done it, but wire cutters were a simpler solution. We waited until the guard was walking toward the north side of the resort, and then I started snipping away at the bottom of the fence. After a couple of snips, Roy pushed me aside and grabbed the wire cutters. He cut through the fence like it was made of string and then pulled open a gap large enough for us to crawl through. I went first, followed by Keane. Roy started to crawl through, but I held up my hand.

"We need somebody out here to keep an eye on the security situation," I said. "I'll call you when we've got Priya."

I could see he wanted to argue, but then he thought better of it. "All right," he said. "But if I don't hear from you in fifteen minutes, I'm going in after you."

I nodded, and Keane and I took off across the lawn toward the nearest structure. We skulked from building to building, while Roy gave us updates on the location of the guard and other employees via my comm. For the most part, the complex was quiet, but occasionally someone would leave the main building to return to what I took to be the living quarters, or vice versa. All the entrances seemed to be protected by palm-print scanners. Our plan was to grab an employee on the way to the main building and use them to get inside.

"Remember," whispered Keane as we watched the entrance to the main building from around a corner, "our priority is the sheep."

"That may be your priority," I said. "It isn't mine."

Thunder rumbled in the distance, and if Keane replied, I didn't hear him. I darted across the grass toward a diminutive young man in a white lab coat who was approaching the main building. Coming up silently from behind him, I put my left hand over his mouth as I pushed the barrel of my SIG Sauer against his neck. I was a head taller than he was, so I had to lean down to speak ominously into his ear. "I'm looking for Priya Mistry," I said. Shorty froze in fear, and I could tell he was thinking about trying to make a run for it. I put the barrel to his temple and felt the fight go out of him. He pointed toward the building, and I gave Keane a nod. "If you scream, you're dead," I said, and gave Shorty a shove forward. I wasn't lying; I'd shoot him if I had to. I didn't know what Shorty's job was here, but he clearly knew about Priya, which meant he had to know she was being held against her will. That made him guilty of kidnapping, at the very least.

Keane came up behind me. I held my gun on Shorty as he swiped his palm in front of the scanner, doing my best to stay out of view of the camera that would undoubtedly be watching the entrance. Protocol with these scanners was to require everyone entering the building to be scanned before entering, but I'd done security long enough to know that protocol was almost never followed. Civilized people held the door for one another, and no silly security protocol was going to change that. Nobody would look twice at a couple of people following Shorty through the door. That was the theory anyway.

The scanner blinked green as Shorty swept his palm over it, and the door swung open. Shorty went inside, Keane and me following closely behind, our faces downcast to avoid being seen on camera. Once inside, I got up close to Shorty, jamming my gun into the small of his back. "Take me to Priya," I said. He led us down a hall to an elevator and pressed the down button. So far, so good: we hadn't yet run into any other employees, and hopefully our luck would hold. We got in the elevator. There was only one button, and Shorty pushed it. I got behind him, keeping my face down and the gun out of sight. Keane stood at my side. I'd given him the backup gun, and he held it hidden inside his coat.

"Where do they keep the sheep?" Keane said to the man.

"Priya," I said. "We're getting Priya first."

"Down the hall and to the right," said Shorty, his voice tight with fear. "Room thirty-six."

"Which one?" asked Keane. "The sheep or—"

But at that moment, the elevator door opened. Standing in front of us was a balding heavyset man with a blotchy red complexion. His name tag read *Dr. Henry Allebach*. The MIT scientist who had written the paper about memory transfer.

"Davis," said Allebach. "I was just going up to . . ." He stopped as he saw Keane and me in the elevator. I gave him about a second and a half before he had time to realize we weren't supposed to be there and yell for security. It was long enough.

I clocked Shorty on the back of the head with the nine-mil and then pointed the barrel at Allebach, stepping over Shorty as he fell. "Not a word," I said to Allebach. "Keane, get that guy out of the elevator." While Keane dragged Shorty's limp body into the hall, I moved a few paces, keeping my gun on Allebach. I tried a few locked doors before I found a supply closet. "Drag him in here. Hurry."

Keane dragged Shorty into the closet. I heard a faint moan, followed by the sound of a gun hitting a head again. Keane emerged from the closet and closed the door. "He should be out for a while," he said.

I nodded. "Okay, Dr. Allebach. Take us to Priya Mistry. Room thirty-six, I believe."

"You don't want to see Priya," said Allebach.

"The hell I don't," I said. "Go."

He shook his head but began walking slowly down the hall. From the outside, the building looked like a hotel, but the inside resembled a hospital: bright-white walls, tiled floors, minimal décor. The place smelled like disinfectant.

"Pick up the pace, Doc," I said, jabbing him in the ribs with the gun barrel. I didn't see any cameras in the hall, but there was a pretty good chance I'd been seen clocking Shorty in the elevator. We had to assume we didn't have much time to get Priya. We almost certainly didn't have time to get Mary the sheep, if she was even here.

We came to a T in the hallway. Allebach went right, and I glanced left to make sure the hall was clear in that direction before following. Whoever else was in the building was apparently busy at work, because the halls were empty. Room thirty-six was the last door on the right. Allebach paused and then turned to face me.

"Please, gentlemen," said Allebach. "Leave her be. There's nothing you can do for her now."

"We'll be the judge of that," I said. "Open it."

Allebach sighed. He waved his palm in front of the scanner, and the door slid open. I shoved him ahead of me into the dark room. "Keane," I said. "Find a light switch." The door shut behind us, and the blackness of the room was complete. I gripped Allebach's arm so I wouldn't lose him, and held the pistol barrel to his back. To my right, I heard Keane scrabbling around in the darkness. "Keane," I said. "Light."

A moment later a bank of fluorescent lights flickered on overhead. We were in a small room completely bare of furnishings except for a bed up against the far wall. Lying on the bed, turned away from us, was a slightly built person with a clean-shaven head.

"It would be better if you left her alone," said Allebach.

"One more word," I said, "and you're joining Shorty in the closet. Keane, watch the esteemed doctor. And keep an eye on the door."

I holstered my gun and went to the bed. As I approached, I could see that it was definitely Priya—or one of her clones; it was impossible to tell. She appeared to be breathing.

TWENTY-FIVE

I put my hand gently on her shoulder. "Priya," I said quietly. She didn't stir. I shook her slightly. "Priya," I said a little louder. "My name is Blake Fowler. I work with Erasmus Keane. We've come to get you out of here."

Still she didn't stir.

I shook her harder. "Priya! Wake up!"

She sighed and rolled onto her back. For a moment her eyelids fluttered open, and I thought her eyes fixed on me. But then her pupils rolled back into her head, and her eyes closed. She didn't look well. She looked tired and gaunt, and several years older than the other Priyas.

"I'm going to have to carry her out," I said. "Bring Allebach over here."

Keane prodded Allebach toward the bed, and I picked up Priya, throwing her over my left shoulder in a fireman's carry. With my right hand, I jerked the sheet off the bed and handed it to Keane. "Tie his hands with this. Shove the pillowcase into his mouth. We need to get out of here. Allebach, hands behind your back." I drew my gun and held it on Allebach so Keane could tie him up.

"We need to get the sheep," said Keane, wrapping the sheet around Allebach's wrists.

"Fuck the sheep," I said, and immediately regretted it. "I mean, we need to forget about the sheep. Priya is a human being. She's our priority. We get her out and then go back for the sheep."

Keane shook his head. "You take Priya to Roy. I'm going after the sheep." He had finished tying Allebach's hands and was working on getting the pillowcase off. I was wishing he would hurry the hell up, because Priya was getting heavy.

"Keane, that's crazy," I said. "You're going to get yourself—"

Behind me, I heard the door open. I spun around in time to see a man in body armor entering the room. It was my old pal Brian, and he'd gotten his hands on another nine-millimeter. The grin on his face told me we'd walked into a trap.

I set Priya down and gave Allebach a kick in the seat of his pants. As he stumbled forward, I grabbed the long end of the sheet hanging from his wrists. He jerked to a halt with a yelp, his arms bending awkwardly behind him.

Two more men came in after Brian, pointing Herstal F2800s at Keane and me. Belgian assault rifles—a nice touch. Keane pointed his gun back at them. I had mine on Allebach because I figured our only chance was if he was worth more to them than Priya.

"Perhaps," said a woman's voice behind them, "I can help solve your quandary." Selah Fiore stepped into view.

"Drop your guns," I said, "or Dr. Allebach gets a bullet in his head."

Selah shook her head. "That would be a shame," she said. "Especially considering the fact that you already killed my other chief scientist, Dr. Guryev. Fortunately for me, though, I don't need Dr. Allebach anymore. In fact, today was to be his last day working for me. He's retiring."

"Please," Allebach pleaded. "I was going to move to Belize with my girlfriend. I never meant to hurt anyone."

Selah smirked slightly at this, and then turned back to Keane and me. "Put down your guns and we can talk about you two getting out of here alive," she said.

"Bullshit," I said. "This whole operation depends on Dr. Allebach. We know about his memory-transfer theories, how you created clones of Priya and gave them her memories. You can't do that without him."

"Actually," said Selah, "I can. You're a bit too late, gentlemen. That was by design, of course. I wouldn't have let you get this close to either Dr. Allebach or Bryn if I still needed them. As you can see, though, Bryn is used up. She'll be dead before morning."

Behind me, Priya—that is, Bryn—lay where I'd left her, not moving. Her breathing was quick and shallow.

Keane lowered his gun. "Forget it, Fowler," he said. "We're beaten."

I held my gun on Allebach for a moment longer, but realized there was no point. If Selah didn't need Allebach any longer, threatening him was useless. Hell, she'd probably kill him herself as soon as she had the chance. Maybe that was what the smirk was about. I let go of the sheet, and Allebach stumbled toward Selah. Brian stepped forward and disarmed us. I wanted to smack the stupid grin off his face.

"What the hell did you do to her?" I asked, looking at Priya. "Lobotomize her? Suck her memories, her personality, her humanity, right out of her head?"

"What I did," said Selah, "is save her."

Behind her, Dr. Allebach was struggling to get his hands free from the sheet. Nobody seemed interested in helping him.

"Save her from what? A normal life? Being human?"

Selah shook her head. "Bryn Jhaveri was never going to

have a normal life. She was destined to be a star. More than a star, even. She was destined to be a goddess, the embodiment of humanity's hopes, fears, and desires. But deification comes with a price. It was too much for her. Too much for any human being to take."

"Because you demanded too much from her," I said. "Because you wouldn't let her be a human being."

"I'm the only reason she lasted as long as she did," Selah said. "Do you really believe the solution to Bryn's problems is to treat her like she's just another nobody and hope she doesn't figure out she's special? You think she's paranoid now? Try telling a goddess she's a nobody, that she's just like everybody else. Lie to her every day, build up an elaborate illusion to explain why men obsess over her, why people she barely knows fall in love with her. How long do you think that would last?"

"Maybe if you hadn't carved her up, made her into somebody's idea of an irresistible sex symbol . . ."

Selah sighed heavily. "You're missing the point, Mr. Fowler. I didn't create Priya Mistry. I saw Priya Mistry in Bryn Jhaveri, the way Michelangelo saw *David* in a block of marble. If I hadn't made Bryn Jhaveri beautiful, she would have been just a freak. She was never going to fit in anywhere but Hollywood. There's no place in our society for remarkable plain women. By making Bryn Jhaveri into Priya Mistry, I allowed her to have something like a normal life, at least for a while. I refuse to apologize for that."

"She never had a normal life," I said. "You used her, built an artificial reality around her. It drove her crazy."

"No," said Keane.

I turned to Keane. "You're not seriously taking Selah's side."

"Not at all," said Keane. "Selah made clones of Bryn Jhaveri in order to capitalize on her investment, without regard to Bryn's suffering, which I think we can agree is morally reprehensible. However, Selah is right about one thing: the clones weren't driven crazy by their circumstances. They went crazy *despite* their circumstances. As I said before, Bryn's paranoia didn't arise from her observance of the conspiracy. It happened the other way around. Bryn's paranoia made the conspiracy necessary."

Selah nodded approvingly.

"How the hell do you figure that?" I ask.

"Bryn Jhaveri always knew there was something different about her," said Keane. "She never fit in, anywhere she went. People acted strangely around her, and she couldn't figure out why. It made her neurotic, paranoid. She was desperate for something to change, for somebody to make sense of what she was going through. So when Selah told her she was special, that she was destined to be a star, Bryn wanted to believe her, and to make that idea a reality. She agreed to become Priya Mistry. Agreed to the surgeries, the gene therapy . . . and even the clones, probably."

"So it's true," I said. "There weren't any other actresses. You didn't modify other women to make them look like Priya. You made clones of the original."

"Correct," said Selah. "I apologize for misleading you, but you have to understand that cloning human beings is illegal. I thought it better to lie, given the circumstances."

"And Bryn knew about it?" I asked.

"Yes," said Selah. "She didn't care. She was willing to do anything to have her uniqueness confirmed, even if it meant making copies of her. Ironic, I suppose."

"But once it was done," said Keane, "the clones couldn't deal with their new reality—the idea that there were others of them out there. So Selah's people manipulated their memories, made each of them believe they were unique."

"That's right," said Selah. "And spent a great deal of

money and effort creating an entire reality around each of them."

"A padded room," I said. "With lots of nice scenery."

"Basically, yes," said Selah. "It was the best place for them. The only place for them."

"If you hadn't created them, you wouldn't have needed to put them in padded rooms."

"True," said Selah. "But we put a lot of money into Priya. We needed the clones to maximize the return on our investment. Without them, we couldn't have justified the expense. So you see, this really was the best possible option for everyone. Especially considering the clones' short life-span."

"Because of the artificial aging, you mean," said Keane. "They burn out quickly."

"In part," said Selah. "After a few months, the clones begin to show their age. We've never been able to fully reverse the process, so eventually the clones have to be . . . retired."

"The word is *murdered*," I said. I was somewhat gratified to have had my initial impression of Selah Fiore born out: she was a complete psychopath.

Selah shrugged. "Their physical bodies are destroyed, yes. But the core problem is more fundamental. No matter how convincing we make the illusion, eventually the paranoia takes over. The clones go crazy, generally much sooner than their bodies wear out."

"So then what?" asked Keane. "What do you do with them once the neurosis has progressed beyond manageability?" Keane seemed more fascinated than horrified.

"We wipe their memories," said Allebach, stepping forward. I'd almost forgotten he was there. At some point he'd evidently managed to get his hands free and remove the pillowcase out of his mouth. "Then we start fresh, same as we do for the new clones. Transfer Bryn's memories to the clone. With some adjustments, of course. We wipe her memories of this place, for starters, and use an artificial memory programming process I developed to fill in the blanks—things that happened after we began duplicating Bryn. This process is different for each clone, depending on her circumstances. They each have to be programmed to know and trust their own bodyguards, for instance."

"Why are you telling us all this?" I asked. I turned to Selah. "Why did you bring us here? That was your plan, right? Lure us to your secret hideout?"

Selah smiled. "I don't like loose ends," she said. "To answer your first question, I suppose I feel you have a right to know, after all you've been through."

"I guess that means you're going to kill us," I said.

"I don't kill when I can avoid it. People disappearing . . . it's messy. No, my plan is to wipe your memories of Priya Mistry and this place and then let you go."

I couldn't bring myself to thank her for this kindness.

Keane didn't seem to even notice what she'd said. He was deep in thought, still trying to solve some element of the mystery. "How long has this been going on?" he asked.

"We first cloned Bryn two years ago," said Selah. "We ordinarily keep two or three of them active at any one time. There have been twenty-eight clones altogether, including the two who are currently active."

"You said the paranoia becomes overwhelming after a few weeks," said Keane. "They all suffer from it?"

"Every one," said Selah.

"But the clones are perfect copies of the original, Bryn Jhaveri," he said, looking at the woman lying unconscious on the bed. "Which means she was insane as well."

"Yes," said Allebach. "She had the same inherent flaw as the rest of them. Every ten weeks we erase her most recent memories and start over. We used to tell her she was taking a break from filming to relieve stress. That's why we bought this resort initially. But we've found it makes little difference what we tell her. Ten weeks later she's a basket case, and we have to wipe her memory again. We've tried to pinpoint the source of the psychosis, modify her memories to prevent the meltdown, but nothing works. Bryn was on the verge of a psychotic break when Selah found her, and she's going to have that break no matter what we do. It's hardwired into her brain."

"Every ten weeks for two years," said Keane. "That's over ten resets. That can't be good for a person."

"It isn't," said Allebach. "Between the resets and the memory transfer process we have to go through every time we activate another clone, her brain is experiencing a lot of trauma. She's begun to have seizures, and we almost lost her last week to an aneurism. The trauma also made her mental state worse, exacerbating her psychosis. Even at the beginning of a reset, we had to keep her on high doses of antianxiety and antipsychotic drugs, and she's begun to experience symptoms of dementia. She was aging nearly as fast as the clones."

"Was?" I asked.

"It's not a problem anymore," said Selah.

"Why is that?" I asked.

"Because," said Keane. "They found a body that can tolerate the resets and memory transfers. A body that regenerates faster than they destroy it."

"Yes," said Allebach. "We transferred Bryn's memories to a host better suited to handle the stress. The procedure was a success, although it seems that Bryn's original body is unlikely to survive it. Her mind is already gone, as you can see."

"You killed her," I said.

"You're not listening, Mr. Keane," said Selah. "Bryn's body was used up. We found her a new one. One that will never wear out. It's not, I suppose, an ideal host, but you work with what you have."

I'd been so focused on the horror of what they had done to the woman on the bed that it hadn't fully registered what she and Keane were saying. "Hang on," I said as I processed the conversation. "You can't possibly be saying . . ."

Selah smiled. "Would you like to see her?"

TWENTY-SIX

Selah and Allebach led us down the hall to another room, with Brian following to make sure we behaved. Selah dismissed the other two men, presumably to free them up to pursue other gun-toting-thug-related duties. We entered a room similar to the one we had just been in, but there was no bed. Straw was scattered on the floor, and in the corner was a trough full of water. In the middle of the room, watching us, was Mary the sheep.

Except it wasn't Mary. It was Priya Mistry. Or Bryn Jhaveri, I suppose. Even if I hadn't known about the memory transfer, I think I'd have noticed something strange about this sheep. An intelligent glint in the eye. Maybe I was imagining it.

"Hello," said the sheep, eyeing us uncertainly.

The sheep's mouth didn't move, and for a moment I thought I was hallucinating again. Then I realized that the voice was coming from a small speaker hanging from a collar around its neck. The speaker was connected to a harness on the sheep's head.

"It's a thought-to-voice translator," said Selah. "A sheep's mouth isn't suited for articulating human speech, so we use this device to allow her to communicate with us. How are you today, Bryn?"

"I'm okay," said the sheep. "I feel a little . . . funny." The voice was generic and vaguely female-sounding, and I was having a hard time accepting the fact that this was really her.

"You conducted the memory transfer process on the sheep," said Keane, staring with fascination at the sheep. "Transferred Bryn's memories and personality to Mary's body."

"We used a somewhat more thorough process than we'd used on the clones," said Allebach. "The sheep had already built up five years' worth of memories, and we needed to make sure we wiped out any trace of them. We also needed to make sure we had a high-fidelity copy of Bryn's memories, because the sheep will be the source of Bryn's personality for all future clones."

"That's why Bryn is dying," I said. "You sucked her brain out."

The sheep shuddered slightly and looked at me with alarm. At least, I think it was alarm. I don't have a lot of practice reading the facial expressions of sheep.

"Try not to upset her," Selah scolded. "Bryn isn't dying. Not ever."

That gave me a bit of a chill as I remembered what Takemago told us about Esper's sheep: they might very well be immortal. Even if nobody ever unlocked the secret of human immortality, in a hundred years Flagship could still be producing original shows starring Priya Mistry, cloned from Bryn Jhaveri's DNA and using memories copied from the sheep.

"But . . . why?" I asked.

"As I said," Selah replied. "Bryn's psyche has a fundamental flaw. That flaw causes excessive stress on any body that hosts her memories. Priya Mistry is too valuable a property to be allowed to burn out. I need her around for at least another ten years, and her body wasn't going to last another six weeks. Fortunately, due to my previous association with Esper Corporation, I knew of a suitable host body that could tolerate the stress—indefinitely. And I figured they owed me."

"I don't understand what's happening," said the sheep.

"Nothing to worry about, Bryn," said Selah. "This is Mr. Keane and Mr. Fowler. They just stopped by to make sure you're being treated well."

The sheep nodded slowly, which I found unexpectedly creepy. I'd never seen a sheep nod before. "I was just thinking about drinking some water and then going to sleep," said the sheep. "I'm very tired today, for some reason."

"You seem oddly unperturbed by the fact that you're a sheep, Bryn," said Keane.

The sheep stared at him for a moment and then looked down at her body. "I am, aren't I?" she said.

"Do you find that fact upsetting?" asked Keane.

"I think I did at first," said the sheep. "But I guess I've gotten used to it. I don't really think about it anymore."

"How could you possibly have gotten used to it?" I asked, astounded. "You've only been a sheep for—"

"Six months," Selah interrupted.

"That's impossible," I said. "Two days ago, the sheep was in a garage in—"

"Two days ago," Selah said, "Bryn was right here. She spent the day eating grass in the sunshine, and then was brought back here at night to go to sleep, just as she does every day. She finds it very comforting. Don't you, Bryn?"

"Yes," said the sheep. "I do. I love grass. And sunshine. What were you going to say about a sheep being in a garage, Mr. Fowler?"

"Mr. Fowler is confused," said Selah. "He's thinking of a different sheep." She shot me a glare that told me I'd better not contradict her. "We'll leave you be, Bryn. Sleep well."

Selah turned and left the room, Allebach following close behind. Brian, his rifle still trained on Keane and me, nodded at the door, indicating we were to leave as well. Keane started toward the door. I paused, taking a last look at the Bryn-sheep. "Good-bye, Bryn," I said. "It was nice to finally meet you."

"Nice to meet you too," said the Bryn-sheep. She held my gaze for a moment, and then walked to her trough and began lapping up water.

We followed Selah down the hall, prodded by Brian.

"How could you do that to her?" I asked.

Selah shrugged. "I've done the best I could for everyone involved. Bryn agreed to this arrangement, knowing the risks."

"You're telling me she agreed to be turned into a sheep?"

"She agreed to have her memories transferred to any host we chose. The fact that in this case the host is a farm animal is immaterial. Of course, legally speaking, the creature you just spoke to is not human, and therefore has no rights. So we no longer have any legal obligation to consider Bryn's opinions on the matter. Once Bryn's body dies, our business relationship will be at an end."

I shook my head, hardly believing what I was hearing.

Selah led us down the hall to another door. She waved her palm in front of a scanner, and we went inside, Brian bringing up the rear. We found ourselves in a vast laboratory that resembled the one we'd met Dr. Takemago in at the Esper building. The walls were lined with banks of ominous-looking equipment and displays, and articulated robotic arms dangled in several places from the ceiling. Several lab-coated technicians milled about the room, engaged in various mysterious tasks.

In the middle of the room were two empty hospital beds. Toward the far wall were twelve vaguely sarcophaguslike chambers. Through a window near the top of seven of the chambers—the ones on the right-hand side of the series—a young woman's face was visible. It was the same woman, Bryn Jhaveri, at three different stages in her development. The three on the far right were identical to the Priya Mistry we knew. The fourth looked almost like Priya, but something was a little off about her. After a moment it registered with me that the clone hadn't yet been subjected to the cosmetic surgery that would perfect her appearance. So that was another bit of truth in what Selah had told us: whatever genetic modifications they'd made to Bryn, they apparently still relied largely on surgery to make her look like Priya Mistry. The one to the left of the "unfinished" Priya looked like a teenager, and the third one was so young that only the top of her head showed through the window. It occurred to me that the other four chambers might not actually be empty; they probably held smaller, younger versions of Priya. *Younger* was a relative term, of course. The real age difference was probably just weeks, or even days.

"So this is where stars are born," mused Keane.

"Just one star, so far," said Selah. "Every one of her."

"And one lab technician," said Keane.

Selah nodded. "Hugo Díaz. Mag-Lev's people needed a corpse to avoid suspicion."

"This is insane," I said. "You know that, right? Why are you doing this?"

"We've been over this," said Selah. "Priya is too valuable a property not to take full advantage of her."

"I get the economics of it," I said. "What I'm wondering is, what kind of twisted individual builds a secret lab under a Malibu resort to make copies of a human being, with the sole purpose of increasing their bottom line? How does that even occur to you?"

Selah shrugged. "It all just sort of came together. We had

originally planned to use only cosmetic surgery to make Bryn into Priya, but there are limits to what surgery can accomplish. I was familiar with Esper's work on gene therapy because of my previous association with them, so I hired Esper's expert to consult on the possibility of using gene therapy to perfect Priya."

"Michael Guryev," said Keane. "God rest his soul."

Selah went on. "Dr. Guryev was very interested in the possibility of making practical use of his work, but he was insistent we keep his involvement secret, because of various legal and ethical concerns. So I created the Tannhauser Institute. When Bryn began developing serious psychological problems, I hired several psychologists to treat her, but the only treatment that had any effect was repressing her recent memories through posthypnotic suggestion. Their hypothesis was that the paranoia was a result of Bryn's experience in the lab, so we assumed that if we repressed those memories, we'd cure her. When the paranoia kept resurfacing, one of my psychologists suggested contacting Dr. Allebach. Dr. Allebach devised a process for thoroughly erasing Bryn's memories, but the problem paranoia continued to resurface. Even creating a buffer of artificial memories didn't help significantly. Every ten weeks, we had to wipe her memories again. It was clear that Bryn's body wasn't going to be able to survive this indefinitely. Allebach and Guryev came up with the idea of artificially aged clones, with Bryn's memory implanted in them. But this was a temporary solution as well, as I've explained."

"Why not just transfer her memories from one clone to another?" asked Keane. "You could keep doing that indefinitely."

"Copies of copies," said Allebach. "The brain is an analog system. Fidelity is lost with each transfer. After five or six generations, the quality would have degraded to a noticeable level. We needed a more permanent solution."

"Dr. Guryev knew about the special qualities of Esper's sheep," said Selah. "He suggested that Mary would be a suitable vessel for Bryn's memories. The idea gave me pause, but we couldn't think of any reason it wouldn't work."

"Clearly, the fact that it's batshit crazy didn't factor in," I said. "And I don't buy your story. You found a young actress with a lot of potential, and somehow on the way to making her a star, you kind of accidentally created a top-secret illegal cloning program? It's bullshit. Something else is going on here."

"Immortality," said Keane. "That was Selah's original reason for getting involved with Esper. And that's still what she's after. Priya Mistry was just a test run, albeit a very lucrative one. Her ultimate goal is a new body for herself. As soon as they solve the problems associated with accelerated aging, she'll clone her own body, transfer her memories to it, and have her current body 'retired.'"

Selah smiled, as if pleased Keane had figured her out.

"Of course," Keane added, "the new version of her will have a critical flaw, much like the Priya clones."

"Oh?" said Selah, bemused. "What's that, Mr. Keane?"

"You'll still be a lunatic," Keane replied. "You realize that your own plan demonstrates you're a sociopath, right? You're assuming that your identity is going to be transferred to your new body along with your memories, but if that's true, then all the copies you've made of Bryn are just as much Bryn as the original, including the sheep. By your own logic, they're all human beings, but you treat them as cattle."

Selah shrugged. "Such abstract philosophical considerations don't interest me," she said. "What matters is that my ideas, my plans, and my memories will live on."

"Narcissistic sociopath," said Keane. "All right, you obviously brought us here for a reason. Are you going to give us the grand tour? What's the deal with the Matryoshka

dolls?" He was indicating the Priyas lined up in the sar-
cophagi.

"The three on the right have already been imprinted with
Bryn's memory," explained Allebach. "They're ready to be
activated at any time. We simply wake them up, subject them
to the artificial memory implantation process that fills in
the gaps from the past few months with a history appro-
priate to that particular iteration of Priya, and then transport her to a hotel. She wakes up the next day and goes to
work."

"I suppose you're going to tell us this is legal as well?" I
said.

"Actually," said Selah, "I can make a compelling case that
it is. There are a number of anti-cloning laws on the books,
but the current prevailing legal theory is that each individual
owns his or her own DNA. DNA is simply information, and if
you own the information, you have the right to duplicate
it—or to sell it to someone else. The principle is no different
than an author giving a publisher a right to make copies of
a book he's written. Bryn Jhaveri gave us a license to repro-
duce her DNA in perpetuity, and since DNA never lapses into
the public domain like other intellectual property, that
means Flagship can keep making copies of her forever."

"I question your legal interpretation," said Keane. "But
whether or not what you're doing is illegal, it's distasteful.
If word got out, Flagship would take a PR beating."

Selah laughed. "Your cards are showing, Mr. Keane," she
said. "Is that your plan? Let me guess: if anything happens to
you and Mr. Fowler, a message goes out to a hundred media
outlets telling them all about the great Priya Mistry conspiracy?"

"Something like that," said Keane.

"Oh, Mr. Keane," said Selah. "You are brilliant, but I'm
afraid you've miscalculated. I own most of the media outlets

in this town. Not all of them, but enough to determine the narrative. All the other news outlets will follow my lead. So if I say the story is how a famed detective's obsession with Priya Misty drove him mad, causing him to devise a bizarre story about a secret underground cloning laboratory, that will be the story. By the time anyone thinks to check any of the details of your crazy allegations, I'll have moved this entire operation somewhere else. We'll have to cut down on Priya's appearances for a few months, but I was planning on doing that anyway. I track public perception of Priya Mistry very closely, and my research tells me we're reaching a point of diminishing returns. Priya needs to make fewer public appearances for a while, or we risk overexposure."

"That would be a shame," I said. "God forbid your brand be damaged."

Selah shrugged. "Cherish your moral outrage as long as you can, Mr. Fowler. An hour from now you and Mr. Keane are going to wake up in your beds at home, with no memory of this place. Dr. Allebach is going to erase everything that happened over the past three days. You'll never have met me or Priya Mistry, and you won't know anything about a missing sheep. They'll also remove any hard evidence they find in your building. And before Dr. Allebach wipes your memories, he's going to extract all your passwords so that my operatives can also delete any notes you've made about this case. He'll insert memories of a thoroughly unremarkable week, so you won't suspect anything. Maybe someday you'll realize something doesn't fit, but you'll never put the whole puzzle together. And even if you do, there will be nothing you can do about it. This whole operation will be gone, and I'll never let either of you get close to Priya again. Sorry, gentlemen. This is where the story ends for you." She nodded at Dr. Allebach.

"This way," said Allebach, indicating the two hospital

beds. I hesitated for a moment, and then Brian pointed his rifle at my head.

"Amnesia or death," said Allebach without emotion. "Your choice."

Keane and I walked to the beds. I glanced at Keane, wondering if he was thinking what I was thinking: Selah could wipe our memories of what had happened and erase all the physical evidence, but we weren't the only ones who knew about Priya. I could only hope Selah wasn't as meticulous as she seemed.

My hopes were dashed a moment later as the door to the room opened. April stumbled in, followed by Roy. Behind them were the other two gunmen.

TWENTY-SEVEN

"April!" I shouted. "Are you okay?" I got up from the bed and made to go to her, but Brian struck me in the temple with the butt of his rifle. I fell to the floor, dazed.

"Blake!" April cried.

I rubbed my head and got a grip on the bed. "I'm all right," I muttered after a moment, glaring at Brian. He smirked at me. I pulled myself to my feet. "Did they hurt you?"

"No," April said. "I'm okay." She appeared harried and tired but uninjured.

"Sorry, guys," said Roy. "They came out of nowhere. I didn't—" His voice faltered as he caught sight of the series of Priyas along the far wall. "What in the hell . . . ?"

"We had a deal," I snarled at Selah. "We gave you the sheep, and you let April go!"

"And then you broke into my top-secret facility," said Selah. "In any case, you can have her back shortly, once her memories of the past three days have been erased. Dr. Allebach, please conduct the procedure on Mr. Fowler and the lawyer first. I want Mr. Keane to witness the results of his failure."

One of the gunmen prodded April toward the beds. As they did, a large robotic arm with four articulated metallic sections slid silently along a rail running the length of the ceiling toward April. I noticed Dr. Allebach was holding a control pad; the arm was responding to the movements of his fingers. As the arm approached, it unfolded, revealing a basketball-sized metal globe at the end of the arm. From the globe, a dozen or so robotic tentacles protruded. The arm paused in front of April, and she screamed as several of the tentacles wrapped themselves around her arms and legs. Her screaming stopped when one of the tentacles coiled around her head, blocking her mouth.

"No loose ends, huh?" I said. "You're going to wipe all our memories and pretend like none of this ever happened?"

"Not exactly," said Selah. "I'm going to have Dr. Allebach wipe your memories and those of Mr. Keane and your girl-friend. Roy, I'm afraid, is a bit more problematic."

"He knows too much," said Keane. Roy regarded him stoically.

"His memories go back too far. I fear he began to suspect something months ago. I can't let him near Priya, but erasing his memories of the past two years will raise too many questions. I'm not going to be able to let Roy leave this facility."

"You're going to kill him, you mean," I said, eyeing Roy.

"I'm afraid I have no choice," replied Selah.

The robotic arm lifted April and carried her to one of the beds. It gently deposited her onto the bed and then began securing her with nylon restraints. When the tentacle left her mouth, she didn't scream, but her eyes were fixed on me, pleading with me to do something. Anything.

I wasn't really paying attention, though, because I was watching Roy, who was quietly seething with fury. It was one thing for Selah to threaten to kill him; it was quite another for him to be exposed to the horrors of what Selah was doing to his beloved Priya. If Selah expected Roy to just give up, she was mistaken. If he was going to die, he was going to do his damnedest to take Selah with him. The only question was whether he would get the rest of us killed in the process.

One thing was certain: whatever Roy did, he'd have a better chance of success if the guards' attention were focused somewhere else for a few seconds. I took a deep breath and made my move.

"Get your hands off her, you sons of bitches!" I yelled, launching myself toward April. I shoved the technician nearest me—a petite brunette woman—out of the way and landed on the bed on top of April. Throwing my arms around her, I continued my sideways roll. The bed slammed into the gunman who had been guarding April, knocking him down. His rifle flew from his hands, skittering across the floor. April's right wrist was secured to the bed frame, so the bed capsized as my momentum carried us to the floor. My right elbow struck first, and I felt something crack. April yelped in my ear, and pain shot through my arm.

"Stay here!" I said to April, gasping, and then scrabbled away from her on the floor. It didn't occur to me in my pain-addled state that she didn't have much of a choice. Letting my right arm hang limply at my side, I looked up to see a rifle barrel a foot from my face. Behind it was Brian, looking downright gleeful at the prospect of shooting me in the head. A split second later, though, Brian disappeared from view, swept aside by the crushing bulk of the juggernaut that was Roy. The guard who had been watching Roy lay unconscious against the wall near the door, blood gushing from his nose. With that one down and Roy taking out Brian, that left only the guy I had knocked to the floor.

Trying to ignore the mind numbing pain in my arm, I pulled myself to my knees and turned to look for the third man. He was on his knees too, about ten feet away, reaching for the butt of his rifle. I launched myself toward him, wrapping my left arm around his ankles, but there was no way I could hold him with one arm. Fighting against the instincts that were screaming at me to protect my injury, I threw my right arm around his legs as well. The guy kicked back, hitting me square in the crook of my elbow. For a moment all I knew was pain. I blacked out.

I was only out for maybe a second, but it was long enough: the guy was getting to his feet, the gun barrel aimed at my head. Behind me, I heard someone roar in anger, and I turned to see Roy barreling toward the man, his face red with rage. The man shifted his aim to Roy.

Ordinarily, this would have been all the opening I needed: I could have tackled the guy while he was distracted and disarmed him. He'd probably have gotten off a few rounds at Roy, but I could have stopped him before he killed anybody else. In my current state, though, I couldn't even get up off the floor. My limbs felt like rubber, and the pain and dizziness were so bad, it was all I could do not to puke.

"Roy, no!" I gasped, knowing he was sacrificing himself in vain. But there was no stopping the juggernaut.

That was what I was thinking, anyway, when the robotic arm shot across its rail and swung down from the ceiling, knocking Roy across the room. The gunman opened fire a split second too late, riddling the opposite wall with bullets. Meanwhile, Roy flew a good twenty feet and landed with a crash against a bank of expensive-looking equipment. He lay, moaning, on the floor.

Allebach tapped the screen, and the robotic arm retracted into the ceiling. Keane, standing nearby, was watching with interest. He didn't appear to have moved during the entire fracas. There were times when a phenomenological inquisitor was downright useless.

"Well," said Selah. "That certainly was exciting. Now, shall we proceed?"

I groaned, my arm throbbing. With me and Roy incapacitated, April tethered to the bed, and Keane content to stand in the middle of the room, doing absolutely fucking nothing, we didn't have much of a chance. The guard who had fired on Roy now had his gun on me again, and the one Roy had tackled was getting to his feet. Roy was a dead man. Keane, April, and I would have our memories wiped. And Selah would get away with everything.

The brunette technician pulled me to my feet, and I yelped as she put her hand on my smashed elbow.

"Arm"—I gasped—"broken."

The woman nodded and looked to Allebach. There was something familiar about her, but I couldn't quite place it.

"We can fix that for you," said Allebach. "You'll wake up with a fully mended arm and no memory of it ever breaking." He smiled. "No extra charge."

"Fuck you," I muttered.

The technician helped me into one of the beds while two others righted April's bed and finished securing her. When they were done with her, they secured me as well, leaving my useless right arm free. Brian had gotten to his feet and was eyeing my broken arm as if he were considering giving it a good squeeze.

But then Allebach tapped a display console, and a machine hummed to life above me. A robotic arm descended toward me, and a sheath opened to reveal a clutch of tentaclelike appendages. The appendages writhed to life, and as the arm extended, their suckerlike ends attached themselves to various points on my skull. I couldn't turn my head, but to my left I heard what I knew was a similar machine descending toward April.

TWENTY-EIGHT

"It's almost too bad," I heard Keane murmur.

I wanted to tell him to go fuck himself, but I couldn't muster the energy. I had nearly been killed, and all he could say was "It's almost too bad"?

Apparently, I wasn't the only one thinking this, because a moment later Selah echoed my thoughts. "Hold on," she said. "What do you mean, it's almost too bad? I'm about to foil your chances to solve this case and erase seventy-two hours of your memory, and all you have to say is 'It's almost too bad'?"

I managed to turn my head enough to see Selah and Keane out of the corner of my eye. Next to me stood the technician who had helped me up earlier. I caught a glimpse of her name tag, which read NIKKI. Why did she seem so familiar? Had I met her somewhere before? The pain shooting through my right arm was making it hard to think.

"I mean, it's almost too bad I can't let you go through with this," said Keane. "It's amazing technology, and it raises all sorts of interesting epistemic and ethical issues. I'd love to witness it in action. But of course I'd retain no memories of the process, so it's a bit of a moot point."

Selah laughed. "You can't *let* me go through with it? How the hell do you think you're going to stop me?"

"I'm not," said Keane. "You're going to stop on your own."

"And why would I do that?"

"One word," Keane said. "Maelstrom."

Selah glared at him. "I don't know what you're talking about."

"Let me refresh your memory, then," said Keane. "After you were kind enough to demonstrate the Feinberg-Webb test for us the other day, I looked into the company that created the test, Empathix. It seems they started out nearly twenty years ago as a marketing research company, with a focus on quantifying the psychological and sociological factors that went into a successful marketing campaign. Part of this involved identifying the traits of effective spokespersons—charisma, essentially. This work eventually led to the creation of the Feinberg-Webb test, and gave rise to the careers of Priya Mistry and Giles Marbury, aka Mag-Lev. But Empathix's work went far beyond identifying personality traits. They also developed algorithms for identifying societal 'tipping points'—for example, when consumers were on the verge of embracing a new product or technology. It was presumably Empathix's research that caused you to cancel lighthearted comedies like *Room for One More* and bet heavily on gritty urban-based shows set in the DZ: Empathix warned you about a shift in consumer taste. Of course, it's impossible to say for sure, because fourteen years ago, you bought a controlling interest in Empathix, and they've been rather secretive about their work ever since."

"Forgive me, Mr. Keane," said Selah, "but I'm still not seeing how any of this speculation is going to make me not want to erase your memory."

Keane continued, "The other clue came when I realized the truth about Mag-Lev—that he was just an actor you had plucked out of obscurity to play a part. Clearly, you have the means to pull off an extremely effective psyops campaign, but I had a hard time seeing how you would gather the intelligence necessary to install a warlord in the DZ. That would take more than a generalized psyops campaign; it would require an intimate knowledge of the internal politics of the DZ. There are only a handful of people with that sort of knowledge, and none of them are likely to run in the same circles as a Hollywood media tycoon. That leaves only people who were involved in a certain top-secret project to control the aftermath of a cataclysmic breakdown of the federal government."

"Maelstrom," I said, realizing what Keane was getting at. Selah bit her lip.

"As I'm sure you're aware, during my previous career I was intimately involved in Maelstrom. We designed the DZ down to the smallest detail," said Keane. "We knew exactly when the breakdown was going to happen, and how it was going to play out. We knew who the key players were going to be in the drama of the Collapse in Los Angeles before they even knew themselves. But there were two things I never figured out. The first was where the forecasting data came from. The predictive model was near perfect, but I could never determine who had devised it. The second was who was paying for the program. The money came from a nonprofit organization called the Los Angeles Future Foundation. LAFF didn't divulge its donors. I spent no small amount of time trying to dig up something on them, but came up empty. The funny thing is, once I thought to look for a connection between Flagship Media and LAFF, it was relatively easy to connect the dots. Easy for me, anyway. I have an eye for patterns. Oh, and a contact in the banking industry."

It was hard to focus through the pain in my arm, but the gist of what Keane was saying gradually penetrated. "You're saying Empathix saw the Collapse coming," I murmured.

"And Selah used that information to set up LAFF to reshape Los Angeles."

Keane nodded. "It's no accident that Selah's net worth skyrocketed shortly after the Collapse, when other billionaires were losing their shirts. She reduced her investment in anything denominated in dollars and put her money in hard assets that could weather a currency crisis. She lost just enough money to cover her tracks, but by the end of the Collapse, she was up nearly a hundred billion dollars. And that's just on paper. What the financial records don't show is that, thanks to the restructuring of Los Angeles, Selah is now uniquely positioned to control the future of the entertainment industry. Her programs set in the DZ are just one small part of it. Selah holds enough interests in media properties in this town that virtually nothing happens without her say-so. And since journalism is essentially a vestigial organ in the entertainment industry these days, it means she also controls the news. Combine that with her ownership of Empathix, and you've got a near-perfect system for manipulating public opinion. The only reason Selah Fiore isn't universally recognized as the most powerful person on the planet is because that's exactly how she wants it."

"Well done, Mr. Keane," said Selah. "I assume your plan is to release this information in an attempt to sully my reputation, and maybe subject me to a tedious SEC investigation. Pardon me if I'm not exactly quaking with fear."

Keane smiled. "That's because you assume you can control the story. No doubt you've got a contingency plan in place for the eventuality that this information becomes public. But there's a problem with predictive models like the ones Empathix uses, and overreliance on such models can create blind spots in your planning."

"Do enlighten me, Mr. Keane," said Selah. She was trying to fake boredom, but she wasn't the actress she once was.

"Individual action," said Keane. "Generally, the consequences of any individual's actions are insignificant, and can be accounted for in the model. But there are situations in which an individual is uniquely situated to disrupt the system in ways the model can't predict. For example, if I don't leave this building with that sheep, two things are going to happen. First, Jason Banerjee is going to release a secret dossier that details the Maelstrom program. His intention is to ruin me, but I've arranged to have the financial records linking Flagship to LAFF sent to him. So he'll get to ruin me and smear you at the same time. Second, Mag-Lev is going to launch an all-out war against you. You might be able to weather a federal investigation or a turf war with Mag-Lev, but not both at the same time. One way or another, you're finished."

Selah took this all in, regarding Keane coldly. "Congratulations, Mr. Keane," she said at last. "You do have a talent for manipulation. It would seem that the only rational option for me at this point is to let you go."

"Indeed," said Keane.

"Sadly," she said, "you've made a miscalculation of your own."

"Really," said Keane flatly. "And what might that be?"

Selah smiled. "I'm not a rational person."

Keane raised an eyebrow at her. "Don't be absurd. You didn't get where you are today by being irrational."

"You conflate strategy and motivations, Mr. Keane. My strategies are rational. My motivations are not. 'The irrationality of a thing is no argument against its existence, rather a condition of it.'"

"Nietzsche," said Keane, shaking his head. I sympathized. It was never a good thing when a bad guy started quoting Nietzsche. "You're seriously going to go through with this just to spite me?"

"Certainly not," said Selah. "Not everything is about you, Mr. Keane. Maybe I will lose this fight eventually, but not because I rolled over when the great Erasmus Keane told me it was my only option. I control my own destiny."

Keane cocked his head at this remark, as if realizing something he'd missed. "Yes," he murmured. "I suppose we all do." He glanced at Dr. Allebach, who frowned at him. Keane then turned to look at me. No, not at me. At the lab technician standing next to the bed. The one I thought looked familiar.

"Fascinating," said Keane.

Selah sighed irritably. "You've made your play, Mr. Keane," said Selah. "It didn't work. Try to accept your fate with some dignity."

"It's not my fate that's in question," said Keane, "It's yours. I'm afraid you've been outsmarted, Selah."

"You expect me to believe you have another card up your sleeve, Mr. Keane? Please. This sort of stalling is beneath you."

"Oh, you haven't been outsmarted by *me*," said Keane. "That honor goes to Bryn Jhaveri."

Selah scowled. "What in the hell are you talking about, Keane?" she demanded. "Bryn Jhaveri is a sheep locked in an underground room. She doesn't have a clue what's going on here. How could she possibly have outsmarted me?"

"See, that's the core of your problem right there," said Keane. "You want to have it both ways. You deify Priya Mistry but think of Bryn Jhaveri as cattle. You want a goddess in a box. It doesn't work like that."

"I'm starting to think your plan is to drive me to suicide just so I don't have to listen to you pontificate anymore," Selah said.

Keane chuckled. "Come on," he said. "I can't be the only one who sees it. Help me out here, Fowler."

"Keane," I said as calmly as I could manage. "I've got a big, horrifying, tentacled mind-sucking machine stuck on my head right now, so maybe you could just get to the fucking point."

"Sorry," Keane said. "It just seems so clear to me now. You said it yourself, Fowler. Priya Mistry is logic Kryptonite."

"Am I supposed to understand what that means?" Selah said impatiently.

"Oh, I think you understand it quite well," said Keane. "You're intensely aware of the effect Priya has on the men around her. Particularly men who spend a great deal of time with her, and who know her every thought."

"Is that what this is about?" Selah asked. "Dr. Allebach's obsession with Priya? I always thought it was harmless. Pathetic, but harmless."

Allebach glared at her but said nothing.

"It's certainly pathetic," said Keane. "But you may want to rethink the harmless part. Have you lost track of any of your clones in the past few weeks?"

"Of course not," said Selah. "We keep very close tabs on them."

"You're certain?" said Keane. "Every single one is accounted for. No accidental deaths?"

Selah shrugged. "Occasionally one of them will develop a mutation as a side effect of the accelerated aging process. If it's serious enough, the clone has to be destroyed."

"And has this happened recently?"

"It's possible," said Selah. "I don't keep track of every faulty clone we incinerate."

"I suspect that if you check your records," said Keane, "you'll find you're one short. A clone that was supposed to be destroyed was never incinerated. And I'm willing to bet that the flaw in this particular clone was an imperfect facial structure. She would still be very pretty, but she wouldn't be mistaken for Priya."

"This is ridiculous," Allebach snapped. "We have strict protocols for keeping track of the clones."

"Protocols you are uniquely suited to subvert," said Keane, "since you devised them."

"I'm a scientist," Allebach growled. "The idea that I would—"

"Shut up, Henry," said Selah. She turned back to Keane. "You're saying Dr. Allebach grew a customized clone for his own . . . use?" She seemed mildly disgusted by the idea, which struck me as a bit ironic. Allebach was turning red with either anger or embarrassment, but he said nothing.

"Exactly," said Keane. "In his defense, he believes he's in love with her. With them. Whatever."

"And how do you know all this?"

"I knew there was someone inside your organization feeding the clones information," said Keane. "Someone slipping letters to them that were signed Noogus. It had to be somebody with intimate details of Bryn's childhood as well as information about your plans for the sheep. Once we determined that the Priyas were clones, the obvious answer was that Noogus was another clone."

Selah seemed dubious. "So Dr. Allebach abducted this clone and then set her loose so she could feed information to the other clones? I'm sorry, Mr. Keane, but that makes no sense. If she wanted to shut me down, why didn't she just send you the address of my lab? Why be so cryptic about it? For that matter, why not just go to the FBI?"

"That's exactly what I couldn't figure out," said Keane. "Until now. You provided the answer yourself. Bryn Jhaveri doesn't just want to expose you. She wants the same thing you do, Selah. The same as all of us, really. To control her destiny."

"Meaning what, exactly?" asked Selah.

"Try to see this from Bryn's point of view. Or points of

view, rather. Bryn isn't a sheep; she's a person. More precisely, she is *persons*. Each has essentially the same personality, but different circumstances and points of view. Imagine what that must be like. How would you react if you found out you were one of many, that what you thought of as 'you' was simply a template for any number of points of consciousness existing in the universe? It's the ultimate philosophical question writ large: What is my relationship as an individual to the *other*? I suspect many of us would react with shock, hate, anger, fear. But that's not how Bryn Jhaveri reacted. When one Bryn met another in my office, there was a moment of shock, but very quickly they were watching bad sitcoms together, like old friends. Sisters, even. Can you imagine having that level of comfort with yourself? The ability to be okay with the fact that somebody else is running around with your personality? The level of empathy each Bryn is capable of possessing for the others is astounding. Now imagine that one Bryn becomes aware of the existence of all the others, and how they are being manipulated and abused. What does she do? How does she express her empathy for them?"

"She tries to shut the operation down," said Selah. "As I said, if she wanted to do that—"

"No!" exclaimed Keane. "I mean, yes, she wants to shut you down, but she wants more than that. What does she do for the clones who are already out there? Remember what you said in your office, Selah? You asked what we would do if we had control over the clones. You said you had to shield them from the truth for their own good. But you don't have their best interests at heart. Bryn does. I'm not asking what *you* would do, Selah. I'm asking what *Bryn* would do."

The answer suddenly hit me. "She'd let them choose," I said.

"Bingo!" cried Keane. "She'd give them just enough information to figure out the conspiracy if they really wanted to. Cryptic notes from Noogus, pointing them in the right direction, but no conclusive proof. We know two of them sought out the truth, but we don't know how many letters Nikki sent. She could only communicate with the ones who were brought back here recently. And maybe some of the clones ignored the warnings, hoping to persist in the delusion."

There was a moment of silence. Then Selah spoke. "Nikki?" she asked.

"Hey?" replied Keane.

"You said, 'We don't know how many letters Nikki sent.' Who the hell is Nikki?"

"Oh!" exclaimed Keane. "I'm sorry. Got a little ahead of myself." He turned to face the technician next to me. "Nikki, why don't you introduce yourself."

The woman took a step back, bumping into the bed. She turned for a moment, and I caught a glimpse of her face.

Jesus. That was why she seemed so familiar. Her face was different, but everything else about her—the way she stood, moved, smelled—was Priya Mistry.

TWENTY-NINE

"How . . . how did you know?" the woman asked.

"I knew Allebach would keep the object of his affections close," said Keane. "And of course you bear a striking resemblance to Priya, if one ignores certain superficial facial features. Also, your name tag."

"Nikki?" Selah asked. "How did that tell you anything?"

"Short for Nicole," said Keane. "Feminine form of Nicholas. The name of her teddy bear. Noogus."

Nikki nodded slightly. "I picked it myself," said Nikki. "Henry—that is, Dr. Allebach—and I agreed I needed a pseudonym. I couldn't very well go by Bryn or Priya."

"Hold on," said Selah, baffled. "The two of you created a false identity so that Nikki could work in the lab? Just so she could sneak messages to the other clones?"

"No," said Keane. "I don't believe Dr. Allebach knew Nikki was going to try to communicate with the other Priyas. She did that on her own."

Allebach looked at Nikki, and she averted her eyes.

"Then why?" asked Selah.

"We love each other," said Allebach. "We wanted to be together." A note of desperation had crept into his voice. He was looking at Nikki, but she still refused to meet his gaze.

Selah shook her head. "No," she said. "I don't buy it. Maybe Nikki alerted the others on her own, but you two were up to something."

"Excellent deduction," said Keane. "A little late to do you any good, but you're exactly right. I imagine part of the reason they stuck around was that they didn't want to leave until Dr. Allebach had received his final payment from you, for transferring Bryn's memories to the sheep. But there is something else as well."

"What?" Selah demanded. "What were they planning?"

"I could make a conjecture," said Keane, "but I don't know the details. It might be better if Dr. Allebach told you."

"Why are you doing this?" Nikki said suddenly, looking at Keane. "She was going to let you and your friend live. You would have no memories of this place. There would be no blood on your hands."

"No," said Keane. "That's where you're wrong. I'd have blood on my hands if I didn't stop you, whether or not I had any memory of the blood being there. I may be straining this metaphor a bit. The point is, I can't let Selah kill Roy, and I can't have her messing with our memories. That's not negotiable."

"I gave you all the answers you needed," said Nikki. "So you could help the others. But you weren't supposed to know about this. You were never supposed to come here."

"Unfortunately for you," said Keane, "you weren't the only one feeding us information. Selah left just enough bread crumbs for us to find this place. I don't blame you for wanting revenge against Selah, but you have to let us go."

"*She* has to let you go?" Selah asked. "She isn't the one in charge here, Mr. Keane."

"You're still a step behind, Selah," said Keane. "Let me spell it out for you. Your chief scientist fell in love with someone who is determined to undermine your cloning operation. Now, do you really think you're still the one in charge?"

A look of horror came over Selah's face. She turned to Allebach. "What did you do?"

Allebach was looking to Nikki, who still wouldn't meet his gaze.

"Might as well tell her now," said Keane. "She's not going to let you out of here until she knows."

Allebach turned to face Selah. "I sabotaged the memory-implantation program. Every new clone will wake up with a complete memory of this place and what was done to her. Whether they'll still want to be famous, I don't know. You'll have to talk it over with them."

"It's their choice," said Nikki. "They deserve to know."

"I created them!" cried Selah. "They deserve nothing!"

Allebach shrugged. "Whatever they deserve, it's done. The program has been encrypted, and it can't be altered."

"You did this for her?" Selah said. "For one of *them*? A *clone*?"

"Don't talk that way about her!" Allebach snapped. "You don't know anything about love."

Selah laughed bitterly. "Love! Hell, Dr. Allebach. She *used* you. Do you honestly believe she's going to run away with you? Where were you going to go? Costa Rica?"

"Belize," said Allebach through gritted teeth. "We're going to Belize. Tell them, Nikki. Tell them what I mean to you."

Nikki bit her lip and then met Allebach's gaze. "I . . . I love you, Henry," she said. "You know that. I didn't tell you about warning the other clones because I didn't think you'd understand. I'm sorry."

A look of profound relief came over Allebach's face. "It's all right, sweetheart," said Allebach. "I forgive you." He smiled reassuringly.

"You've got to be kidding me," said Selah. "He created you

in a lab and brainwashed you. Whatever phony memories he stuck in your head, you have to be aware of that."

Nikki shrugged. "I can't explain my feelings," she said. "All I know is how I feel."

"The heart has reasons of which reason knows nothing," said Keane. I recognized the quote. Pascal. I wasn't sure it was an improvement over Nietzsche.

Selah shook her head. "Well, it doesn't matter. Neither of you are leaving here until Dr. Allebach rewrites the memory-implantation program."

"I told you," said Allebach. "The program can't be altered. It's encrypted, and I threw away the key."

"Then you'll start over," said Selah. "You'll rewrite the program from scratch. Don't play me for a fool, Doctor. I know you can do it."

Allebach shook his head. "I destroyed everything. I never planned on writing another transfer program. To reconstruct all that work . . . it could take weeks. Maybe months."

"I don't care if it takes you ten years," said Selah. "You're not leaving here until you rewrite it. You understand me, Doctor? You are of no value to me if you can't rewrite the program."

Allebach thought for a long time, glancing back and forth between Nikki and Selah. "If I rewrite it," he said at last, "if I give you a program that works, you'll let us go? Both of us?"

Selah scowled. "I should have you both killed on principle," she said. "But in the interest of getting this program back up and running, I'll agree to let you go. Run off to Bora Bora or wherever. All I care about is Priya Mistry."

"How do I know you'll live up to your word?"

"You don't," said Selah. "But you can take your chances or you can rot in a cell next to a sheep for the next fifty years. You're not getting a better offer."

Allebach nodded slowly, considering what Selah had said.

He turned to Nikki. "It's up to you," he said. "If I rewrite the program, we can be together. I think . . . maybe if I can recover some of the files, I can do it in about six weeks. But I know how important this is to you. I will understand if you don't want me to do it."

Nikki regarded Selah. "What if he refuses?"

Selah shrugged. "I'll keep you both locked up until he changes his mind."

Nikki turned to face Keane. "Damn you!" she said. "Why did you have to come here? I had everything under control. Henry and I would have been on a plane to Central America before Selah knew anything was wrong."

"Sorry," said Keane. "We had a lost sheep to find. Foiling elaborate cloning plots is just a side effect."

"And what did you gain by exposing our plan?" Nikki asked. "You know Selah's still going to wipe your memories. Did you expect her to be grateful?"

Keane shrugged. "I'm an optimist," he said. "I always hope everyone will get what they deserve."

"And what do I deserve, Mr. Keane?" Nikki asked.

"I don't envy you," said Keane. "You didn't ask to be created. To be put into this situation. But then, none of us did. I guess you have to decide for yourself what you deserve."

Nikki regarded him for a moment, and then nodded. She turned to Allebach. "Do it," she said.

"Are you sure?" Allebach asked.

"I'm sure," replied Nikki. "I want us to be together. It's what we deserve." She looked into his eyes, and he smiled.

"Thank you," said Allebach. "You know all I want is to be with you."

"I know," said Nikki. "We'll be together soon. Away from this place."

Allebach approached, spreading his arms to embrace her. It was a little hard to believe, but I found myself hoping that love really could transcend their bizarre circumstances. That was when Selah screamed.

"She's got a knife!" Selah cried. "Stop her!"

Selah was right: Nikki had pulled something silvery from her pocket, possibly a scalpel. It glinted in the fluorescent light as her hand arced upward, plunging the blade into Allebach's neck. Gunshots rang out, and Nikki stumbled against Allebach and slumped to the ground. Out of the corner of my eye, I saw Brian, his rifle trained on her.

Allebach fell backward, clutching at the handle protruding from his neck. As the blade slipped and fell, a geyser of blood erupted from where it had been. Allebach gasped and gurgled, flailing helplessly on the floor. Nikki lay, slumped across his legs, unmoving, blotches of red growing across her lab coat.

"Stop the bleeding!" shrieked Selah. "We have to save him!"

One of the technicians ran to Allebach's side. He tried to stanch the bleeding with a lab coat, but it was clearly hopeless. At the rate blood was gushing from his artery, Allebach would be dead in minutes. Keane went to Nikki, dragging her off Allebach and laying her flat on her back.

Her eyes fixed on Keane's for a moment. A smile flickered across her lips as she gasped, "Everyone gets . . . what they deserve." Her eyes went dead, and her head lolled to the side.

Keane pressed his fingers to her neck, and after a few seconds he shook his head. He closed Nikki's eyelids and stood up. "She's gone," he said.

Meanwhile, the technician looked helplessly up at Selah as the white coat turned crimson. "I can't save him," he said. "She cut clean through the artery."

"No," said Selah. "No, no, no. He's the only one who can rewrite the transfer program. Without him, I'm finished."

"That was the plan," said Keane.

We watched in silence as the life drained out of Allebach. After some time Selah spoke.

"So she didn't really love him after all."

Keane sighed. "No, she didn't. You were right the first time. She was using him. Allebach was seriously deluded if he thought he could brainwash Bryn Jhaveri into loving him. For Allebach, love was all about control. For Bryn, it was about letting go. She was just pretending to love him. Acting, I suppose. She just needed him to get close, one more time."

"And you knew," said Selah. "You knew what she was planning."

"I hoped," said Keane. "Getting her to kill Allebach was the only way we were going to get out of here alive and with our memories intact."

Selah stared at him. "You can't be serious," she said. "There's no way in hell I'm letting you out of here, after the stunt you just pulled."

"She was going to kill Allebach anyway," Keane said. "Probably as soon as he got her outside the facility. That's why she had the scalpel. I just coaxed her to take advantage of her current opportunity. And as Nikki said, if I hadn't intervened, she'd have been long gone by the time you realized you'd been had. You can hardly blame your misfortune on *me*."

"And this is supposed to convince me to let you go?"

"No," said Keane. "The fact that you're completely out of options should do that. Remember what happens if I don't leave here tonight with my memories intact. Banerjee exposes Maelstrom, prompting a federal investigation into Flagship Media, and Mag-Lev declares war on you. Maybe it was worth the risk when you still had your clone operation up and running, but now Flagship is all you have. You're not going to risk losing it just to spite me, no matter what Nietzsche has to say on the matter."

Selah glared at Keane, but I could tell she knew she was beaten. "Go," she said, her teeth gritted.

"We'll also need the sheep. And Bryn. The original one."

"What the hell do you need the sheep for?"

"If we don't return it to Banerjee, he'll blow the lid off Maelstrom. Your choice."

"Fine," said Selah, defeated. "Take the sheep. And Bryn. Just get out."

Keane detached the machine from April's head and then undid her restraints. April got up and helped me get free while Keane helped Roy to his feet. Roy seemed dazed but not seriously injured. We were a sorry-looking group, but we were all alive, our memories intact. We were going to be okay. And we had Nikki to thank for that.

I wondered what Nikki had planned for herself, after she'd gotten out of Selah's facility and killed Allebach. Had she really intended to run away and live happily ever after? How would she have fared in the outside world? As a paranoiac, she thrived as a captive, plotting against her keepers. But would she have been able to survive in an environment free of persecution? It was impossible to say, but I suspect she had accepted the likelihood of a tragic end some time ago. She deserved better than this, but she had at least died quickly, without suffering the torment experienced by the others. Maybe she was the lucky one.

April finished with my restraints and helped me sit up. Trying to ignore the throbbing in my arm, I got to my feet. April and I made our way to the door, Keane and Roy close behind.

"One more thing before you go, Mr. Keane," I heard Selah say.

I stopped and turned, seeing Keane regarding her suspiciously. *Here it comes,* I thought. She was just toying with us. She never had any intention of letting us go. She's going to kill us all, just for the fun of it.

"Since we're disclosing all our past foibles," Selah said, "I assume you've told Mr. Fowler all about your work on Maelstrom?"

I sighed. "Can we do this another time?" I asked. "I get it. Keane was involved in some pretty fucked-up stuff. But right now—"

"Oh, we can certainly discuss the details of Mr. Keane's sins another time," Selah said. "But that's not what I'm talking about. I'm not referring to what Mr. Keane did, but rather who he did it *with*."

Keane stared at Selah coldly but said nothing.

"You never told him, did you?" asked Selah, with a smile. "How long has it been? Three years? You see Mr. Fowler every day, and you've never told him. And people call *me* a sociopath."

"God damn it," I said, beginning to feel dizzy. "Out with it. What are you talking about?"

"What was her name?" asked Selah. "The one you consulted with all the time. She was some kind of liaison with the city. You know who I mean. That pretty blonde who used to work for the planning department. What was her name? Gail?"

April looked at Keane, then at me. Keane averted his eyes.

"Gwen," I said, my blood going cold. "Her name was Gwen."

THIRTY

Somehow I wasn't surprised. Maybe on some level I had known it for some time.

April was right: although she was too nice to say it in so many words, she had always suspected I had gone to work for Keane because I thought he could help me find Gwen. But after three years, and repeated assurances that Keane was doing everything he could, the trail was as cold as ever. The thought had nagged at me for a while now: Why was Gwen's disappearance the one case Keane couldn't solve? And the answer was completely obvious, now that I forced myself to consider it: Keane had been the one behind her disappearance.

"Fowler, I can explain," Keane said as we made our way down the hall.

"Don't fucking talk to me," I replied. My arm was killing me, and the last thing I wanted was to be subjected to another one of Keane's explanations. I stopped and turned to face April. "Go with Keane and retrieve the sheep. Roy and I will retrieve Bryn." April nodded. Keane looked like he wanted to say something, but then thought better of it. They took off down the hall, and Roy and I continued to Bryn's room. I cradled my right arm with my left while we walked;

the break seemed to be in the humerus, just above the elbow. Roy looked dazed but not seriously injured, and the four of us had reached an unspoken agreement: to get the hell out of there before Selah changed her mind. I didn't even bother to get our guns back from Brian. Let the jerk keep them.

Roy carried the unconscious Bryn down the hall to the elevator, and I followed. When we were back upstairs, I called Pavel and told him to meet us with the Suburban just outside the resort entrance. The rain was coming down hard now.

Pavel pulled up just as we got there. Roy laid Bryn down in the backseat. She didn't move, and seemed to be barely breathing.

"What did they do to her?" Roy asked softly, crouching on the ground next to the Suburban, oblivious to the rain. He had been unconscious nearly the entire time we'd been in the lab, and it was going to be just about impossible to get him up to speed on everything that had happened. And probably unnecessary.

"They used her up," I said softly. "Sucked her soul out."

"So she's dying," he said, stroking her cheek with his hand. "Again."

"I'm afraid so," I said. "Selah said she wouldn't last the night."

"Jesus," Roy said, tears welling up in his eyes. "Why did we even take her out of there?"

"I didn't think you'd want her to die in there," I said.

He shook his head, blinking away the tears. "No, you're right," he said. "It's just . . ."

"It's rough, I know," I said. "Nobody should have to lose the woman he loves twice. I'm sorry, Roy."

"I need to get out of here," said Roy, burying his head in his hands. "Away from this town. Because she's still out there. All of her. It's too much to take. I can't turn on my fucking TV without seeing her. Knowing my Priya is dead, but at the same time she's still alive, and she doesn't even know who I am. How is anybody supposed to deal with that? It's too much. It's just too much."

I nodded sympathetically. Right now getting as far away as possible from this fucked-up city—and from Erasmus Keane—seemed like a very good idea. It was starting to seem like nothing in Los Angeles was real. The news was propaganda, the fearsome warlord Mag-Lev was some third-rate actor, Priya Mistry was a fictional character, the creation of the DZ had been completely choreographed . . . and then there was Erasmus Keane.

Who the hell was he? I still didn't even know his real name. Erasmus Keane was a fabrication, like Priya Mistry. Were the cases we had "solved" together even real? Was he really a brilliant detective, or had he simply used his unearned reputation and knowledge of the DZ blueprint to create the illusion of amazing deductive prowess? It certainly explained the showboating and "phenomenological inquisitor" label. As I watched April and Keane—or whatever his name really was—approaching with the sheep, I found myself wondering if he was more con man than investigator.

"Roy," I said. "There's something else I need to tell you."

Roy looked up at me and laughed bitterly. "More bad news?" he said. "You've got a truckload of dead Priyas to deliver to my door?" His cheeks were damp with tears.

"Nothing like that," I said. "But—"

"What? Jesus, Fowler, just tell me. Things can't possibly get any worse. I wish you'd have let Selah kill me back there."

I sighed. How did you break news like this gently? "I'm sorry the woman you love is dead, but let me ask you this: if her consciousness was to live on in a farm animal of your choice, which animal would you pick?"

April and Keane came around the corner of the Suburban

with the sheep. They were both soaked from the rain, but the sheep seemed to be bearing it better.

"Oh hell," moaned Roy as he saw the sheep. "The sheep again? What the fuck is the deal with the sheep? Can't I have a moment alone with the woman I love without having to share it with the fucking livestock?"

The sheep regarded Roy with a puzzled expression.

"Roy," I said. "There's something you should know about this sheep."

"No!" howled Roy, getting to his feet. "I don't care about any fucking sheep! Jesus, it's all the same to you people, isn't it? Misplaced your TV superstar? Can't find your car keys? Lost a farm animal? Call Fowler and Keane! We'll find whatever you're missing, and probably kill it while we're at it! Maybe two or three times, because that's how fucking thorough we are!"

"Keane and Fowler," said Keane. "Also, killing someone's car keys would be a neat trick."

April smacked Keane on the back of his head. "Shut up, Keane," she said.

"It's not like that, Roy," I said. "We did everything we could to save Priya."

"Yeah, well," said Roy bitterly, "she's still dead. But you've got your sheep, so I guess you can chalk another one up in the win column, right?"

"That's what I'm trying to tell you, Roy. The sheep—"

"Don't fucking talk to me about the sheep!" Roy howled. He turned toward the Bryn-sheep, raising his hands over his head. "Get out of here! Nobody wants you! The only reason anybody cares about you is because you're a freak. Some mad scientist's wet dream, built in a laboratory so people can carve pieces off of you. Cut you apart, piece by piece, your kidneys, your liver, your lungs, your heart. But they won't stop there. They'll make more of you. Hundreds, thousands of you, and cut your heart out, over and over and over. No matter how much they take, they'll always want more. It will never, ever end. So go! Get out of here! Run right off that cliff. It's probably the only chance you have to escape." Thunder rumbled in the distance, as if to punctuate his point.

The Bryn-sheep was trembling. She had backed a few steps away from Roy and averted her gaze, unable to endure the full weight of his wrath. But now she looked up at him, pain and fear in her eyes. Roy seemed to sense something was wrong, that this wasn't how a sheep was supposed to act. He had expected it to run away or maybe to attack him. He hadn't figured on the sheep bearing his assault and then looking him straight in the eye. Roy met the sheep's gaze, and the two remained that way for some time, each of them trying to make sense of what the other was doing.

"Did I do something wrong?" the Bryn-sheep asked at last.

Roy's eyes rolled into his head, and he passed out.

Pavel produced some smelling salts from a first aid kit, and we managed to get Roy more or less conscious and ambulatory enough to get into the front seat of the Suburban. April and Keane helped the Bryn-sheep into the back, and then we all crammed in after her. I sat between April and the human Bryn. We made Keane ride in back with the sheep. He told Pavel to head toward the DZ, and then he called Mag-Lev, telling him we'd be there within an hour with the "package."

"You've got to be shitting me," I said to Keane. "We can't give Mag-Lev . . . the package." The Bryn-sheep was sitting, her head toward the rear of the Suburban, looking out the back window, so fortunately I didn't have to look at her while referring to her as "the package."

"No choice," Keane said. "We made a deal. Mag-Lev may be a poseur, but he's also got half the gangbangers in Los Angeles working for him."

"We didn't know the nature of the package when we made

the deal," I said. "You can't seriously be considering handing over a human being to that psychopath wannabe gangster just to save your own ass." I could only hope Bryn-sheep was too confused by this entire situation to understand what we were talking about.

"I question your characterization of the package," Keane said in a triumph of euphemizing.

"Just to be clear," I said, "you retrieved the package from Selah in order to give it to Mag-Lev so he could use it for leverage against Selah, right? But Selah doesn't want the package anymore. So what's the point of handing it over to Mag-Lev?"

"I know you don't want to hear this right now," said Keane, "but you have to trust me on this, Fowler."

I groaned but didn't reply. I didn't have the energy for this conversation. My arm was killing me, and I was damp, cold, and exhausted. I just wanted to lie down and sleep.

Keane turned around and began talking to the Bryn-sheep, but over the sound of the rain and thunder, I couldn't make out what he was saying. The two of them conversed quietly for most of the ride back to Los Angeles.

We were met at the DZ checkpoint by Mag-Lev's people, who searched us for weapons. I yelped and nearly passed out as one of the goons insisted on straightening out my arms. Satisfied we weren't packing guns, they escorted us to Mag-Lev's headquarters. The five of us, along with the Bryn-sheep, met Mag-Lev in the lobby of the building. Roy carried the human Bryn. Neither he nor the Bryn-sheep had spoken a word since we'd left Malibu.

"As promised," Keane said. "We've rescued Priya and retrieved the sheep."

"My God," said Mag-Lev, approaching Bryn's limp body cradled in Roy's massive arms. "What did they do to her?" He pressed his fingers against her neck. "She's dead," he said after a moment. Roy didn't flinch. I think he must have known. He set her body down in a plush chair.

"You call this a rescue?" Mag-Lev said to Keane, crouching next to Bryn.

"She was near death when we got there," said Keane. "We did what we could."

Mag-Lev was silent for a while, stroking Bryn's cheek. At last he said, "God, she was a beautiful woman."

"She *is* a beautiful woman," replied Roy, glaring at Mag-Lev.

Mag-Lev regarded Roy quizzically for a moment but didn't reply. He sighed and walked to the Bryn-sheep. Reaching out and patting her head, he said, "You've caused a lot of trouble, you know. What's so special about you anyway?"

"I wish I knew," said the sheep.

Mag-Lev screamed and staggered backward as if he'd been struck. The Bryn-sheep started in fear.

"What the?" Mag-Lev exclaimed. "It can talk!"

"She's not an it," Roy growled. "She's a person."

Mag-Lev was silent for a moment, and then he began to laugh. "So that's why everybody wants this thing. It's some kind of biological anomaly. Fuck me, a talking sheep. What, is Selah planning some kind of televised freak show? What else does she have up her sleeve, a pig that does crossword puzzles? A trombone-playing monkey?"

"Shut up!" Roy growled. "Don't talk about her like that!"

Mag-Lev took a step forward and bent down to inspect the device around the Bryn-sheep's neck. "How does it work?" he asked. "It translates the sheep's thoughts into human speech?" He looked the Bryn-sheep in the eye. "Are . . . you . . . hungry?" he said loudly and slowly, the way Americans tend to talk to people who don't speak English.

"Not . . . particularly!" yelled the Bryn-sheep, mimicking Mag-Lev's mode of speech.

"Ha!" Mag-Lev barked, causing the Bryn-sheep to start. "It has a sense of humor! Or is it just programmed to respond that way? Mimic the speech pattern of the person it's talking to, to make the illusion of intelligence seem more real? God, if I didn't know better, I'd think there were actual thoughts going on inside that stupid sheep skull."

Roy moved toward Mag-Lev.

"Easy, Roy," I said, eyeing Mag-Lev's armed thugs, who had us surrounded.

But Roy brushed Mag-Lev aside and knelt down in front of the Bryn-sheep. "I'm sorry, Priya," he said. "I didn't know."

"It's okay," said the Bryn-sheep, looking into Roy's eyes. "I'm a little confused by it myself."

"Priya?" said Mag-Lev. "Hang on, are you saying . . . ?"

"The sheep has all of Priya Mistry's memories and thought patterns," said Keane, "and therefore her personality. For all intents and purposes, that sheep is Priya."

"No," said Mag-Lev, taking a step away from the Bryn-sheep. He no longer seemed amused. "It's a trick. That device just translates a few basic animal thoughts into human speech. Stock phrases that don't really mean anything."

"Priya," Keane said, and the Bryn-sheep turned her head to face him. "Can you tell me who Noogus is?"

"Noogus?" the sheep asked in a puzzled tone. "Well . . . he was my teddy bear. When I was very little. Why do you want to know about Noogus?"

Mag-Lev continued to back away. "That doesn't mean anything," he said. "Noogus is probably some kind of trigger word, like when you tell a dog to fetch or play dead."

The sheep turned to Mag-Lev. "Why are you talking like that, Giles?" she said. "I thought we had something together. Why are you trying to hurt me? I didn't ask to be made this way."

"H-how . . ." Mag-Lev stammered. He turned to Keane. "You told the sheep about me?"

"Afraid not," said Keane. "Congratulations, Priya actually remembers you. You should feel honored."

"But . . . she's a sheep!" Mag-Lev said.

"I'm still me, Giles," said the Bryn-sheep. "I just look different. I'm the same inside."

"No," said Mag-Lev. "You're not her. You're an animal. You're not Priya!"

"It's me!" the Bryn-sheep pleaded. "Please, you have to believe me. It's me, Bryn. You still love me, don't you, Giles?"

Mag-Lev shook his head, backing away from the Bryn-sheep. "Stop it," he said. "You're not her! Stop talking!"

"Giles, please!" cried the Bryn-sheep, walking toward Mag-Lev. "You're all I have. I thought you would be happy to see me. Now we can finally be together!"

"Get that thing away from me!" Mag-Lev howled, drawing his gun. "Get it out of here before I shoot it!"

The Bryn-sheep backed away, frightened. Roy stepped in between her and Mag-Lev. "Don't you dare!" Roy growled.

Mag-Lev backed off. "Just get it away from me! Get it out of here!" he screamed.

The Bryn-sheep trotted out the door, followed closely by Roy.

"Get out of here," Mag-Lev growled. "All of you!"

The rest of us made for the door, Keane bringing up the rear. As he reached the door, he stopped and turned to face Mag-Lev. "We're square," he said. "I met the terms of our deal."

"Just get out!" Mag-Lev screamed. "Get out!"

I walked outside and Keane followed, closing the door behind him. I looked back to see Mag-Lev crouched next to the chair in which Bryn's corpse reclined. He was holding the dead woman's hand and staring at her face, as if to erase the thought of the Bryn-sheep.

Roy and the Bryn-sheep were already almost to Pavel's Suburban, parked just down the street. I walked as fast as I could without jarring my arm.

"Hurry up," said Keane. "I can't guarantee Mag-Lev isn't going to realize he's been had."

It took me a moment to figure out what he meant. "You coached her," I said.

"Bryn deserves most of the credit," said Keane. "She's actually a hell of an actress."

"I wondered how she'd recognized him," I said. "So all that stuff about them finally being able to be together . . ."

"She didn't even remember Giles Marbury," he said. "I told her the only way Mag-Lev would let her go was if she pretended to be in love with him."

"How the hell did you settle on that strategy?" I asked.

Keane shrugged. "Mag-Lev is all surface. Appearances are the only thing that matter to him. He was never in love with Priya. He was in love with the idea of being the guy with Priya. So you give him Priya without the image of Priya, and he loses his mind. He couldn't process it."

"What if he'd shot her?"

"It was a calculated risk," said Keane. "I guessed that his need to delude himself about his love for Priya would outweigh his revulsion toward her."

"Did you tell Bryn about this 'calculated risk'?" I asked.

"I didn't have a lot of time," Keane replied.

"You're an asshole," I said.

Just then my comm chirped. It was Dr. Takemago. I groaned. I had almost managed to forget that we'd also promised the sheep to Jason Banerjee at Esper. We may have escaped Selah Fiore and Mag-Lev, but we still needed to deal with Banerjee. Out of the frying pan, into the fire.

"Dr. Takemago," I said. "We've got your sheep, but there have been some . . . complications."

For a moment I heard nothing but a sort of rustling sound. Eventually I realized Takemago was crying.

"Dr. Takemago, what's wrong?"

"Mr. Fowler," Takemago said, gasping. "They're dead. They're all dead."

"Who?" I asked. "Who's dead?"

"The sheep," Takemago said. "He's killed them. Said it was too dangerous, that someone would find out what had been done. Mr. Fowler, Mary cannot be brought back here. Please, promise me you will keep Mary safe from Mr. Banerjee."

"I promise," I said, without taking a moment to think about it. "I'm not letting that son of a bitch near Mary."

"Thank you, Mr. Fowler," Takemago said. The line went dead.

"I mean it, Keane," I said. "We can't let Banerjee have the— have Bryn. He'll kill her."

Keane regarded me silently for a moment. "Let's get you to a hospital," he said.

THIRTY-ONE

Pavel drove the Suburban to the hospital, where I spent most of the next three hours waiting for a doctor to set my arm. I don't remember much after that.

I woke up in my own bed to the smell of freshly brewed coffee. April was standing over me, a mug in her hand.

"Time to get up, sleepyhead," she said. "Keane's been bugging me for two hours, but I told him to let you sleep. I don't think I can hold him off much longer though."

I groaned and slowly sat up, using my left arm. My right was in a cast. The arm ached a bit, but the excruciating pain from the previous night was gone. "What time is it?" I asked.

"Just after nine," said April. "Keane says you have a meeting with Esper's vice president of research and development. What's that about?"

I took the mug from April and sipped the coffee. "The sheep," I said. "Technically it belongs to Esper. Legally, we're obligated to deliver it to them."

"You can't be serious," said April. "She isn't just a sheep. She's a person. I've spent the past hour talking to her."

"She's here?" I asked.

"She and Roy slept in the lobby. He's head over heels for her. It's kind of adorable."

"How is Bryn doing?" I couldn't help thinking she was due for some kind of psychotic break once she became fully aware of what had been done to her.

"Surprisingly well," said April. "Roy seems to be helping. I get the feeling this is the first time in quite a while anybody has treated her like a person."

I couldn't think of anything to say to that. Had Bryn really been so thoroughly objectivized as Priya Mistry that taking the form of a farm animal really was preferable? Or was her quiescent demeanor simply the result of Allebach's memory implants? Allebach had given her the memory of having gradually adjusted to being a sheep, as a sort of cushion against the jarring nature of the transition. But if she figured out that memory was fake, would she be forced to come to grips with what Selah had done to her? Or would the power of the memory hold, even after it was revealed to be an illusion? I couldn't begin to guess.

"Whatever Bryn may look like," said April, "she's a human being. You can't give her up to Esper. You don't know what they'll do to her."

I sighed. Actually, I was pretty sure I did know. "That's what I told Keane," I said. "But it's complicated."

"How is it complicated?" asked April. "You agreed to retrieve a sheep, not a person. Circumstances have changed. Tell Banerjee you were unable to solve the case. Return his money. Problem solved."

"It's not just the money," I said.

"Then what is it?" she asked.

"Fowler!" I heard Keane yell through the door to my apartment. "Time to go!"

"I need to get dressed," I said.

"What did Keane mean when he said Banerjee would blow the lid off Maelstrom? Jesus, Fowler. You need to stop protecting him. I heard what Selah said about—"

"I'm sorry, April," I said. "I've got to go."

Keane and I took a cab to the Esper building, leaving Roy and April to watch Bryn. Keane instructed Roy to keep the doors locked and shoot anybody who tried to get in. Keane said he didn't trust Banerjee not to send the cops to smash in our door and try to take the sheep by force. I didn't either, but then I wasn't sure I even trusted Keane at this point. We rode to Esper in silence, except for the sound of the rain.

"Gentlemen," said Banerjee as we walked into his office. "Any luck finding my sheep?"

"Oh yes," said Keane. "It's been quite a productive couple of days. We've learned, for instance, why you're so concerned about getting Mary back. I had a nice conversation with her about it this morning, in fact."

Banerjee regarded Keane coldly. "That sheep belongs to me," he said. "I demand you return it."

"So you can kill her like the others?" I said.

"Look," said Banerjee. "Whatever you think you know about Mary, the fact is that she's just an animal. An animal that belongs to me, to do with as I see fit. Hand her over, Mr. Keane, or the truth comes out."

Keane studied Banerjee for some time. "No," he said at last. "I don't think I'll be doing that."

"Why?" asked Banerjee. "What possible use do you have for a sheep?"

"None," said Keane. "But as far as I can tell, Mary has never hurt anyone. You, on the other hand, are a murderous psychopath and, quite frankly, a huge asshole. I don't like you, and I don't like being blackmailed." Banerjee glared at Keane but said nothing. I appreciated Keane standing up to Banerjee, but I sure hoped he had more up his sleeve than insults, because otherwise we were in serious trouble. "You know," Keane went on, "I'd hoped that by the time I walked in here, I'd have figured out an angle to use on you, some way to outmaneuver you. I already outsmarted Selah Fiore and Mag-Lev, and I figured it couldn't be too difficult to find some leverage to use against you as well. But to be honest, I've got nothing. Maybe I'm slipping, I don't know. I'm not in a position to dictate terms to you. Right now the sheep is in the lobby of my building. Yours for the taking."

I stared at Keane, not believing what I was hearing. After all we had gone though, he was going to cave to Banerjee?

"Good," said Banerjee, with a smile. "I appreciate your willingness to be reasonable on this matter. I'll write you a check and send someone to fetch the sheep."

Keane shook his head. "You misunderstand me," he said. "I'm not taking your money, and I'm not giving you the sheep. Here's how this is going to play out, Banerjee. Mr. Fowler and I are going to walk out of here, and we're going to get that sheep somewhere safe. Somewhere you will never find her. Mary is going to live the rest of her life, however long that may be, out of the spotlight. The fact is, you and Mary want the same thing: to keep her out of the news. So if you're smart, you'll leave things be. If, on the other hand, you're more vengeful than smart, you'll break into my building and take her. If you do that, I'm going to make sure you and Esper get plenty of headlines. Everyone in the world will know Esper genetically engineered sheep with human brains—and then killed them to destroy the evidence."

"You have no proof of any of that," said Banerjee. "And you're forgetting about Maelstrom."

"Listen to me, you moron," said Keane, leaning over the desk. "I know full well you can destroy me. What I'm telling you is that *I don't care*. If I let you play that card once, you're going to get it in your head you can play it whenever you like. That isn't going to happen. So destroy me if you like, but understand this: there is no upside for you. If you take that sheep, you're going to spend the next five years doing damage control—if you manage to keep your job, which I seriously doubt. Release the Maelstrom information if it will make you feel better, but your threats aren't going to factor into my decision. You already got what you wanted: leave us alone, and nobody will ever find out about your illegal research. Fuck with us, and you're in for a world of trouble. We'll see ourselves out."

Keane got up and made for the door. I followed.

"Nice doing business with you, Banerjee," said Keane, turning to smile at Banerjee. "Try to be good."

THIRTY-TWO

Keane and I grabbed a cab outside of the Esper headquarters. We rode in silence most of the way, the rain having subsided to a slight drizzle. Finally I spoke. "I appreciate
your standing up to Banerjee," I said. "I mean, Selah and
Mag-Lev, too, but Banerjee had you over a barrel."

Keane shrugged. "Threatening to expose Esper's illegal
research seemed like the best strategy, given the circumstances."

"No," I said. "The best strategy would have been to turn
Bryn over to Banerjee. When you played Selah, you needed
the sheep to bargain with Mag-Lev, and when you played
Mag-Lev, you needed the sheep to pay off Banerjee. But you
don't need her anymore. You had no good play against Banerjee, and no reason to put yourself at risk like that other than
concern for Bryn. You're still an asshole, but I wanted to let
you know I appreciate your standing up for her."

Keane seemed uncertain what to say to that. Finally he
said, "I didn't know they were going to kill everybody in
Maelstrom. I should have figured it out, but I didn't. I got so
wrapped up in the project, I didn't think about the implica-
tions."

"Clearly," I said. "I mean, you worked on a top-secret project to deal with the aftermath of a cataclysm in Los Angeles, and you never considered that the people signing the checks were up to no good?"

"Sometimes my desire to solve a problem . . . clouds my judgment," Keane said. "But I've never killed anybody. I tried to stop them, but I barely got out myself. Creating the character of Erasmus Keane was my only way out. And I swear, Fowler, I had nothing to do with Gwen's death."

I swallowed hard. "So she is dead?"

Keane looked down. "As far as I know, yes," he said.

"Why didn't you tell me?"

He was silent for a moment. "I . . . couldn't."

I snorted. More non-answers from the non-person, Erasmus Keane. I was getting really tired of this shit.

"Look," said Keane after a moment. "I know you're still mad at me, and I don't blame you, but we have more pressing matters to worry about."

"More pressing than you conspiring with my missing girlfriend to destroy Los Angeles? Really? Like what?"

"Like the fact that we don't know for certain that Banerjee didn't send the police to pick up Bryn while we were out."

My chest tightened. I'd been so preoccupied with Keane's sins, I'd forgotten Banerjee still presented a very real threat. I had been counting on him to make the rational decision, but there was no guarantee he would. If Banerjee was angry enough with Keane, he might kidnap Bryn and ruin Keane's life after all, just to spite him.

These fears were confirmed when we got out of the cab in front of the office and saw that the door had been smashed in. It was only open a few inches, as if someone had tried to close it again, but the wood had splintered around the locks.

"Wait here," I said to Keane, drawing my gun. I ran to the door and shoved it open. The building was eerily quiet, and

I moved inside, gun at the ready. Brian still had my SIG, but I'd retrieved a Glock from the office. It took my eyes a moment to adjust to the dim light of the lobby, and at first I didn't notice the giant fuzzy mass lying in the corner of the room. It wasn't moving. Near the sheep's head was a large, dark stain in the carpet.

"No," I murmured, moving slowly toward the sheep. "Please." For some reason I had assumed Banerjee's people would abduct Bryn and dispose of her in some cold, sterile fashion in the Esper lab—not shoot her and leave her for dead in my lobby. But Banerjee was relying on the LAPD to be his muscle, and they weren't known for their finesse. And if Banerjee wanted to send us a message, this was the way to do it. I could only hope Roy hadn't been killed trying to protect Bryn. And April. Jesus, I had no idea if April had been here as well. Banerjee would have told the cops to be thorough.

I knelt over the sheep and held the back of my hand in front of her nose. I felt warm breath. Then she licked me. Her eyes opened.

"Hello, Mr. Fowler," she said. "Did you take care of everything at Esper?"

I nodded dumbly, and quietly holstered my gun. It occurred to me the stain on the carpet she was lying on had been there since we moved in. "What . . . happened?" I asked after a moment, gesturing vaguely toward the door.

"Cops broke down the door," I heard Roy say. I turned to see him entering the lobby from the back, carrying a bucket that appeared to be full of water. "Came through the front, the back, the roof. Must have been twenty of them. I'd have started shooting, but we didn't have a chance. Figured if we didn't resist, at least some of us might get out alive." He put the bucket down in front of Bryn.

"Thanks, Roy," she said, and nuzzled his hand affectionately. She put her head in the bucket and began to lap up the water.

"You did the right thing, Roy," I said. To my right, Keane walked in, taking in the situation.

"Yeah, well," said Roy, "it didn't do any good. They gathered us all together in the lobby. Me, Bryn, April, and Pavel. I knew what was coming next. None of us were getting out alive."

"So what happened?" I said.

"All the sudden they backed off. Seemed like they got an order to stand down. Left without a word."

I glanced at Keane, and he gave me a knowing nod. Banerjee's thugs had been there and let them live.

Just then, April walked in, carrying several large bags. "I wasn't sure what kind of salad you wanted, Bryn, so I got three Caesars and four—Blake!"

"Good to see you, April," I said. She dropped the bags and ran toward me. She threw her arms around my waist. "Easy!" I said, holding my injured arm out of the way.

Roy emptied the bags April had dropped, revealing several sandwiches and an ungodly amount of salad. "Hungry, Bryn?" he said.

"Famished," Bryn replied.

Roy opened the salad containers and set them down before Bryn, and she began munching enthusiastically at the greens. "God, this is good," she said, without pausing in her mastication. The fact that the only thing that creeped me out about this scene was Bryn talking with her mouth full was a testament to just how far out of whack my sense of the uncanny had gotten over the past few days. I guess you can get used to just about anything eventually.

We sat down on the floor of the lobby and had a sort of impromptu picnic. We could have moved to a room with some furniture in it, but Bryn seemed content to remain in the relatively open space of the lobby, and the unspoken consensus was that she deserved a break after everything she'd been through. Keane wisely remained silent while we ate. He must have suspected I was in no mood to listen to him pontificate after Selah's revelations about Maelstrom and Gwen. To be honest, I was tempted to walk out and never come back, but there was still something I needed to see through with Keane.

"What about Bryn?" I asked. "What are we going to do with her?"

"I've got an idea about that," said Keane.

THIRTY-THREE

After lunch, Keane called an ex-client who owned a ranch near Bakersfield and convinced him to take Roy on as an on-site manager and handyman. The client owned dozens of properties all over Southern California; Keane said the ranch was just a tax write-off for him. The house on the property was small and rundown, but Roy insisted he was up to the challenge of renovating it. Bryn promised to do her part as well, although I wasn't sure what she could actually contribute other than mowing the lawn and producing wool. Still, it was something. I don't think Keane mentioned to the client that Roy's girlfriend was a sheep. There were some things best left unsaid. The two of them were downright giddy about the idea of getting out of Los Angeles and having a real life for once. They made for a very strange couple, but I gave them better odds than most. The way I figure it, if you can get past the fact that your partner is of a completely different species than you, you're already ahead of the game.

We never had a chance to warn the final Priya Mistry clone, who had been brought in to replace the one who had been killed in the explosion on the *DiZzy Girl* set. She was found dead of an apparent suicide in her hotel room at the Four Seasons later that night. Selah had evidently decided

that the risk of prolonging the charade a little longer out-
weighed the benefits. *DiZzy Girl* was canceled, but Flagship
Media's coverage of Priya's "troubled life" and suicide went
on for months, garnering record ratings. Figures. We also
never found out what happened to the unfinished clones in
Selah's lab. Mostly, I tried not to think about it too much,
but I supposed they probably met the same fate as Esper's
sheep. Slaughtered like cattle.

The mysterious Maelstrom file had burned up completely
when Mag-Lev's thugs blew up Keane's car, so whatever
other secrets it contained were going to remain secret for a
while longer—assuming Banerjee was cowed by Keane's
threat. Our financial situation was worse than ever at the
close of the Case of the Missing Sheep and the Case of the
Concerned Teddy Bear, owing to the fact that we weren't
likely to get paid for either of them. We'd failed to deliver on
the former, and our client on the latter was not, legally speaking, a person, and therefore unable to cut a check. On top of
that, it wasn't at all certain that the insurance company was
going to pay for Keane's exploded aircar. This was a tricky,
dangerous, and often unrewarding business. But it was all
worthwhile to give Roy and Bryn a chance at happiness.
That's what I told myself, anyway. Who the fuck knows?

After our impromptu picnic in the lobby, Pavel left to
take the happy couple to their new home, and April left
shortly thereafter. Keane went up to his office, and I spent
most of the rest of the day in bed. My arm was throbbing,
and I was just plain worn-out from everything that had
happened over the past few days. Thoughts of walking out
on Keane gave way to thoughts of sleep. I was in no shape to
make a life-changing decision anyway. I figured I'd revisit
the matter in the morning.

It was dark when I woke up, and I knew immediately there
was someone in the room with me. I had locked the door to

my apartment, but it was an old lock, easy enough for a pro to pick. We hadn't had a chance to fix the doors of the building yet.

"April?" I asked. She was the only person besides Keane who had a key to my apartment, and somehow I knew it wasn't Keane.

"Sorry to disappoint you," said a woman's voice. It was familiar, but it wasn't April's. I knew I should know who it was, but for some reason I just couldn't place it. That had been happening a lot lately. But this time it wasn't Priya Mistry. It was a voice out of another time, one that just didn't fit somehow. In my sleep-addled state, I couldn't quite figure out why, but I knew that voice was impossible. It couldn't be here.

The light went on, and I saw the face that went with the voice. Her hair was shorter, and had been dyed brown, but there was no mistaking that face. The wide lips, high cheekbones, the pale, flawless skin. She stood next to the door, wearing a long coat that concealed most of her tall, angular form. In her hands was a large envelope, which she handed to me. Somehow I knew what the label was going to say before I even looked at it.

MAELSTROM.

"What the hell happened to you, Gwen?" I asked.

Gwen sighed. "You got any coffee, Blake?" she said. "This could take a while."